Tall, rich, ha...
Prince, king...
men need...
honour...

Royal

ENGAGEMENTS

By

REBECCA WINTERS,
MEREDITH WEBBER &
MELISSA JAMES

Three brand-new royal romances
Three glamorous royal weddings

Royal

ENGAGEMENTS

REBECCA WINTERS
MEREDITH WEBBER
MELISSA JAMES

M&B™ and M&B™ with the Rose Device
are trademarks of the publisher.
Harlequin Mills & Boon Limited, Eton House,
18-24 Paradise Road, Richmond, Surrey TW9 1SR

ROYAL ENGAGEMENTS
© Harlequin Enterprises II B.V./S.à.r.l. 2010

A Royal Bride of Convenience © Rebecca Winters 2010
Expecting the Cascaverado Prince's Baby © Meredith Webber 2010
Too Ordinary for the Duke? © Lisa Chaplin 2010

ISBN: 978 0 263 88026 7

009-0410

Harlequin Mills & Boon policy is to use papers that are
natural, renewable and recyclable products and made from
wood grown in sustainable forests. The logging and
manufacturing processes conform to the legal environmental
regulations of the country of origin.

Printed and bound in the UK by
CPI Mackays, Chatham ME5 8TD

A Royal Bride of Convenience

REBECCA WINTERS

Dear Reader,

I find royal stories irresistible because they represent life in another universe that's right here on earth. They appeal to my love of fantasy, yet they're grounded in reality.

I lived with several 'real' princesses when I attended boarding school in Lausanne, Switzerland. Like me, they were students there, but I was aware they lived a life of privilege. When the holidays came, their 'highnesses' were whisked away from school in limousines with royal crests in order to reach the airport in Geneva where they would fly on their royal planes to reach their royal households.

My own headmistress, good friends with a lady-in-waiting to the Queen of Spain, often went to the apartments of the Queen when she was in residence in Lausanne. That was a long time ago, yet my experiences abroad still creep their way into my romance novels.

A Royal Bride of Convenience, based in Geneva, might be a flight of fantasy to provide reading pleasure, but the fact remains that the fictitious Prince Niccolo and Princess Francette do exist in real life somewhere.

Enjoy!

Rebecca Winters

Rebecca Winters, whose family of four children has now grown to include five beautiful grandchildren, lives in Salt Lake City, Utah, in the land of the Rocky Mountains. With canyons and high alpine meadows full of wild flowers, she never runs out of places to explore. They, plus her favourite vacation spots in Europe, often end up as backgrounds for her Mills & Boon® Romance novels because writing is her passion, along with her family and church.

Rebecca loves to hear from her readers. If you wish to e-mail her, please visit her website at www.clean romances.com

Look for an exciting new novel from Rebecca Winters,
Miracle for the Girl Next Door,
available from Mills & Boon® Romance in June 2010.

CHAPTER ONE

"I RELINQUISH my time to Prince Raimondo Niccolo Giancarlo di Castellani."

"Thank you, Mr. Secretary General."

Nic leaned forward to speak into the microphone so he'd be clearly heard. Though his parents and the majority of people who knew him called him Raimondo, to his closest friends in his military unit he was simply Nic, the name he preferred.

"For three days now, the discussion going on before this council of the United Nations has done little more than incite rancor from every side.

"We're all assembled *seemingly* for the same goal—to decide how our world body should act to stop crimes against humanity, prevent genocide and end war crimes. Yet instead of putting our heads together to come up with a plan to enforce this doctrine, there are those among you once again debating the policy's validity!

"As the chosen delegate from the Enclave of San

Ravino, and personal envoy of my father, King Leopoldo, I'm making a formal protest and walking out of this conference until such a time as a majority of you can find the courage to act for the welfare of the oppressed." His black eyes flashing, he said, "I call on any delegates in this room who feel as I do to walk out with me, as a show of solidarity against this sort of shameful filibustering."

Before his anger turned to rage, Nic shot to his six-foot-three height and headed down the aisle to the nearest exit, carrying his attaché case. To his satisfaction other members, maybe sixty of them, got up at the same time he did. Not as many as the hundred he would have liked to see, but it proved he wasn't a lone voice.

More suited to freefall paratrooping than sitting in a chair listening to parsed rhetoric going nowhere, he burst through the doors to his waiting limo. The heat was surprising for early June. His driver maneuvered him through New York's heavy noon traffic to the airport.

While en route, Nic called his father's personal secretary on the satellite phone and asked to be put through to him so he could make his report. Knowing the U.N. proceedings were being televised, no doubt someone on the staff had been keeping his father updated. By now King Leopoldo probably knew his hot-headed, thirty-three-year-old son had made an explosive departure from the world stage today, upsetting the entire proceedings.

Never let it be said he hadn't warned his parent he was a military man, not a diplomat. However, he'd agreed to represent San Ravino at the assembly in order to appease his father, who believed in talk. He was of the old school. Nic, still to be convinced, was a man of action, not words.

For the last nine years Nic had been a part of the Raiders, a secret special operations force working in Africa, the Middle East and elsewhere. He loved what he did. The Spartan lifestyle appealed to him enormously. The only time he took leave from his unit was at the royal request of his father, and couldn't be disregarded.

Nic wasn't unaware that the days were ticking away until July, the dreaded time when he'd promised his parents he would get out of the military and take up his duties at home.

He made furrows through his straight black hair, anxious to jettison his suit for his fatigues. Comfort was what he craved on the flight to San Ravino, its own country within the borders of central Italy. With his duty accomplished, he could kick back and relax before he took another flight to rejoin his unit in the Middle East. As soon as he could connect with his father, he was prepared to listen, mostly, while the older man reamed him out for displaying his temper in public. Instead he heard something quite different.

"Raimondo? Where are you, exactly?"

Nic blinked. Not even a greeting? "I'm in the limousine, on my way to the plane."

"Are you alone?"

He frowned. "Yes?"

"Good. I've caught you in time."

Nic, on the verge of telling his father he wouldn't go back to the assembly, heard the older man say, "Your superior has been in contact with me. Your orders are to fly to Africa for a dire emergency. Someone will meet you at the plane. Don't bother to come home first."

Surprised, Nic gripped the phone tighter. He hadn't heard his father this intense since he'd told him of his plans to enter the military. "Were you given any details?"

"According to him there's been another outbreak of violence in northeast Chakul. Some missionaries have already been killed. They need your particular expertise."

"It's a hot spot," Nic muttered. Especially after the floods, when the clans had battled over water points for their livestock. As soon as humanitarian efforts were made to stave off hunger and disease the hostility escalated, and lives were lost. The drill was all too familiar to him.

This was the reason diplomatic chitchat didn't get the job done—which reminded him of the gridlock he'd just left behind in New York. "Did you happen to see what went on in the general session this morning?" Better get official business out of the way while they were still on the phone.

His father made a strange sound in his throat. "I thought you would have walked out on them yesterday. You showed admirable patience under impossible circumstances."

"*Grazie*, Papa." Nic couldn't be more pleased at the way this conversation was going.

"I was proud of you." After a distinct pause, "About your mission—take care, my son. Come home safe." The entreaty sounded gruff. He hung up before Nic could assure his father he was always careful.

Not only the choice of words, but the tremor in his father's voice caught him off guard, causing his throat to swell. Normally his parent didn't reveal his emotions. This was one of those rare moments when guilt caught up to Nic. He clicked off.

Another son might have been all the things his father had dreamed of. Instead, his parents had got Nic, their only offspring, who continually disappointed them with choices that in their mind put him in physical jeopardy on a twenty-four-hour basis. He felt even guiltier that they'd never tried to pressure him into doing his royal duty.

Since his betrothal to the Princess Francette de Norestier of the Principality of Haut-Leman on his fifteenth birthday—a nightmarish memory for him—he'd never seen her again, and his parents had never spoken of her. But as the night followed the day, he realized it was only a matter of another month before her name surfaced.

Not for the first time did a certain thought enter his mind—albeit suggested jokingly by his closest buddy Aldo. "Why not remain hidden in the mountains after one of our raids and not emerge again for years and years?"

After enjoying a round of beers one night while on leave, the idea had sounded good to him. Unfortunately it sounded even better right now, and he was stone-cold sober, but he refused to let it spoil his life while he still had a month of freedom left.

Before long the limo pulled up to the royal jet and Nic got out.

"*Buongiorno*, Your Highness."

"It *is* a good day now that I've been liberated," he said to Bruno, the dark blond steward who came down the steps to greet him. They'd been friends a long time. "Tell Rocco we have a change in plans and will be flying directly to Tangiers."

"Very good. Will you be wanting lunch?"

"*Si. Grazie.*" He walked down the passageway to his suite, jerking off his tie and suit jacket. As soon as they gained cruising speed he'd take a shower, then pore over his maps to reacquaint himself with a region that was always volatile.

It didn't take much for the clans to end up causing chaos that would develop into full-scale warfare. Too many innocents suffered. A burst of adrenaline seized his hard-muscled body as he contemplated his imminent mission.

A baby was crying.

As Lise Belard began to regain consciousness she grew more aware of her surroundings and realized her assailants had dumped her in the Fillouxes' hut with Celeste. It was pitch-black inside. Her hands and ankles had been bound. The blanket over her head had been removed, but someone had gagged her with a foul-smelling piece of burlap and had thrown her on her side, where pains shot through her arm and hip.

By some miracle the three-month-old infant who'd been sick for the past ten days was still alive, but her pitiful, continuous whimpers wrenched Lise's heart. Tomorrow Adam Brown, the doctor from Nairobi, was due to be here with his team, to check on the baby and bring medicine.

The village was in short supply of antibiotics and AIDS medication to prevent pregnant mothers from passing the disease on to their children, but Lise feared he and his staff would be ambushed and killed en route, all the fresh supplies confiscated.

Right now she couldn't help herself, let alone comfort the baby, who had to be in pain from hunger by now. Even if Lise were to inch over to the crib she wouldn't be able to reach for her. The ropes had been tied too cruelly tight.

Shudder after shudder swept through her body. For the first time in her life she knew true terror. She had the real conviction that before the night was over she and the baby would be dead.

Celeste's missionary parents, Jean and Marie Filloux, from Neuchatel, Switzerland, had in all likelihood been murdered, and Lise was next. She could taste her fear. The sickening rate of her heartbeat sent the blood in surges against every pulse-point of her body. When she'd started this work five years ago, the risks to her life and health had seemed negligible when compared to the suffering she'd witnessed here. Someone had to try and make a difference, no matter how little.

Most of the first-aid supplies sent to the war-torn borders of Chakul never made it this far north. If it weren't for the latest on-going bike fundraiser she'd spearheaded at home, she wouldn't be able to give the amount of help she did.

Purchasing motorbikes for the locals allowed them to penetrate the far reaches of the various settlements with supplies. It was one of the quickest ways to bring immediate relief to the suffering after the spring rains. However, she feared that the arrival of the bikes had enflamed the warring clans and they had a special punishment ready to mete out to her.

Today Lise had made a hazardous bike trip to take the last of her supplies of drugs and food to the makeshift tent town eight miles from the village.

The route was almost impassable in spots. She'd been grateful to get back to the safety of the compound by nightfall without a serious problem.

But, except for Celeste's baby cry coming from the Fillouxes' hut a hundred yards away, she'd been aware of an eerie silence. Of course everyone was indoors for the night. Still, that kind of quiet had been unnatural. Having shut off the motor that doused the headlight, she'd been shrouded in darkness.

As she'd walked her bike to the side of her hut, the hairs had stood up on the back of her arms and neck. Something had told her not to go inside. She'd immediately turned the bike around and started the motor up again to head for the sentry post.

The next thing she knew something had been thrown over her head, suffocating her. After being knocked down, she'd been bound and dragged for what felt like a long distance before she knew nothing more.

Lise had survived many local uprisings, but this was the first time one of the rebel factions hating foreigners, and missionaries in particular, had ventured this far from the border to slaughter innocent people.

Her family had begged her to find another way to do good. There were thousands of charitable causes that wouldn't put her life in danger. But on a photo safari to Chakul she'd discovered the people were loving and peaceful, grateful for any kindness from a stranger.

The tour director had told everyone to bring extra paper and pens to give out to the children. Those were treasures to them. When Lise had discovered how delighted they were with the merest trifle, despite their great impoverishment, it had touched her heart and set her on her particular path. At the time it had been an easy choice to make, considering she'd been running away from pain for years.

But as she lay there, trussed up like a prized fowl to be butchered, she was aware the consequences of those choices had caught up to her. Certain death was coming. Her senses could feel it, smell it.

Celeste had finally stopped crying. The poor little thing was too ill. With no mother to hold and kiss her, she'd given up.

The quiet had an unearthly quality now. Her captors were outside, planning something. Lise broke out in a cold sweat. If she'd known how and when she was going to die, would she have still chosen to work in this part of the world?

Of course she already knew the answer to her own question, or she wouldn't be here, but she could still grieve for certain experiences she would never know—like marriage to a soulmate, like being a mother to her own baby.

Lise had to dig back a long way to understand how she'd come to do her life's work in Chakul. She supposed it had started as a form of rebellion against the life she'd been born into. Not against her parents, who were wonderful people, but against the royal institution itself, with its archaic betrothals, used as a sole instrument to aggrandize wealth and property.

Her betrothal had been sanctified in the church on her tenth birthday. To this day all she could remember was a fifteen-year-old beanpole, with an evil smile and black coals for eyes. Afterwards in the courtyard she'd heard him call her a royal pudding behind her back—in Italian, no less. She'd swung around and thrown pebbles from the fountain at him, screaming that she would never, ever marry anyone so mean.

That was a lifetime ago. As far as Lise was concerned, marriage was the most individual, sacred matter on earth. To enter into it for any reason but love was anathema to her.

She'd always believed that if she ever met a man she truly loved, she would seek out Prince Raimondo in secret and end their betrothal. It would kill her parents. She would be forever diminished in their eyes for putting love before them and the crown, but she knew herself too well. A marriage based on anything less would never work.

Lise knew her betrothed felt exactly the same way. Not once in eighteen years had he tried to make contact. She suspected he nursed the hope she might even have died by now. He was probably going to get his wish.

As tears trickled across the bridge of her nose, her

ears picked up a sound. It wasn't Celeste. Someone was moving inside the hut with great stealth. *Dear God, please help me.*

CHAPTER TWO

WITH the aid of night-vision goggles, Nic took in the interior of the last hut to be inspected. Aldo was right behind him. There was a body on the floor, another body in the crib.

While his buddy dealt with the baby, Nic crept over to the mother, who'd been bound and gagged. He knelt down and felt for a pulse at her throat. She was Caucasian. Her dark hair was worn in a braid on top of her head, the typical missionary coiffure.

She was still alive, but unconscious. No sign of her husband. If she'd worn a wedding ring, it was gone now. Thankfully the air assault had scared off the attackers before they could do her any more harm.

He removed the gag, then took out his knife to free her hands and feet. Once that was done, he easily swept up her khaki-clad body from the mat covering the floor, noting she was long-legged. Carrying her in a fireman's lift, he followed Aldo out the door.

They half ran through the compound to the area where an open-air bush vehicle filled with wounded locals was waiting. The other one had already gone.

Time was of the essence to meet the military helicopters at the designated rendezvous. Everything had to be accomplished under the cover of darkness. When the dawn came, there could be no indication that the Raiders had ever been here.

After setting her on a banquette next to a group of women, one of whom reached for the baby, he and Aldo signaled the driver to take off. They, along with others from the unit, stood on the running board, with their assault rifles positioned in case they met with hostile fire.

By the time they reached the clearing, one helicopter had taken off. The other one was waiting for them, its blades rotating. As soon as the vehicle stopped, Nic jumped off and started ushering people toward the opening. When he saw that the missionary had recovered enough to hold the baby, he realized she'd only been pretending to be unconscious. She'd done a good job of it.

Nic helped her into the helicopter. Aldo followed and closed the door for the short flight to El Wak, where the displaced people and missionaries would be given shelter and food. With their mission accomplished, Nic's unit would board military transport and fly to the Middle East.

Counting the minutes until the helicopter landed,

Nic was first out the door, where he was met by the commander of his unit. It came as a big surprise that he was here rather than with the rest of the unit. Something was up for him to be on hand for a one-night maneuver. After they saluted, he took Nic aside, away from everyone getting off the chopper.

"We have a desperate situation here that requires your help. We've already obtained your father's backing, but of course it's up to you. It's asking a lot of you, Nic, but because of who you are, and your outstanding record of service, I'm going to ask it."

"Go ahead."

"Intelligence indicates that the woman on board with the baby was going to be held hostage and used as a bargaining tool for the enemy, to gain concessions from the Chakul government. You got here before they could kidnap her."

"Barely in time," Nic muttered.

"I understand she's been working in the bush for a number of years, crusading for human rights. They want her silenced."

"Naturally," Nic bit out. The missionaries were an amazing group of human beings. "What about her husband?"

He shook his head. "We don't know anything about him, but we'll find out soon enough. From all the chatter, it's the woman they're after. Since she's been targeted, and we've rescued her, neither she nor the baby will be safe until she's well out of the country. Unfortunately, we've learned through our sources that the government has now decided she has inside information that could be of vital use to them, and won't grant her permission to leave once they find her. Our night raid has foiled the enemy's plans, but it has put her in the middle of a sticky political situation unless we get her out. Either way, her life's in danger."

The potential to be held as a hostage by any terrorist group put all missionaries' lives in danger. Nic could only admire them. "What do you want me to do?"

"Your father's jet is standing by at a nearby town." Nic sensed where this was going. The nearest town was a couple of hundred miles away. "Officially it landed for emergency repairs before continuing on to South Africa. Unofficially…"

He got it.

"We'll fly the three of you there in the helicopter. It will land on a deserted road near the airport. A car will be there to drive you to the jet. You'll shed your uniform and leave it in the helicopter before you change into civilian clothes."

"Am I to play the Prince on vacation, then?"

"Whatever comes to mind. If the car is stopped, you'll have to get creative."

"As long as I have a free hand…"

"Absolutely."

"Bene."

"By the time you arrive at the jet let's hope we're still one step ahead of the authorities. Your pilot is standing by, ready to assist."

Rocco had been a fighter pilot at one time. This kind of intrigue would definitely appeal to his love of adventure.

"Once you're on board, you'll be cleared for take-off. If the Chakul authorities should get word of this, it will be too late for them to do anything. She'll have diplomatic immunity because she'll be under King Leopoldo's protection, and a major international incident will have been averted."

It sounded easy enough in theory. "What's our destination?"

"Word has reached the head of the mission in Geneva. They plan to meet her there and see to her needs until they can get hold of her family. Are you willing to do this? Remember you don't have to."

They eyed each other soberly. "Was there ever any doubt?"

"Thank you, Nic. There's more riding on this than you know."

He'd already figured that out. To go to these lengths meant this missionary was important for reasons not even his commander knew, or he wasn't telling him.

"Publicly you'll never be acknowledged for what you're doing, but behind the scenes you and your father will have the gratitude of many governments working for peace in this area. From my standpoint, the Raiders won't be the same once you're out for good next month."

"Thank you." Nic saluted him and headed for the chopper, but his commander's last comment put him in a dark place where he couldn't bear to go.

So far no one had spoken to Lise. She was still strapped to the seat of the helicopter with the baby. Everyone else had got out. There was one soldier who stood guard at the entrance.

She had no idea who these men were, or where she was, or what was going to happen to her. It was still the dead of night. All she did know was that she was at their mercy—she and Celeste, who was too sick to cry. She held the baby close to her heart and hummed some little tunes like Marie did to comfort her.

Any second now she expected to be bound, gagged and suffocated by a blanket thrown over her head, before they transferred her to another location to be executed.

While she bent over Celeste's little body to kiss her cheek and neck, she heard men's voices outside the helicopter. Until now no words had been spoken, but it didn't matter. They were too indistinct for her to know what language the men were speaking, let alone what they were saying.

As she lifted her head, she watched the one soldier

leave and another one enter. This one closed the helicopter door and made his way toward her, filling her with renewed terror. In the semi-darkness he appeared to be the same soldier who'd carried her from the hut to the bush van.

She held the baby tighter, while her heart hammered with sickening speed. He was tall and powerfully built. In his helmet and uniform, he looked so tough it made the horror of this night all too real.

"What's your name?" He spoke English to her in a deep masculine voice. It didn't sound British or American. She pretended not to understand. He switched languages. *"Como se llama usted?"* When she still did not answer him, he said, *"Parli Italiano?"*

When she continued to rock the baby, she heard him exhale, and realized her lack of cooperation was angering him. Good! She'd had it with being the helpless victim.

"Eh bien, vous êtes française?"

No, she wasn't French, but since she was going to her death anyway, she refused to give him any information about herself. When she flew to and from Chakul, she traveled incognito, on commercial flights.

Everyone assumed she was French. The fact that the customs officials saw she was a native of French-speaking Haut-Leman, a principality on the south side of Lake Geneva, didn't raise any eyebrows. To make it easier for the locals she'd told them to call her Lise, a shortened version of the name of her *grandmère*, Analise Belard, and it had stuck.

Though Lise might have lost everything else in the raid including her passport, she still had pride. Since her life was about to come to an end anyway, why give him the satisfaction of thinking he could intimidate her further.

"Ecoutez, madame." He continued in French, which he could have learned in any one of the French-speaking European countries, or the countries of Maghreb in North Africa. It was impossible to tell. "Your husband could be dead or not. For your safety, we're going to take a small flight and then set down again. When we do, we'll get into a car that will drive us to an airport where a plane is waiting."

For what? Was this a group involved in white slave trafficking? She couldn't bear it.

"You will speak to no one unless I tell you exactly what to say. *Vous comprenez?*" he demanded, in such a menacing tone she shrank from him. His dark voice added to the layers of fear paralyzing her.

Lise nodded, not willing to enflame him further. He thought she'd been torn from her husband, that she was Celeste's mother. The probability that the Fillouxes were dead made her want to cry out in agony. Instead, the scream of the rotors pierced the quiet.

Her captor moved to the front of the helicopter. After saying a few unintelligible words to the pilot, he strapped himself in. Before long they were airborne.

Celeste made little cries now and again. The poor darling missed her parents. Lise felt her cheeks and forehead. The baby was running a temperature. She needed to be in a hospital, but that wasn't going to happen.

Flying to her doom in the darkness, the next hour felt like an eternity. She'd been alone many times in her life, but this was a different kind of alone... All she could do was cling to the baby and absorb her warmth while she prayed for a miracle.

Suddenly the helicopter was dipping. Her heart thundered, sounding out shockwaves through her terrified body. This was it.

Her captor moved like lightning to undo her straps and whisked her to the entrance with Celeste. After opening the door he jumped out, before taking the baby from her.

"Allez, madame. Into the car!"

Lise could see it parked several yards away. Maybe she should just start running in the opposite direction and hope he shot her dead, but she couldn't leave the baby defenseless.

Everything became a blur as she got in the back of an old, dark, four-door sedan whose engine was running. She didn't recognize the make. Her captor handed her the baby, then shut the door. The driver turned his head to stare at her. By now her body was soaked in sweat from fear.

She clutched the baby against her shoulder. In a

matter of seconds the soldier joined her in the back-seat and the car took off. He'd discarded his uniform and was now wearing a T-shirt and khakis. Without his helmet, the transformation was quite startling, but a change in clothes couldn't disguise the evil in him.

Convinced her life had been preserved for a fate she considered worse than death, she couldn't forget for a moment her captor had likely been paid a lot of money to carry out orders. He was going to turn her over to some filthy monster living in the darkest reaches of the continent, where she would no doubt be raped before she was exterminated.

Celeste, Celeste. What are we going to do? How can I get us away?

Another long drive in silence with twists and turns made her dizzy. She hadn't had food or drink since she'd left the tent settlement. Her body had grown weak and was dehydrating. So was Celeste's. Without nourishment, the baby was going to die.

Maybe it would be better if she died in her arms. At least then Lise would know what had happened to the precious infant before they were brutally torn from each other.

In a few minutes the car started to slow down. The driver spoke to her captor in rapid Swahili, but she followed it. Swahili had been an easy language for her to learn. They'd come to a police checkpoint outside the airport and had to stop while the car was searched.

Her prayers for help had been answered!

But when the car came to a full stop, she almost went into shock when the soldier holding her captive pulled her and the baby into his arms in an unexpected move. She half lay against his chest, imprisoned. As the driver opened the door, the light from outside allowed her the first real glimpse of her captor.

Impressions of a man in his thirties with bronzed, rugged features flew at her like colors through a prism. Beneath straight black hair, eyes blacker than the night stared down into hers, impaling her. Their intensity sent a thrill of alarm through her shivering body.

"Kiss me like you mean it if you want your freedom, *madame*," he muttered fiercely, before his hard male mouth covered hers.

Did he really say *freedom*?

The word caused her heart to slam against her ribs. Maybe this man wasn't her enemy. She didn't know anything, but on the slightest chance that he meant it, she cooperated by not fighting him.

Her lukewarm response didn't appear to be enough. While the police shone a flashlight on them, he urged her lips apart to drink deeply. No one would know the baby was sandwiched between them.

What had started out as a cold and calculated diversion to send the message that nothing of importance was going on in the backseat, became something else. His kiss of refined savagery grew more intimate and prolonged.

With the release of adrenaline, she found herself getting into it—a kind of mindless response, because she'd never known a kiss like this before. Lise had never been made so compellingly aware of her womanhood. There was something primitive about what they were doing. It had to be the fear of losing her life that was causing her to lose her mind and her control right now. His kiss had ratcheted up her pulse-rate till it was off the charts.

Somewhere on the periphery she heard the policeman and the driver passing muffled jokes back and forth before the door closed. As the car moved on, she wrenched her mouth from the soldier's. Out of breath, she slid across the seat with Celeste.

He'd told her to cooperate if she wanted her freedom. Well, apparently she'd passed the first test, but she still had no idea what was going on. In all likelihood he'd used the age-old ploy to escape the government's radar because nothing was going to deter him from carrying out his mission.

His kiss should have repulsed her. Instead she was more terrified of him than ever because— because in a purely physical way her body seemed to have recognized a force coming from deep within him. Though her mind had screamed for her to stop, her senses had bent to his will. But how could that be possible, or acceptable? It wasn't!

This soldier was capable of anything, and thought his sensual mastery had produced the results to silence her. That was what his corrupt male ego got for thinking! The next time the car stopped she would open her door and jump out, screaming for help. They weren't locked. Airport security would *have* to hear her and come running.

She gathered Celeste against her shoulder to make it easier to run with her. Her fingers slid to the handle. Even before the car came to a complete stop, she would make a run for it.

It was taking forever to get to this plane. Naturally it belonged to some grotesque junta leader and his henchmen, who committed hideous crimes against women and children.

While she was damning them all, the car slowed down. This was her chance. She flung open the door, but her captor checked her movements. While he pulled her back against his broad chest with one arm, his other snaked around to clamp his hand against her mouth. She couldn't have made a sound if she'd tried. Lise started to feel sick. There was a ringing in her ears.

With frightening ease he dragged her and the baby from the car. She was so weak she couldn't fight him. He picked her up like she was a piece of cotton and started running with them toward a gleaming white private jet parked in the distance.

A tribal leader who possessed that kind of money could have her flown anywhere in the world for his personal pleasure. She would never be seen again. A moan escaped her throat.

CHAPTER THREE

NIC could hear sirens in the background. No doubt the guard at the checkpoint had received word from his superior that a Caucasian woman the government was looking for might be trying to escape the country. But he'd got the warning too late and had alerted other security forces to stop Nic.

He hurried up the steps with the woman and her baby. Their bodies were so limp, he feared for their lives. The moment he was on board, his steward closed the door and Rocco started the engines. He would already have done the pre-flight check.

"Bruno? Quick! Secure her baby while I fasten this woman in her seat." There were four in the club area facing each other, with a table in the center.

"*Si.* I have everything on hand to feed the *bambino* once we reach cruising speed."

The baby had its mother for that, but until she was well enough again…*"Grazie."*

They worked at triple speed. Then the steward

moved forward while Nic strapped himself in the seat for take-off. The engines whined. Rocco didn't have to taxi around. He had a straight ribbon of runway before him, but it was bumpy because of the potholes. Worse, it was dangerously short. Nic had been here before.

Avanti, Rocco. Muoviamoci!

As the jet thrust forward he heard rapid machine gun fire and could have sworn they'd been hit. The sound caused the woman's eyelids to flutter open for a moment. This was the first time he'd seen her in the light. His breath caught. Through inky lashes as dark as her fragrant hair and finely arched brows, he saw orbs more beautiful than the most exquisite cobalt crystal.

When she closed them again, Nic's gaze wandered over her features. She had high cheekbones, and a proud nose with a dusting of tiny freckles. No woman of his acquaintance would dare wear her hair—more black than brown—pulled tightly away from her face like that. She probably hadn't seen make-up in years, but she didn't need any with her honey complexion. There was an earthiness about her that appealed to the male in him.

His eyes roved over her supple curves. Living in the bush kept her tall body toned and fit in a way a pampered lifestyle could not. Beneath well-worn khakis, her legs went on forever.

He waited until the last breathless moment to study her wide mouth. Ever since he'd tasted her, it had been calling to him like a siren. The passionate flare of her lips was no mirage. Their shape could have been made expressly for him. Maybe because she was a missionary, he'd known a tantalizing forbidden fruit moment as her mouth had brought his senses to pulsating life.

But it was a one-time experience, carried out for their survival. Under no circumstances was it to be repeated. The raid last night had robbed her of a husband. Her baby was now fatherless. As soon as Nic delivered them to Geneva, his mercy mission would be at an end. Her grief was only beginning...

While they were still gaining altitude, he tore his gaze away from her to study the baby. When the missionary's day in the bush had started out, she'd dressed it in an undershirt and overalls. Whether boy or girl he couldn't tell. A light cap of brown hair covered its head. But on closer inspection he stirred in alarm, because the infant's complexion had a sick pallor even though spots of flame marked its drawn cheeks.

He knew little about babies, but he'd been around thousands of starving and dead infants. This one looked well cared for, but it was ill.

The second the seat belt light shut off, he jumped out of the chair to meet Bruno, who was just coming from the galley with a towel and some diapers. His other hand carried a baby bottle full of milk. Their eyes met.

"How much damage was done to the plane?"

"Rocco said there's a small leak coming from the fuel tank. Depending on how bad it is, we may not make it to Geneva. He's checking for possible places to land."

Nic had been afraid of that. "Whatever happens, she's not to know who I am. *Ever*." This operation was classified for the protection of many people and countries.

"Capisco."

Knowing her thirst must be fierce, Nic grabbed a bottled water from the fridge and hurried back to the club area. "Bruno? You wake the mother and help her to the restroom." After the experience in the car, he felt it best his steward take charge of her. "Give her anything she wants to eat or drink. She's been through a horrendous experience and is still in shock. I'll take care of the baby."

"Bene."

Nic undid the straps and laid the baby on another seat. He undid the overalls to change its diaper. It was a girl! Her diaper was dry. That had to be a bad sign—she was dehydrated.

He used the other diaper for a model and hoped he'd put it on right. Then he cradled her in his arms and put the nipple in her mouth. She was out like a light and sick. He knew that, but she needed nourishment.

At first she didn't respond. Speaking in French, he urged her to drink. "Come on, *petite*. Swallow some for me." Like a miracle, her little mouth began to react. She made some baby sounds. Before he knew it she began sucking, even though her tiny eyelids were closed.

She was so perfect. Everything about her from her retroussé nose to the cuticles of her nails delighted him. Encouraged to find she wanted her bottle, he let her keep drinking. But all of a sudden she started to cry, and began spitting up all over him and herself. Frantic, he grabbed for the towel and put her against his shoulder.

"What do you think, Bruno?" He'd reverted to Italian. "Should I try feeding her again?"

"I wouldn't if I were you," the woman muttered in kind. "She can only handle small increments."

Nic turned around, stunned to find she was back, and speaking fluent Italian. She stood a little ways apart from him. Already she'd drained most of the water from her bottle.

"Sit down, *signora*, and I'll hand her to you." She did his bidding.

He placed the baby in her arms and gave her the bottle. "I'll get you a clean towel."

"I have some here." Bruno had come from the galley with more supplies and a tray of sandwiches and fruit. He put everything on the table.

The great African sun had come up over the horizon, spilling sunlight through the windows of the jet. It reached her head and shoulders, creating a nimbus around her. She had a certain compelling presence. Nic realized he was staring at her like before, only this time she was awake and didn't like it.

He didn't like that he couldn't take his eyes off her.

While she nestled the baby against her and tried feeding her again, he handed her an apple. She shook her head. "Would you like a sandwich?"

"No."

Nic could see this was going to take time. He bit into the fruit. "What's her name?"

"It doesn't matter." Lise put a towel on her shoulder and burped her. "We didn't expect to be alive this morning." She kissed her cheek.

"Your baby's ill," Nic spoke quietly.

"How observant you are," she mocked, before lines marred her features. "Last night's raid ensured no doctor would get through today."

If and when he did arrive, he wouldn't find anyone there. When things quieted down, those who had been displaced would return to their homes. As for the fate of the missionaries, of her husband in particular, his commander would know that information and relay it to Nic at a later date.

Shock still had hold of her. Until she talked about her husband, he decided it would be wise not to bring up the horror of last night. "As soon as we land you can take her to a hospital. After what you've been through, you should be checked out by a doctor too.

Those are some pretty bad abrasions on the side of your arm. I assume you have them elsewhere?" The bloodied sleeve of her khaki blouse ended above the elbow. She had wounds from the hem to her wrist. "If you'll allow me, I'll clean them for you."

Her jaw hardened. "No, thank you. Where are you taking me?"

"We've received word the mission people are waiting for you in Geneva, but the pilot might have to put down sooner for repairs."

"Of course," she muttered with dismissive sarcasm, refusing to look at him.

"Obviously you don't believe me. If I were in your shoes, I wouldn't either."

Her mouth formed a pencil-thin line. Had it really given him cardiac arrest a little while ago?

"My name's Nic. What's yours?"

"Since you're going to turn me over to the monster you work for, it doesn't matter either."

His curiosity got the better of him. "Which monster is that?"

"The name's not important. They're all the same. Human trafficking has gone on for centuries and always will."

It was a grim fact of life. No one knew it better than Nic, who was sickened by it every time his unit saw action. She knew it too. This woman had no reason to trust him.

She had fire. You wouldn't see her roll over and

die without a fight. It wouldn't surprise him to hear months from now she'd returned to the bush with her daughter to carry on without her husband.

"If we have to put down soon, you'd be wise to eat now, to preserve your strength for the baby." His suggestion went ignored. "You're welcome to shower. It will make you feel better."

She threw her head back. "Better for whom? The criminal who pays you enough money to carry out works of abomination? No, thanks. I know what my fate is, but until it happens I refuse to provide footage for the camera installed."

He took a fortifying breath. There was no reaching her. "I'll say this once. I'm not your enemy. If we have to put down in unfriendly territory, you're going to need my help to survive."

Though her eyes flamed a hot blue, her look was glacial. A fascinating dichotomy. "I'll take my chances."

Beneath all that incredible beauty she was tough as nails. But she would have no defense against butchers who beheaded their own kind, sometimes for no reason at all.

While he'd been talking to her, or rather talking at her, he noticed Rocco had made a course correction that put the sun on the other side of the plane. They were heading into clouds. Nic gave her one more encompassing glance before moving forward past the galley to the cockpit.

Rocco spoke the second he saw him. "We're losing fuel fast. I decided to head for Moroni and have already notified them."

"You made the right decision."

Moroni was the capitol of one of the Comoros islands, and a relatively safe place for the time being.

"What's the weather like there, Rocco?"

"Heavy ceiling. No rain yet."

The airport only had one short runway. You could land there if weather permitted. Even then you hoped you could stop before you ran out of asphalt. "What's your ETA?"

"Twenty minutes, give or take the wind off the ocean."

"I hope you feel lucky today. We need to get the repairs done fast. There's a sick baby on board."

"How sick?"

"She needs to be in a hospital." To Nic's chagrin there were few services for tourists in the ancient Arab town of Moroni, farther away. The makeshift clinic was good for bandages if they didn't run out.

Rocco nodded. "I feel lucky."

"Then let's do it."

CHAPTER FOUR

WHILE Lise continued to feed Celeste a little bit of milk at a time so she'd hold it down, she surmised there'd been a coup of some kind last night. She couldn't tell if her captor—a mercenary well-placed in the hierarchy of some powerful junta leader—was taking her to the man who gave him orders, or had decided to keep her for himself. Now that he had control of this jet, he could do whatever he wanted.

If he'd decided he wanted *her*, then she would have to outwit him. She wasn't so naive she didn't realize he'd enjoyed playing the ardent lover for those few minutes while the police showed up. Lise had kissed quite a few men in her life with a great deal of pleasure, and had enjoyed romantic relationships with several of them. She knew when a man wanted her.

Adam, the divorced British doctor working at the government hospital in Nairobi, was the last in a succession of men who'd wanted her so much he'd asked her to marry him. Too bad they always had to ruin a good thing. She'd told Adam she wasn't the marrying kind, and she hadn't seen or heard from him since. That was a month ago.

This rogue assassin who'd seized her in the night was another story altogether. In his evil world a woman only had one place. Lise knew he would have gone on devouring her if his goal hadn't been to get them aboard the jet ASAP. The fact that her husband had just been slaughtered and her child was dying meant less than nothing to him. How traumatic would *that* have been if it had been true?

He took his opportunities where and when they came, even in the backseat of a car in some Chakul backwater. He would use her for his pleasure until he tired of her, then decide if he would kill her or turn her over to the big *jefe*. But before either of those things happened, she would get away from him or die in the attempt.

Having made up her mind, she helped herself to a sandwich and some fruit, knowing she'd need all her strength for what lay ahead.

He'd warned her they might have to set down before reaching Switzerland, a destination he'd never intended to reach. Her anxiety escalated when she saw the "fasten seat belt" sign flash sooner than she'd anticipated, but it didn't matter. She was determined to sabotage his plans and escape after they landed.

Before she could get up to strap Celeste in her

REBECCA WINTERS   45

own seat, he entered the club compartment. Lise took an involuntary breath at the sight of his blatantly masculine physique, shocked he had that effect on her. She couldn't pin down his nationality, but his dark coloring combined with aquiline features possessed a definite Mediterranean flavor.

Once again his black eyes took their time wandering from her bush boots to the braid secured on her head, missing nothing in between. She swallowed hard, because he didn't bother to hide what he'd like to do to her once he'd got business accomplished. "I'll take care of your baby while you fasten yourself in." He plucked Celeste from her arms.

Comply with his wishes. That was the way to let him think he was winning this particular war. Later on she'd catch him off guard and make her break.

Not long after he'd strapped himself in, the jet began a fairly steep descent through the clouds. Maybe they would crash, foiling his plans. Maybe this was how God was answering her prayers. If so, she was ready.

In the end the wheels touched down on solid ground, with water to the side of them. The jet glided to a stop close to a building she could see out the window. There was a sign in French and Arabic. Prince Sai Ibrahim Airport. That meant they'd landed in the Comoros, on the Indian Ocean. She remembered flying over the volcano that had erupted here maybe five years earlier.

It was a place of white beaches and coconut palms, but few facilities. Adam had talked about a recent outbreak of cholera here. Her glance darted to Celeste. The plan to lose herself in a crowd was out. Depending on how long they had to wait for repairs, she might manage to get on board another plane when one flew in.

While she was deep in thought, the jet taxied to the front of a nearby hangar. The forbidding male who called himself Nic got out of the seat. He shot her a warning glance. "Don't even think about trying to get away from me."

Heat crept into her cheeks at realizing her thoughts had been so transparent.

"You have no money or ID and could end up in the hands of men more unscrupulous than myself. At least aboard the jet there's food for you and the baby. You can trust it won't give you parasites. While I'm gone, Bruno will see to your needs."

Bruno was just another henchman!

Beneath her lashes she watched his powerful body disappear down the aisle and leave the jet with the pilot, whose brown mustache matched his hair. She judged him and Bruno to be in their early forties.

On cue, the steward came out of the galley. "The repairs could take until evening. If you'll follow me, I'll show you to the bedroom, where you and the baby can rest."

Much as the mere mention of the word *bedroom*

made her cringe in the context of her captor, she needed sleep desperately. Celeste could lie on the bed with her. When she got hungry, Lise would be able to feed her in comfort.

"Thank you," she murmured, deciding it would be best to cooperate until there was another opportunity to get away. She released the baby from the straps and carried her down the aisle to the suite with its private bathroom. Despite her precarious circumstances, she welcomed the luxury if only for Celeste's sake.

"I'll bring a fresh bottle for the *bambina*."

A few minutes later he returned with supplies. When he left again, she planned to lock the door, but there wasn't one. Even if there were, it wouldn't keep her captor out if he wanted in.

She gave the baby a quick bath in the bathroom sink and put a fresh diaper on her. After feeding her again, she put her down near the center of the bed. While the baby slept, she took advantage of the toiletries to brush her teeth and wash her hair while she showered.

If there was a hidden camera, she didn't care at this point. It was heavenly to wash off the grime and the blood. Her arm was sore. She had abrasions on her hip and thigh, but nothing too serious.

After stepping out of the shower, she covered herself in lotion. A white terry cloth robe hung on the hook. She wrapped herself in it and wound another towel around her hair to dry it. Unbound, it fell below her shoulders. She'd let it hang loose for an hour, then rebraid it.

When she emerged from the bathroom, the bed called to her. Lise sank down on top near the baby, thinking she would just close her eyes for a few minutes.

With the help of two mechanics, Rocco and Nic had made the necessary repairs so they could take off again. They came on board and washed their hands in the galley sink. Nic reached for a towel to dry himself.

Bruno had food and coffee waiting for them. Nic eyed him as they ate. "How are the passengers?"

"They've been sleeping for hours."

"Bene." Rest would help the shock to wear off. "I'll go back and let her know we're about to take off again."

He left the galley. In a few long strides down the aisle he came to the bedroom door and knocked. There was no response. He tapped again before opening it a crack.

The sight of the robed woman lying on her back with her long dark hair splayed across the pillow robbed him of breath. He could still smell the mango fragrance from the shampoo she'd used.

His gaze took in the mold of her beautiful female form. She reminded him of a goddess in repose. The baby lay next to her. She was awake. Her brown eyes caught sight of Nic. Something about her helplessness tugged at his emotions before she started to cry. The noise woke her mother.

In that first second when she saw him standing there, her eyes launched fiery blue missiles at him. The next second she scrambled to her feet, cinching the belt of her robe tighter before she gathered the baby off the bed.

While she used her daughter for a shield, her glistening hair settled about her shoulders in enticing disarray. Color seeped into those classic cheekbones. She was by far the most gorgeous woman he'd ever laid eyes on in his life. Considering the number of incredibly attractive women he'd come across in his thirty-three years, that was saying a lot.

"I *did* knock," he assured her, "but it appears you needed your sleep. I came to let you know the plane has been repaired and is now able to continue on. If you'll dress and come to the club compartment with the baby, we'll be able to take off."

"I need to feed her a little more milk first."

"Take the time you need."

"Grazie."

"Prego." He closed the door. Though she'd thanked him, he knew she didn't trust him as far as she could throw him and would try to disappear the moment he turned his back.

While Nic walked forward, he was imagining her surprise when he actually delivered her to the safety of missionary staff waiting for her in Geneva. She would receive immediate help for her baby. Like any loving mother, she would make certain her sick child's needs were taken care of before she gave in to her grief for her lost husband.

A few minutes later, the woman he couldn't get off his mind came to the club area dressed in her bloody, dirt-stained outfit. Yet, because of her carriage and poise, the clothes didn't matter. Neither did the way she wore her hair. It was in a braid now, hanging down her back.

She had unforgettable looks and an indomitable will. He feared the combination was going to haunt him indefinitely. Fate had played a cruel trick to place her in his path this close to the imprisonment he'd been dreading since he was fifteen.

As he watched her fasten the baby down and strap herself in, he found himself remembering the way her mouth had opened to the urgent pressure of his. For those earthshaking moments while he discovered he couldn't get enough of her, she'd clung to him.

Though her response had been out of fear for her life, he knew in his gut she'd sensed the chemistry between them, even if she was a married woman. He should be feeling guilt for that moment of unexpected, indescribable pleasure, but so help him he couldn't summon any. Just thinking about it forced him to suppress a groan.

Once again the "fasten seat belt" light came on.

The jet taxied to the runway. In moments they were airborne. When it went off again, Nic unfastened the baby's straps and cuddled her while Bruno served dinner to her mother.

Nic liked the way the baby clung to him, almost as if she recognized him. In all probability she was used to her father holding her and wondered where he was. At least she didn't cry and was willing to let Nic comfort her.

She smelled sweet. Her mother must have washed her hair with the same shampoo. He walked her over to the window. "Do you know where we're going, *petite*? It's far away from your bush home, but you wouldn't be safe there."

"No thanks to men like you," her mother lashed out. When he turned around, he saw that she'd finished her dinner and had put it on the table. "I'll take her now."

The baby was so sweet Nic didn't feel like relinquishing her yet. "Why? She's content with me for the moment."

Her rage had made her eyes suspiciously bright. He'd wanted to give her a little break, but he could see she didn't want one. The baby was all she had left in the world. Nic sensed she needed her daughter to cling to right now.

Without saying anything else, he handed the baby over to her and went back to the galley to pour himself another cup of coffee. While he drank it, black, he stared blindly into space.

She'd lost her husband and feared for her own life. He would like to provide her with the answers she sought, as without being able to trust Nic her self-imposed silence was only escalating the horrors in her mind. Her grief had to be excruciating.

He didn't want to add to her terror, but there was one thing he *could* do that he felt sure she would welcome. It went against all the rules, but he didn't care. This woman didn't deserve to suffer like this any longer.

CHAPTER FIVE

THE next time Lise opened her eyes, the cabin lights had gone on. It was night again. Had it really been twenty-four hours since the village had been attacked? They'd stolen her watch from her so she didn't know the exact time.

She nestled the baby closer and gave her some more from the bottle, but she barely sucked on the nipple. Her color wasn't good. Lise feared she was slowly dying. "Don't worry, little darling. Just as soon as we land, we're going to get away from these terrible men and go straight to a hospital," she vowed.

To her shock, Nic was standing right by her. He must have heard her talking to Celeste because he lifted her out of her arms. Exchanging the bottle with his phone, he said, "While I take care of her, go ahead and call whomever you want. Tell them you're safe and will be arriving in Geneva within the hour."

Lise stared at it for a moment. The military were

known to have special satellite flight phones, but such highly technical equipment had built-in tracking devices. Whatever number she called, he would know who it was.

She didn't dare phone her parents. If it put them in danger, she couldn't stand it. Her thoughts flew to Adam. If she tried to reach him—assuming he was still alive—it could put him and the whole clinic in jeopardy. The last thing she would do was contact the people helping her with the motorbike fundraiser.

What she felt like doing was throwing it in his striking face, but she resisted the impulse for fear he'd retaliate in ways that sent chills through her body. She held the phone out to him. "If we're going to be touching down soon, then there's no need to call anyone. You said I was being met. Seeing is believing."

His black brows furrowed before he took it from her.

"Please give me back my baby."

He lowered the little girl to her arms. "How long has she been sick?"

"Too long."

"I'll arrange for an ambulance to take you and your baby to the hospital the minute we land." She didn't act as if she'd heard him. Nic couldn't help but admire her grit. "Is there anything I can get for you? Do for you?"

Her features closed up. "Leave me alone?"

The question couldn't have been plainer than that. Except for his betrothed, who'd screamed at him and thrown rocks on the day of their betrothal years ago, no woman had ever rejected him under any circumstances. It rankled, even though he knew she was in mourning and terrified of him.

Oddly disturbed, he went to the galley. "Keep an eye on her until we land, Bruno." The other man nodded while Nic moved forward to the cockpit.

The pilot eyed Nic as he slipped into the co-pilot's seat. He needed to get his mind on something else besides the tantalizing female and her baby. Lack of sleep had to be the reason for his preoccupation with their mystery passenger.

"She must be someone *molta importante*," Rocco murmured, tapping into Nic's wavelength.

"You're right. For my father to offer his plane, you'd think she was a head of state." She had the bearing of one. Nothing seemed to faze her. Her fluency in two languages led him to believe she was fluent in more. She spoke continental French with a definite refinement. Her Italian could have been learned in Milan.

If she'd been in Chakul for a long time, her Swahili was no doubt impeccable too. It implied an upbringing and education beyond normal bounds. She kept the grieving over her husband to herself, but it was nothing to do with him.

Nic frowned, determined to stay away from her. He had to keep his identity secret.

His part in this emergency evacuation was done.

When they landed, he'd hand her over to the person sent from the mission headquarters before flying on to San Ravino. Once he arrived at the palace, his father would fill him in on the details and reveal her identity before he rejoined his unit.

"Lise? Over here!"

As she stepped off the plane with Celeste, she recognized Assistant Secretary Laval of the mission standing next to an ambulance parked nearby. His thatch of sandy hair stood out in the semidarkness. Because she'd been so convinced her captor had lied to her, she thought she must be dreaming.

"Giles?"

He ran up and gave her a big hug. "Welcome back. *Dieu merci* that you and the baby were flown out of there before you were killed." He put a hand on her elbow and ushered her toward the ambulance. "I understand she's very sick. Get in the back. We'll have you to the hospital in five minutes."

The relief of knowing Celeste was going to receive help caused her eyes to film over. But before climbing in she looked back at her imposing captor, who lounged against the opening into the jet. A shiver raced over her body at feeling his eyes narrowed on her.

She'd been horrible to him, but she hadn't known. *She hadn't known.* "Just a minute, Giles. I need to go back and thank the soldier who saved my life!"

"There's no time. The pilot is already signaling they have to leave."

Lise could see that. She needed to do something. *"Merci, monsieur!"* she cried from her heart.

He nodded his dark, handsome head before disappearing inside the body of the plane. When the door closed, the sound bounced off every chamber of her heart. He'd risked his own life for her and Celeste. If he hadn't pretended to be her lover at the checkpoint, she shuddered to think what their fate might have been.

To say thank-you didn't begin to convey her overwhelming gratitude. She wanted to call him back, but it was too late now. The jet's lights were flashing and it was already taxiing toward the runway. For a moment she glimpsed a logo on the side, but the plane was too far away for her to make it out.

By the time she'd climbed inside and they were off, the paramedics were already working on the baby. Lise turned to Giles. "What's the word on the Fillouxes?"

"Nothing yet, but as long as there's no news, that gives us hope. Tell me what happened."

Her throat constricted. "It was terrifying."

By the time they'd reached the emergency entrance at the Hôpital Saint-Pierre, she'd finished relating what she'd lived through.

"Do you know the name of the man who rescued us?"

"No, but he was part of the covert operation called in when the boundary war broke out."

Her gaze fastened on the baby, lying so still. "At first I thought it might be a coup."

"Not this time."

"Do my parents know what's happened to me?"

"I informed them you'd been rescued from an uprising and were safe, but since you were being flown home, it would be up to you to contact them."

"Thank you. I'll call them after I know the baby's condition. I'm so afraid she's going to die." Her voice trembled.

One of the paramedics looked at her. "She's very sick and dehydrated, but luckily for her she was flown here in time for us to get an IV going at least." That was thanks to the courageous soldier who'd snatched them from the jaws of certain death. "Just keep praying."

"I haven't stopped since I woke up in the Fillouxes' hut. Poor little Celeste. They can't be dead, Giles. They just can't be!"

He patted her arm. "Our sources are doing everything they can to feed us information, but I'll tell you this much. You can't go back there again or you'll be killed. Until the Chakul government makes fundamental changes, we've recalled all our missionaries from the area."

She took a fortifying breath. "I realize it's too dangerous. My plan now is to care for Celeste so your people don't have to worry about her. I'll stay here at the hospital with her and take her home if I have to."

"Bless you for that," he murmured as the door of the ambulance was opened. "We've been inundated with other emergencies and are short-handed at the moment. In case the worst has happened to them, be assured we're looking for the baby's next of kin."

Lise shuddered to think of the Fillouxes really being dead.

She and Giles followed the paramedics who guided the gurney through the emergency entrance. "The infant ICU is on the third floor. They're waiting for her."

While they stood at the elevator she gave him a hug. "Thank you for everything you've done, Giles. I'll handle things from here. You're needed in a dozen places, so you go."

A tired smile broke out on his face. "You're a very special person, Lise. If anything had happened to you…"

"But it didn't."

"I'll call you tomorrow. Hopefully with good news."

"Hopefully," she whispered, before getting on the elevator with the baby.

As the door closed, she was reminded of Nic, who'd disappeared behind another door a short while ago. She knew the jet was spiriting him away to a new hot spot somewhere on the globe. The thought of it gave her a strange sense of loss.

How long before he was killed during a daring airdrop into enemy territory? A man who did that for a living wasn't made of the stuff of ordinary men.

* * *

Nic had just pulled on a sport shirt and trousers when his butler came in the bedroom with his morning coffee. "Did you sleep well, Your Highness?"

No. Last night he'd relived that kiss in the backseat of the car so many times he'd awakened feeling like he'd never been to bed.

"Well enough, *grazie*," he muttered. "How are you, Guido?"

"Except for my back giving me trouble now and again, I can't complain. Their Majesties would like you to join them for breakfast in the morning room at nine."

"Please tell them I can't. I'm leaving the palace in a few minutes."

"On another one of those missions I suppose? They'll be disappointed."

He slipped into his Italian loafers. "We enjoyed a late supper together before going to bed."

"Need I remind you how much they long for your company?"

"No, but you will do it anyway," he teased the butler, who'd been his friend since childhood.

"They're living next month."

"I know." Nic didn't want to think about next month, when his whole world was going to change. Right now he couldn't think about anything except the woman who'd called out her thanks to him last night, before climbing into the ambulance with the baby.

Finally he'd gotten a kind word out of her. It had

taken all the willpower he possessed not to go after her, but he had no right. Not on any score. She was someone else's wife. He wasn't free.

"Will you have the limo brought around to the east entrance, Guido? I'll be right down."

"*Si*, Your Highness. Please take care of yourself."

"I always do."

"Yes, but the time is so close to your getting out of the special forces. Your parents couldn't take it if anything happened to you now." He left the room as quietly as he'd come in.

Nic reached for his coffee, wishing Guido hadn't brought that up. While he drank, he phoned one of the pilots to alert them he was on his way. After the hours Rocco had put in, he would be dead to the world. It didn't matter who flew Nic to Raiders headquarters outside Rome. His father kept a small fleet and crew ready for business flights.

Twenty minutes later the pilot welcomed him aboard. "Is Your Highness headed for Rome this morning?"

Ignoring the nagging voice of his conscience, he said, "I have a detour to make to Geneva first."

"United Nations business?"

"*Si*," he lied, without compunction.

During the short flight he phoned his commanding officer, who praised him for getting the VIP to safety. There was still no news about the fate of any missionaries from that area. Nic was told things were quiet for the moment, but to stand by for a new assignment. One always came.

"Bene." He'd just been given enough time to do what he felt like doing. After he hung up, he phoned for a limo to pick him up at the airport.

Before long he was climbing into the backseat. *"Hôpital Saint-Pierre, s'il vous plaît."* Nic had seen the logo on the door of the ambulance. At the thought of seeing her again, a spurt of adrenaline spilled into his bloodstream, electrifying him. Terrifying him… because he'd never had a reaction like this to a woman in his life.

His terror doubled when he located the baby's private room and saw her standing next to the crib. Her fabulous dark hair hung loose about her shoulders. She was singing to the baby with the look of a mother's love on her face. Nic tried to dislodge the lump in his throat, but couldn't.

So deep was her concentration, she didn't know he'd entered the room, or else she'd assumed he was one of the nursing staff and didn't take notice. It gave him time to study the exciting mold of her feminine attributes clothed in an elegant tailored suit the color of a ripe apricot. She wore bone-colored sandals. Neither item could have come from the mission's hand-me-downs.

Whether in bush khakis or more formal clothes, she was so stunning tight bands constricted his lungs. Because of her VIP status, she was more of a mystery than ever. He shouldn't have given in to the temptation to see her and the baby again.

His glance darted to her daughter, who was hooked up to half a dozen monitors and an IV. Flashes of the scene inside the hut when he'd first scoped it out filled his mind. His rage at finding the two of them in such a perilous condition still threatened to choke him.

If the air assault had happened five minutes later, there wouldn't have been anyone in that hut. Nic didn't want to think about what their fate would have been. All he knew was that she and the baby were safe now. Her little girl was still holding on, *grazie al Dio*.

As he sucked in his breath she must have heard him, because she turned her head in his direction. When she realized who it was, he could have sworn the color of her remarkable blue eyes deepened. By the rise and fall of her chest, he could tell her breathing had grown more rapid. So had his!

He fought to control his emotions. "I had to come and see how she was doing. What's her name?" he asked in French.

"Celeste. On the jet I—I thought your tenderness to the baby was feigned," she stammered. He could see her swallowing hard. "Now I know you weren't pretending." She shook her beautiful head, causing her hair to swish against her shoulders. "How do I thank you for jumping into hell to save us?"

"It's my job," he quipped, "but if you want to thank

me, why don't you tell me your name. Let's start again, shall we? I'm Nic Tozzetti." He always used Aldo's last name in a situation like this. "And you are…?"

A half-smile broke out on her features. "Lise Belard."

CHAPTER SIX

LISE was incredulous. When she'd first seen him standing there in an expensive-looking cream sport shirt and tan chinos, her heart had run away with her. She'd thought she might hyperventilate. Now she was having trouble calming down.

Not only was he the most attractive man in existence, she owed him her life—and that put him in a category of one. This incredible man would always be unforgettable to her. But he was beyond reach, because she was chained to another until the end of her days and there wasn't a thing she could do about it—not after her parents had given her this much freedom to enjoy a normal life.

He moved closer. Like black fire his eyes swept over her, igniting every atom of her body. "I'm glad to see your arm has been doctored."

"They fixed me up last night."

"Have they put you on an antibiotic regimen?"

"Yes."

"That's good. I've tried to find out about your husband through my sources. I'm sorry to tell you there's been no word yet."

This was the time to tell him the truth, but as long as he thought she was married it was her best defense against the feelings he brought out in her. "Giles said the same thing," she murmured. "I just have to keep praying." She *was* praying for Celeste's parents.

He moved to the other side of the crib to look at the baby. "What's the diagnosis on her condition?"

"The pediatrician came by a little while ago. They found eggs in her stool sample. The little darling has hookworm." Since her last bottle, she'd fallen asleep.

Nic frowned. "How do you think she got it?"

"I'm not sure. Probably through her hands. It's possible someone had been playing with her who'd been in contact with soil filled with worms and she didn't wash her hands before touching Celeste."

"But we know it's treatable," he assured her.

"Yes. The doctor has already started her on a drug regimen. She'll have to be in the hospital for the next day or two. Besides dehydration, her blood count's a little low. They're going to give her iron to ward off anemia."

Her gaze lifted to his. She could feel her eyes filling with tears. "If it hadn't been for you, she'd be dead one way or the other. I'm so ashamed when I think about how terrible I was to you on the plane."

A tiny pulse throbbed at the corner of his hard male mouth. The memory of the way it felt and tasted sent an unbidden thrill through her body. She couldn't stop what she was feeling any more than she could stop breathing.

"I could have been the enemy. You had every right to fear me. A woman like you… Well…let's both be happy you and Celeste are in safe hands now."

"Yes." She bit her lip. "You're very kind. I'm so glad you came to see her, otherwise I wouldn't have known how to reach you to apologize and thank you properly."

He cocked his dark head. "Since she's sleeping so peacefully, why not have lunch with me in the cafeteria and I'll consider it a proper thank-you."

Her pulse sped up. "I'd like that." A part of her knew it would be dangerous to get to know him any better. But another part was desperate to be with him a little longer. A quick meal around other people couldn't get her into too much trouble. Yet even as she reasoned that way, she knew she was only lying to herself.

He followed her out of the room. They moved past the cot propped against the wall. "I see you slept in here last night."

"Yes. I want to be close by when she opens her eyes." On the phone, her parents had begged her to stay at the palace last night, but she'd told them she couldn't leave the baby right now. However, she had gone home long enough to shower and pack a bag for a few days' change of clothes.

"She's a lucky little girl to have a devoted mother like you."

Guilt smote her for keeping up the lie. "Celeste is an angel."

One of the younger nurses passed them in the hall. Lise told her where they were going. The nurse said she'd keep an eye on Celeste, then indicated the cafeteria was on the second floor to the right of the north elevator. While she spoke, her eyes remained fastened on Nic. He was such a gorgeous man—no woman was immune.

Once they reached the cafeteria, they pushed their trays through the line to get the food they wanted. Female heads turned at the sight of Nic, who paid the bill and found them a table for two over against the wall.

He ate part of his *croque monsieur* while she started on her *omelet au jambon*. After he drank some coffee he said, "Where's your home?"

"In central France." Another lie, but it was close enough to the truth that she didn't cringe. "What about you?"

"Central Italy." That covered a lot of territory. A man doing secret missions for the military didn't dare give away anything he didn't have to.

She sipped her coffee. "Your French sounds so authentic, I wouldn't have known."

His lips twitched, causing her blood pressure to skyrocket. "As does your Italian." He finished off the rest of his sandwich. "How long did you work in the bush?"

"It's been five years now."

He studied her until she averted her eyes. "You know you can't go back there. They've got your husband. Now they're looking for you. I'm talking about your attackers and the government itself."

"I know." More tears slipped down her cheeks. She dashed at them with her hands. Nic would think she was suffering over her husband. In truth, her deep sadness had to do with the Fillouxes, and the fact that she couldn't go back to Chakul.

When she'd told her parents what had happened, they'd been shocked but relieved she was back in one piece and told her it was time she stayed home for good. It was code for one thing: they expected her to get acquainted with her betrothed. Gutted by the realization of the duty awaiting her, she'd returned to the hospital and had cried all night while she watched over Celeste.

A bronzed, hard-muscled arm reached across the table. His hand founds hers and squeezed it to comfort her. She felt like the biggest fraud on earth. "What can I do for you?"

She looked across at him. "You've done more than enough for us already. I should be asking you that question." Her voice throbbed as she eased her hand from his. "How soon do you have to go back?"

"When my superior contacts me."

"That means you're on call twenty-four hours a day?" He nodded. "Are you a career officer?" Maybe she was wrong, but she thought he hesitated for a moment before he slowly nodded again. "Evidently you love what you do."

He leaned forward. "When there's an outcome like yours, I'm reminded of what it's all about and realize no other job satisfaction could come close."

"You're right. It couldn't." She buried her face in her hands. "Thank heaven for unselfish men like you."

Lise realized she was a disaster. She reached for the napkin to wipe her face and eyes. No more tears. "There are those who think I'm the most selfish, ungrateful excuse for a man who ever lived," he muttered, sounding far away.

She smiled. "Then they haven't talked to me." Lise was enjoying this too much. Better not get in any deeper. Making a decision, she stood up. "Thank you for lunch and the talk. Now I need to get back to Celeste."

He took a last sip of coffee. "I'll come with you. She's so cute I'd like to see if I can make her smile." Why did he have to say things like that?

Her legs felt less than substantial as they left the cafeteria. Their arms brushed getting in the elevator. Touching any part of him sent a jolt of electricity through her nervous system. When the doors opened to the third floor, she practically ran to Celeste's room to put distance between them.

* * *

Nic shouldn't have taken her to lunch. He shouldn't have flown to Geneva today! But a fire had been started when he'd first glimpsed her face in the backseat of that car. Holding her in his arms had felt right. The kiss they'd shared had done amazing things to him.

If he believed in magic, he would say she'd cast a spell over him. Feeling the way he did now, he didn't know how in blazes he was going to put it out.

When he entered the hospital room, Lise was already bent over the crib, changing the baby's diaper. At his approach she said, "Celeste? Nic Tozzetti is here. Can you smile for your guardian angel?"

As he took his place at the other side of the crib, the baby's brown eyes stared up at him. *"Bon après-midi, petite."* He rubbed his hand over the top of her head. Her brown hair was softer than silk. Nic tried to pick out Lise in her tiny features, but decided she must look like her father.

Celeste's father could still be alive. If so, he would come for his family. Nic had no business being here. The baby wouldn't smile for Nic, not even when he tickled her under the chin. *Because you're not her papa.*

Why hadn't he got that through his brain yet? Time to get out of the room now and never come back.

Lise sent him a rueful smile. "I think Celeste is still too sick to smile."

"She's missing her father." Nic had to say it. *"Au revoir, cherie."* He leaned over and kissed her forehead. When he rose up, his eyes engaged with a pair of impossibly blue ones. *"Au revoir*, Lise Belard. Let's hope you're soon given good news about your husband."

He didn't get a chance to hear her response because the same sandy-haired man who'd met her at the plane had come in the room. "Lise? How's the baby?"

"She's got hookworm, but she's going to be fine."

"That's wonderful."

"Giles? Let me introduce you to Nic Tozzetti. He's the man who rescued me and Celeste. Nic? This is Giles Laval, one of the directors of the mission here in Geneva."

They shook hands. "You did a great thing, Monsieur Tozzetti."

"Your mission has done remarkable things for the Chakul people over the years. Let's hope you'll be able to go back there one day soon."

"We live in hope." The man transferred his attention to Lise. "I came by to tell you we tracked down Marie's aunt, Marguerite Casalle. She lives in Neuchatel too. This is her address and phone number." He handed her a card. "I think it best she hears the news from you. When she learns what happened, I have no doubt Celeste will be welcomed."

Lise nodded without looking at Nic.

Something was going on. He'd been ready to walk

out the door, but Monsieur Laval's news combined with Lise's odd behavior didn't sit right with Nic, prompting him to remain in the room.

He watched the other man give the baby a little pat on the head before he said goodbye and left on another mercy errand.

When they were alone again, Nic could feel a certain tension coming from her. Alarmed, he trapped her gaze. "It appears you're looking for some missionary in your organization to take care of your baby when she's released from the hospital. If you're thinking of going back to Chakul to find your husband, I won't let you. You as much as step off a plane or a boat and you'll never make it back home again."

She clung to the crib railing. "I'm not planning any such thing."

"But you want to," he fired back. "When I leave, I'll get in touch with my superior. Maybe a group of us can go in and look for your husband. I'll need a picture. If you don't have one on you, I'm sure Monsieur Laval has one at headquarters."

"No!" she cried out in panic.

He inhaled sharply. "Why not? It's what we do." When she didn't make a move to give him one, he headed for the door. If he stayed any longer, he'd never want to go.

"Wait—" She hurried toward him.

Nic might not have known her long, but he sensed she was holding something back. Maybe her husband was the VIP, in a much bigger political scheme, and she was trying to warn Nic off without giving away the score.

"It's truth time, Lise," he ground out. "Who's your husband? Since I was asked to get you and your baby out of Chakul in the dark of night, I have a right to know."

She moistened her lips nervously. "I agree, but this isn't what you think."

"Then enlighten me!"

"I—I'm not married." Her voice faltered.

Not married?

His body tautened. All this time she'd *lied* to him? What were all those tears about?

Not only had she just dealt him a blow on a deeply personal level, he'd been prepared to do something unprecedented by trying to find her husband! Her lie had basically shattered him.

"I presume Monsieur Laval doesn't know you're not married to the father of your baby. Is that why you didn't want me to go to mission headquarters for a picture?"

"No—" She shook her head in despair. "You don't understand. I'm not a missionary."

The revelations flew at Nic so fast he had trouble processing them, yet it was all making an odd kind of sense. Missionaries weren't normally labeled as VIPs. "What were you doing in Chakul if you weren't with the mission?"

She threw her head back. "I was there on my own, to help."

"For five years?" At this point Nic was incredulous.

"Yes."

"Do you have medical training?"

"No, but I've learned to do a lot of things. One of the missionary couples, Jean and Marie Filloux, became my good friends. Celeste is *their* daughter, not mine. If they're dead, my heart is broken for her."

Nic passed a hand over his face. Because of the love she'd shown for the baby, he would never have guessed Celeste wasn't hers. His thoughts were running all over the place. When he remembered the way she'd kissed him back in the car, the memory took on new meaning now that he knew she was a single woman. In fact, his heart gave a distinct kick, rocking his whole body.

"How did you come to be with the baby?"

"While I was out delivering medical supplies to the tent village, the uprising started. I had no idea what had happened until I got back to my hut and was attacked. I didn't know anything else until I woke up bound and gagged in the Fillouxes' tent with Celeste."

He rubbed his chest absently. "I was surprised to find anyone alive."

She moaned. "It was the most terrifying experience I've ever lived through. Since you assumed she was mine, I let you believe it, because I wanted to be with her when the end came."

"Like I told you earlier, you were inordinately brave."

"The baby gave me courage I don't possess." He heard her deep sigh. "She needs her parents."

"Don't give up on them yet." He wanted to say something more comforting, but couldn't. In all likelihood they were dead.

She stared at him. "In case they're gone, Giles knows the law and has been looking for her closest relatives. He's found one aunt living in Neuchatel."

"That's not very far from here." Against everything his conscience was doing to warn him, he said, "I'll drive you there tomorrow and we'll tell her what's happened. The hospital staff will watch over Celeste. She'll be in the best of hands while we're gone."

"I know that." A sad look crept into her expression. "When she's better, her aunt will take one look at her and want her."

"I don't doubt it. She's very precious. Anyone would want her." Lise would be the first in line.

She eyed him solemnly. "You might get a call tonight and have to fly out of the country."

"True, but I'm not planning on it." Right now Lise was the only thing that mattered to him. No crisis, no person, no royal betrothal was going to keep him from being with her tomorrow. He couldn't think beyond that.

Since the baby had fallen asleep, Nic didn't kiss her for fear he'd wake her up. He darted a glance at Lise. "I'll be here in the morning. We'll grab some breakfast on the way. *Ciao, signorina*."

Even with so much more at stake he couldn't deny that it was liberating to know she wasn't *signora*.

CHAPTER SEVEN

THE next morning, when the nurse came for Celeste to do some lab work, Lise was allowed to take a shower in one of the staff's own facilities. After having to wear her hair in a single braid in the bush, it was sheer luxury to let it hang loose from a side part, without fear of creeping, crawly things making it a target.

With the addition of some pink frost lipstick and an application of cherry blossom body lotion—also taboo in Chakul, to prevent the insects from dive-bombing her—Lise felt ready to take on the day.

She dressed in a smoky-blue silk blouse with cap sleeves and a denim skirt. When she returned to the hospital room in her sandals, Nic was standing at the window with his hands on his hips. She got a fluttery sensation in her stomach. He was dressed in a black polo shirt and jeans that molded his powerful thighs; his male appeal reached out to her like a living thing.

"Bonjour, monsieur."

Their gazes collided. *"Buongiorno, signorina."* His deep voice sounded even lower this morning. She felt its gravelly tone permeate her body. "Where's our *petite* Celeste?"

Lise knew he didn't mean "our" in the literal sense, but she found herself fantasizing about it anyway. An ache passed through her body. During the night she'd had a huge talk with herself. She would enjoy this day with Nic—a memory she would treasure like a rare book. And in the years to come, when she needed to remember she'd once experienced joy, she would open it.

"Getting some bloodwork done. I think we'd better go before she comes back or I won't want to leave her." She reached for her handbag on the table and they walked out to the elevator.

Nic studied her while he pushed the button. "I've made inquiries this morning. There's still no word about her parents."

Their eyes held. "The dark continent of Africa," she murmured. "The people are so sunny, I never liked the term. I like it even less now."

He grimaced before the doors opened and they got in the elevator. "You're going to miss Chakul, aren't you?"

She looked away. "You can't imagine." Being of real service to people had helped her forget what the reality of her royal birth had in store for her. But no matter how ghastly her marriage to Prince Raimondo would be, she would find a new way to help people and throw herself into it.

They rode to the main floor and headed for the hospital entrance. "My rental is parked across the street." He cupped her elbow while they dodged the busy traffic. Long after he'd helped her in the car, fingers of delight still ran up her arm. To be with him like this brought her pleasure-pain almost too intense to bear.

Geneva, the ancient town the Romans took from Helvetia in 121 B.C., and now one of the great financial cities of the world, sat at the west end of Lake Geneva where it met the Rhone. To reach Neuchatel, they followed a route bordering the northern side of the lake. As they drove, they made desultory conversation, something she badly needed after the horror she'd recently lived through.

They stopped at a charming lakeside restaurant in Saint-Prex, where they feasted on hot chocolate and warm, mouth-watering croissants. The sweet butter and homemade *confiture*, made from the grapes of the surrounding vineyards, added to their delectation.

Like a good omen, the warm sun broke through the mist evaporating off the placid blue waters of the lake, promising a day of enchantment like no other.

Lise was with a man like no other. She hugged the excitement of it to her heart.

Once back in the car, they reached the turnoff at Lausanne and headed straight for Lake Neuchatel, farther north. En route she phoned the Casalle woman. Another woman answered.

When Lise explained she was a close friend of Marie Filloux from Chakul, and wanted to meet with her, the woman told her to come to the apartment. Marguerite would be waiting for her.

After she'd hung up, she answered the question in Nic's eyes. "I imagine it was a housekeeper who picked up. She said to come. Apparently Marguerite lives in an apartment."

One black brow lifted. "Why the anxious look?"

"I don't know. It's all so surreal. Celeste's in the hospital, the status of her parents is unknown, and we're about to ask a perfect stranger to consider raising her niece's baby if worse comes to worse—" Lise hated it when her voice shook like this.

Nic's hand reached out to grasp hers. "It's going to be all right. The only thing to do is take this a step at a time."

For a minute she clung to it, needing his strength before letting go. "I presume that's how you've made it through your years of service in the military? It's good advice. I'd better adopt it or I'm not going to make it."

They pressed on toward their destination. He seemed deep in thought, but there was a comfortable silence between them as she stared out the passenger window. Soon Lake Neuchatel came into view.

Lise hadn't been here since her late teens, when

she and her friends had ridden bicycles through the Jura Mountains and ended up covering the lake from one end to the other. It was another universe of luscious vineyards and ancient villages clustered at the water's edge.

After her teens she'd studied economics at UCLA in Southern California. Her father had insisted that one day, when she was ruler of Haut-Leman, she would need a fundamental grasp of world business and finance in order to make the right decisions for its future. An American university would give her a new perspective.

For graduation, she and her roommates had taken a trip to Africa, and she'd fallen in love with the country. Until a few days ago she'd led a fulfilling life there. Now suddenly it had all fallen apart, and she'd met a man who'd set her on fire. He was the only man who held that distinction and always would.

He's forbidden to you, Lise.

It wasn't fair, but then life hadn't been fair to Jean and Marie. Or dear little Celeste.

She'd promised herself she wouldn't cry anymore. Still dry-eyed, she reached for the card in her purse with Marguerite's address and handed it to him. They were entering the city, with its old town of one hundred-plus fountains built in the sixteenth century. She and her friends had ridden around them on their bikes, fascinated by the town's history.

That was when she'd been a carefree girl. She had to admit her parents had been wonderful to let her sow her oats, wild and otherwise, all this time. But she'd done all the dancing there was to do. Now she was a woman with royal responsibilities. The moment she'd dreaded all her life was finally upon her.

While her emotions were in chaos, Nic put the coordinates in the car's global finder, and it didn't take long before they pulled up in front of a small apartment building. He sent her a penetrating glance. "Are you ready to go in, or do you need more time?"

The man had X-ray vision, and seemed to know what she was thinking and feeling without a word being said.

"Let's do it," she said with false brightness, and got out of the car before he could come around to help her. Marguerite's apartment was on the main floor. Lise approached it first and knocked.

The unsmiling dark-haired woman who opened the door betrayed her Italian heritage with her first greeting in broken French. Lise responded in Italian. With an immediate connection made, the woman's relief changed her demeanor. She introduced herself as Olivia, Marguerite's companion.

Then came the explanation that Marie's aunt was very ill with Parkinson's disease. "She has trouble swallowing, but today is a better day than some." Lise exchanged a loaded glance with Nic, who squeezed her upper arm before they followed the wiry caregiver into the salon.

The frail woman in a wheelchair with a blanket over her legs lifted one hand a little in greeting. "Come over here. How's Marie?" Because her body shook so hard, she spoke with great difficulty.

"Marguerite hasn't seen her niece in over a year," Olivia explained. "She writes letters, but it's not the same as a good visit. They're the only family each other has."

About now Lise needed all the inspiration possible in order to know what to say to this frail woman. She kissed her on both cheeks.

"*Enchantée*, Madame Casalle." Nic took over while Lise tried to gather her wits. "I'm Nic Tozzetti. We've just flown in from Africa for a short visit before going back. Lise offered to bring their little Celeste for her yearly medical checkup. She's just fine."

"Yes, she is!" Lise found her voice at last, thankful for this amazing man who always understood what to do. "I have a picture of all of them in my wallet." With shaky hands she opened it, and held up half a dozen photos for the older woman's perusal.

"Ah." A smile broke out on her drawn face.

"Isn't she adorable? I think three months is the cutest age. Her smile lights up the world," Lise said softly. "Jean and Marie both look wonderful too, don't you think?"

Marie's aunt nodded.

"You keep these pictures. Did Marie tell you how well the motorbikes have worked? See both of them on their bikes?"

"Oui."

"They're amazing. You can go everywhere on them, even in the rain when the roads are impassable or there's no road at all. With the bikes I had shipped in, we've been able to deliver medicine and food all over the flooded areas. The people are so grateful for anything we do for them. Marie and Jean have never been happier in their lives." It was the truth. Especially if they were in heaven now.

The older woman looked tired. "Celeste will be wondering where I am, so we're going to leave. The minute I see Marie, I'll tell her to phone you. Even if you have a hard time talking, you can listen while she fills you in on the latest news."

Her warm brown eyes dimmed with tears. *"Merci."*

They kissed again before Olivia accompanied her and Nic to the door. She beamed. "Thank you for coming. Those pictures have done her a world of good."

"Bless you for taking such good care of her. *Arrivederci*, Olivia."

Lise didn't remember the walk to the car. Everything was a blur. Once they were both inside, Nic drew her into his arms.

"Oh, Nic—" Lise swallowed the sob in her throat. "I couldn't tell her the truth. Thank you for showing me the way." But the second the words came out, she realized the temptation to cling to him was too great.

She sniffed and pulled away from him before she couldn't. Afraid of her lack of self-control, she hugged the door. "That's twice you've saved the day."

"I only said what you would have."

"Maybe Marguerite will pass away before there's official word of Marie and Jean. In the meantime—"

"In the meantime—" he echoed her words "—let's call the hospital and see how Celeste is doing. If all is well, I'd like to spend a few hours on the lake with you." His suggestion caused her heart to thud so hard it couldn't be healthy. "I want to hear more about those motorbikes you had shipped in. They're not exactly cheap. I saw you on one in that last photo. You looked like a pro biker."

Uh-oh.

"To be truthful, I haven't had a real vacation in years. Have you?"

"No," she answered in a quiet voice.

"I think it's time we both had a break from all our worries. Use my phone." He handed her his cell.

A few more hours with him. Would it be so terrible when she knew that after today she could never see him again?

With the blood pounding in her ears she made the decision, right or wrong, to phone the hospital. First she had to call Information. Once connected, the woman at the switchboard rang the third-floor nursing station.

The day nurse looking after the baby was called to the phone. "This is Toinette."

"This is Lise Belard. How's Celeste?"

"She's doing fine. Her labs were all good. Her color's good. She was hungry for her bottle. That's always an encouraging sign. I just put her down and now she's asleep."

Lise heaved a sigh of relief. "Thank you. I'm going to be away a few more hours, then I'll be back."

"If you don't return until time for bed, no problem. Everyone is crazy about her."

"You're very kind. I'm going to hand the phone over to Monsieur Tozzetti. He'll give you his number in case you need to get hold of me."

She handed Nic his cell. The nurse shouldn't have told her she could stay away till late. Lise was out of willpower.

CHAPTER EIGHT

N IC called ahead to the port of Neuchatel to reserve a cabin cruiser rental, one totally outfitted for their pleasure. On the way to the dock he drove them to a sporting goods store for some swimwear and beach towels. They made their last stop at an *epicerie* to stock up on snacks and drinks.

Once they reached the port and parked, they were shown aboard the cruiser. Unlike other women he'd known, she knew her way around a boat. Happy to do tasks with him, she pulled her weight. He could tell she was no stranger to work or the water.

Other than a few sailboats, they seemed to have the lake to themselves. Near the middle he shut off the motor and lowered the anchor. By tacit agreement they changed into their swimsuits. He'd purchased black trunks.

Lise, who'd braided her glistening hair, emerged from the bedroom in a one-piece emerald-green outfit. With those long, gorgeous legs and stunning figure, he had to force himself not to stare. She bathed herself in sunscreen, then with a laugh tossed the tube to him.

"What has you so amused?" he drawled.

"Our farmer tans."

"Come again?"

"That's what they call them in California. We're both bronzed on our faces and arms while our legs look pale in comparison."

He answered with a slow smile of his own. "What were you doing in the U.S.?"

"I went to college there." On that note she dove over the side of the boat and started swimming around it like a mermaid.

Everything she said and did was a revelation to him. He waited until she came around the other side, then plunged in to intercept her. The big splash caught her in the face as she raised her head. Instead of being upset, she let out a laugh before chopping the water, forcing him to take a mouthful.

"So it's war you want—" Enticed by her sense of fun, he slapped the water again. Time and time again they bested each other until he slowly wore her down.

She finally lay back on top of the water. "Enough—no more—I should have remembered you're trained for underwater warfare."

He trod the water next to her, filling his eyes with her beauty. "You're welcome in my unit anytime."

Her eyes blazed a shocking blue in the sunlight. "No, thank you. I know my limitations."

"I bet you're a hot cyclist."

"The traffic is so bad in San Diego, I learned to ride one to get around campus. They're the only way to navigate under impossible conditions."

Nic moved closer so their legs got tangled. "Like the bush for example."

"Yes," she answered in a shaky voice, because he'd caught her around the waist with one arm while he kept them afloat with the other.

Her mouth was so close he could taste it. "You know what I want to do, don't you?"

He felt her body quiver. "If you don't kiss me, I think I'm going to die."

"Lise—" he cried as his mouth closed over hers. His hunger had been building since the first time he'd seen her. Now that he was able to give in to his desire, he never wanted this rapture to end.

The waves from a speedboat caused them to cling. While they rode the swells, every generous kiss she gave him grew into another, until he realized he was a prisoner of his own insatiable need of her. "I want you so much I'm in pain."

"I didn't know it could be like this, Nic," she half gasped. "I didn't know." Her haunting admission told him she was in the same euphoric state he was.

"Come with me, *squisita*," he urged in a husky voice, guiding her toward the ladder at the rear of the cruiser. When they reached the rungs, she couldn't lift herself up.

Nic sensed she was powerless and scaled the steps first, before pulling her out of the water into his arms. Once on deck, he wrapped them tightly around her. Now there was no water, no air between them. They melted into each other while their mouths feasted in reckless abandon.

Driven by the passion she'd aroused in him, he lowered her to the towels he'd spread out to warm in the sun. Finally he could carry out one of his fantasies. He undid her braid and plunged his hands into her dark, silky mane.

They took turns covering each other's face and throat with kisses. Every thrilling touch sent ripples of ecstasy through his body.

On the verge of carrying her below deck, he heard his cell phone ring. His entrancement was so complete he ignored the repeated summons and crushed her mouth once more. But his mind couldn't disengage completely. Only his father, his superior or his pilot could reach him on this line. They could wait. He had more important things to do.

But the persistence of his caller finally caused Lise to tear her lips from his. "That might be the hospital. Maybe something's wrong with Celeste."

The baby.

Nic had forgotten they'd left his number with the

nursing staff. If this call had anything to do with her, then it couldn't wait. He got to his feet and grabbed it from the lounge chair, tortured by having been forced to relinquish Lise for even one second.

A quick glance at the caller ID and he groaned. On her feet now, she stood in front of him, drying her glorious hair with a towel while she waited for the verdict. Anxiety had replaced the glazed look of desire in her eyes.

His gaze locked with hers. "It's not the hospital."

The good news about the baby not only didn't take away her fear, it changed her expression to one of agony. "You're going to have to leave on a new mission?" Even as she said the words, he watched some of the color drain from her gorgeous face.

He tossed the phone on the lounger and cupped her cheeks in his hands. "I'm not going to answer it." Starving for her, he plundered her mouth once more, needing her beyond life's necessities.

To his chagrin, she wasn't with him in the same way any longer. The ringing of the phone had shattered something so intensely beautiful and rare, and he wanted to rage at the injustice.

"You have to respond," she spoke against his lips. "You're Fireman Dan."

With that puzzling remark she pulled away from him, flashing him a heartbreaking smile. "I can see you've never heard of him. Fireman Dan is on the children's network in San Diego. When there's a fire, he has to go. He's made that promise, and the children know he *never* breaks his promise because he's a real live superhero."

"Lise—"

"While you take the call, I'll go downstairs and get dressed." She tried to slip out of his arms, but he held her fast.

"You can't go yet. We have to talk."

She kissed the corner of his mouth where an old scar was throbbing. "If I stay here we won't talk, and you know it."

"I swear I won't touch you." He let go of her. "See?" His hands remained in the air. "Trust me."

Nic swore she grew unsteady because his entreaty had gotten to her. She slowly sank down on one of the padded benches, clutching the towel to her chest. He pulled a lounger in front of her and sat facing her. With her hair in disarray and her eyes glowing a hot jewel-like blue against the emerald of her suit, she was a sea goddess come to life.

"Say something—" she begged softly.

He grasped her hands and kissed the palms. At his touch he felt her tremble. Already he'd broken his promise. He let go of them. "I never know how long I'm going to be away. Sometimes it's weeks. You'll be long gone from the hospital by then. Where will you be?"

"I—I'm not sure," she stammered. "It all depends on Celeste."

"Olivia told us Marie didn't have any other relatives. What will you do?"

She took a deep breath. "I plan to take care of her at home. If I get word her parents are dead, then I'll go through the legal means to adopt her."

Nic wanted to hold her, but he'd just claimed he wouldn't. "Where's home? Don't tell me it's in central France. Where do you really live?"

In a surprise move, she shot to her feet and put distance between them. He reached her in a few strides and slid his arms around her waist from behind. "Answer me, *squisita,*" he implored, kissing her neck. "I have to know where I can find you."

At hearing that endearment from his lips a second time, Lise's emotions were thrown into chaos. She grew weak with longings new to her. This was torture. She finally cried, "I can't do this!" and twisted away from him. But he caught her hand and forced her to face him. She looked panicked.

"*What* can't you do?"

She shook her head. "I don't know how to say this—not after the way I've behaved with you."

Already Nic didn't like this conversation. "You mean there's another man?"

"Yes," she fired, so fast he felt gutted.

"You *couldn't* be in love with him," his voice grated.

She rubbed her arms in what seemed like a frantic gesture. "Surely I don't have to tell you there are all kinds of love, Nic?"

His emotions were boiling to the surface. "Without what you and I have experienced every time we're in each other's arms, anything else couldn't be called by the same name."

Her throat was working hard. "He and I have known each other for a long time."

Jealousy consumed him. "Is it the doctor from Nairobi?"

"No, Nic. I'm talking before I went to Africa. This man and I have a bond."

"Then why didn't you marry long before now?" he demanded in fury.

"Because we don't want to get married."

"Say that again?"

Her jaw hardened a trifle. "Is that really so difficult to understand? You're not married. With your line of work I'm not surprised. Not everyone's cut out for it."

The truth of her words hit Nic like an exploding grenade. He'd had a series of relationships with women over the years, but being betrothed had drawn a line for him he'd never crossed. *Because no woman had ever brought him to the point where he'd wanted to throw away tradition for her.*

Now that it had happened to him, the shoe was on the other foot. Like his love life, *she'd* been operating hers by the same rules. She had every right, but he found he couldn't prevent what started pouring out of him.

"So between periods of living together, you and

this man go your separate ways, flinging hearts and body parts right and left, without regard for the trail of devastation you leave behind?"

She took another step backwards. "It's for that very reason I told you I can't do this anymore."

Her logic only enflamed him. "How many men have come close to selling their souls for you?"

"My relationships with other men have never gone this far!" she defended.

He'd been right the first time. She'd put a magic spell on him. Otherwise how could he find himself wanting to believe she'd just told him the truth?

"Does the man who has this hold on you possess so much money you're afraid to leave him? Was he the one who funded your motorbikes?"

"Does it matter, Nic?"

With that question she'd admitted her guilt. Except that she didn't feel guilty. She was one of those rare women who lived the life she wanted, and damn any man who tried to pin her down.

Just like you, Nic.

What had he and Aldo always said? If it looks too good to be true, it is!

His hands formed fists. "What's he going to say when you bring Celeste home and you tell him you want to adopt her? Will he fund that too?" he lashed out, in so much pain he felt turned inside out.

A shadow stole over her features. "I don't honestly know how he's going to react when he sees her. He's the kind of man who, if he wants a child, probably won't settle for anything less than one from his own body. To be honest, we've never had that conversation."

Wild with pain, he warned, "If you take the baby home with you, I can guarantee you'll have it."

She closed her eyes, obviously unable to look at him.

"What if he says no to all financial help if you insist on raising her?"

"Then I'll come up with the money myself."

"You mean you'll leave him?"

Her eyelids flew open. "If he can't bring himself to take a full role in being there for Celeste, then it will be a case of him leaving me."

That last remark said it all. Her dagger had hit the jugular.

She didn't want to be free of this other man. Nic didn't even figure in the equation, never mind that she could never fit into his. He had nowhere to go with his pain because he couldn't live with any part of this conversation.

In abject torment he reached for his phone to listen to the message from his superior. When he hung up a minute later, she'd disappeared below. Needing to channel his energy with something physical, he changed into his clothes before raising the anchor.

A day that had started out with such promise had just

imploded with the going down of the sun. There was nothing left but grist. He moved to the captain's seat to start the engine, realizing July had come early this year and he'd already begun living his dreaded nightmare.

Out of the corner of his eye he saw Lise walk on deck, her hair neatly braided once more. While they headed for port, she tidied the boat. By the time they reached the dock she had everything packed and ready for them to disembark.

The silence in the car during the drive back to Geneva was deadly. When they reached the outskirts he heard her say, "I'm sorry, Nic."

"Not as sorry as I am."

She stirred restlessly in the seat. "I don't want us to part this way. Please don't be bitter. We've lived through a life-and-death situation together. I'm never going to forget your sacrifice."

He ground his teeth. "It's all in a day's work."

"I didn't mean for it to go this far. If we hadn't kiss—"

"Let's leave it alone, shall we?" he cut in brutally. That kiss would haunt him forever.

Her fingers clawed the armrest. She lowered her head. "How soon do you have to fly out?"

"An hour ago."

"I was afraid of that." He detected a slight tremor in her voice. "Thank you for driving me to Marguerite's. Your being there made all the difference."

Nic needed her to stop talking. He turned into the

drive that took her to the hospital entrance. Though he pulled to a stop, he didn't shut off the motor.

She undid her seat belt and opened the car door, but she hesitated before getting out. He didn't know what she was waiting for. All he knew was that his agony had reached its zenith.

"*Adieu*, Mademoiselle Belard."

CHAPTER NINE

GOODBYE forever.

Nic's last words chased her all the way through the hospital to Celeste's room. She rushed over to the crib and looked down. There was no more IV tube. The baby was awake. When she saw Lise she smiled, and her little hands moved excitedly.

Celeste was so much better already, and it was the balm Lise's broken heart needed.

After washing her hands, she picked her up and walked around the room with her, holding her close against her neck and shoulder.

"It's you and me from now on, my little love."

An hour later the night nurse came in the room with a bottle. "Ah, you're back. She's been much brighter this evening. The medicine is doing its job."

"I can see that." She kissed the top of Celeste's head. "Do you think I'll be able to take her home soon?"

"The doctor said she'd improved so much he would release her tomorrow if everything stayed the same."

"That's wonderful." Lise thanked her, then sat down in the rocking chair and fed Celeste, whose appetite was back. In the bush she'd been perfectly healthy until she'd come down with hookworm. "Did you hear that? I'm taking you home tomorrow and you're going to be all better soon." Hot tears dripped down her cheeks. "I'll take care of you as if you were my own daughter."

She kissed her cheeks before putting her to her shoulder. "I know I'm not your mother, but I'll try to be the best mama there is. Would you like to be my precious *fille*?"

Celeste gave a big burp in response. Lise laughed through her tears and rocked her until she fell asleep. After she'd put her to bed, she picked up the phone over against the wall and called Giles.

She got his answering machine and left a detailed message about her visit to Marguerite and the outcome.

"When Celeste is released tomorrow, I'll take her home with me. To make things legal, and save you further headaches, I'll ask the palace solicitor to draw up a foster care application to file with the Swiss authorities. I know you'll let me know of any developments where Jean and Marie are concerned. We just have to keep praying. *A bientôt*, Giles."

With that taken care of, she got ready for bed and put down the cot for the night. There'd be no hope of sleep. Lise had no one but herself to blame for her crisis state. She'd always prided herself in treating men fairly, never allowing them or herself to step over the line she'd established years ago.

It had worked until Nic.

His very existence had erased all the rules. She hadn't seen him coming. She'd had no defense to counteract his effect on her.

Regardless of her betrothal, she wanted him with every fiber of her being. During the agonizing drive from Neuchatel, when Nic had reverted to the forbidding man who'd rescued her, she'd formulated a plan.

Tomorrow she would tell her parents to go ahead and make preparations for her to meet Prince Raimondo and his parents. She didn't want it put off any longer. Since her parents would welcome Celeste at the palace as long as they believed the situation was temporary, she'd say nothing about her intention to become a foster parent.

She was counting on her mother's heart being so touched when she saw Celeste and knew her plight that the baby would win her over and she'd understand why Lise couldn't possibly give her up.

When the Prince and she could be alone, she would tell him the truth: that she planned to adopt Celeste if it turned out the Fillouxes had been killed. If he could accept the baby as part of the marriage contract, then she'd marry him and swear to give him children if it was within her power to conceive. That way there'd be future Norestier-Castellanis to preserve the future of the two crowns.

But if Raimondo refused, and she would certainly understand if he didn't want to start out their marriage with another couple's child, then he could break the betrothal in good faith and find another princess to marry, without his reputation being tarnished in the slightest.

Lise had spent all last night debating whether to call off the betrothal outright. She could do that, and then the onus would be on her rather than Raimondo. But she'd been raised to do her duty. That meant sacrifice. She had to try to do what was expected of her. She *had* to. But one thing was certain. She wouldn't compromise where Celeste was concerned.

If their marriage was called off because of the baby, then it would mean Lise would no longer be in line for the succession and it would fall to her first cousin, Louis-Pierre, her uncle's eldest son, who'd recently turned eighteen.

Her parents would be wounded. But when she reasoned with them that at the time the betrothal had taken place, years earlier, no one could have foreseen Celeste's advent in Lise's life, would they be able to deny that fate had been in charge of the extraordinary circumstances?

She hoped her logic would defeat them because, having achieved her freedom, she intended to seek out Nic wherever he was. She planned to offer herself to him in any capacity he wanted, *if* he still wanted her and Celeste after what she'd done to him.

Call it infatuation, lust, desire, gratitude, hero-worship, adoration, admiration—whatever combination of feelings you could name or think up—meeting Nic Tozzetti had been a life-changing experience for her.

Of course this would all remain a fantastic fantasy if he never made it back from his next mission…

Enveloped in fresh pain, Lise turned over on the cot and buried her face in the pillow where she could smother her sobs.

It was after 10:00 p.m. when Nic walked down the palace hall to his parents' bedroom unannounced and knocked on the tall paneled door. "May I come in?"

"Raimondo?" his mother called out in a surprised voice.

"*Si*, Mama."

"Well, of course you can come in!" his father blurted.

"*Grazie.*" He entered their sumptuous suite and found them both in bed. They'd been reading, but the moment they saw him they put their books aside.

His mother held out her arms to him. "We didn't know you were home." He embraced her and kissed her on both cheeks before sitting down on the bed next to her.

His father shook his head. "Why didn't you tell us you were back?"

"I'm doing it now, Papa."

"Are you leaving again in a few minutes?" His mother had long since become resigned to his nocturnal comings and goings, although she'd never pretended to like it. Nic had been blessed with exceptional parents.

He eyed both of them solemnly. "I just got off the phone with my commanding officer and wanted you to know I resigned my commission in the Raiders, effective immediately."

The joyful response he'd expected would follow didn't come. They simply stared at him in disbelief.

"Don't both speak at once," he teased them.

His father cleared his throat. "It isn't July yet."

"No, but I've suddenly realized time is fleeting and I'm not immortal. For the last nine years I've been able to indulge my selfish interests to my heart's content, all due to your generosity. Now it's time to show you my gratitude."

Nic got to his feet. "I'd like you to arrange for the three of us to meet with my betrothed and her parents as soon as possible. Despite the fact that neither of us has acknowledged each other's existence in all these years, I've been unconscionably cruel by not making the first overture. It's time I did something about that before real harm is done."

"What's happened to you?" His mother looked dazed.

"When Papa feels it's safe, he'll tell you about my

last mission and his part in it." Nic took a steadying breath. "The experience taught me life can be snuffed out in an instant. I'm ready to take on the responsibilities I've put off for too long. Now, if you'll excuse me, I'm dead on my feet and will see you in the morning. *Buonanotte*."

Shock did strange things to people. He left his parents' bedroom, knowing they'd need the rest of the night to process everything he'd told them. As for himself, he'd had the last few hours to sort through his chaotic emotions and had come to a decision.

The first moment he got Princess Francette alone, he'd be totally honest with her and tell her that he was deeply in love with another woman. If she was the kind of person he hoped she was, she wouldn't want to marry him knowing theirs would be a loveless marriage, doomed from the beginning.

In convincing her that there was no possibility of his ever coming to love her, he had to hope she would call off their betrothal. No self-respecting woman would sacrifice herself that way. He had to believe Francette possessed enough pride and could be honest enough to admit she didn't want to marry Nic under those circumstances.

She could end it with dignity and hold her head high. Given her freedom, she could meet another royal and fall in love with him.

Nic's parents would be crushed, but there'd be nothing they could do about it if she chose to reject him. With the betrothal broken, he could go after Lise and break her down, because he knew in his gut she desired him. That other man wouldn't stand a chance if Nic told her he wanted to marry her and be a father to Celeste.

The only other option would be for him to marry the Princess and keep Lise on the side for his lover. But she wasn't that kind of woman. Neither was he the kind of man who would betray his wife. Francette deserved to be loved.

Somehow he had to make his plan work. Any happiness in his life depended on it.

Three days later Celeste sat in her carrycot in the middle of the bed, playing with a rattle. She was watching Lise finish dressing for the meeting with Prince Raimondo and his parents. The baby's sparkling brown eyes followed her every movement as she dashed back and forth, putting on the final touches.

Lise's personal maid had informed her they'd already arrived at the palace from San Ravino and were awaiting her in the *petit salon*. With that announcement, Lise's frazzled nerves were off the chart.

The tiara her mother had sent to her room still sat in its case. She chose not to wear it. This was only an informal meeting of the six of them. Lise preferred to dress down. She didn't care if Raimondo had shown up in full ceremonial garb. There'd be no audience, no press taking photos.

She'd been waiting three days and nights for this event, but it had felt more like three years. Her gaze flashed to Celeste, who looked adorable in a new pink-and-white dress. The baby stockings were white with little pink and red hearts. On her tiny feet she wore white shoes with straps.

Over the last three days she'd become Lise's little girl. When the time came for Raimondo to meet Celeste, if his heart didn't melt at the sight of her, then he would leave the palace a free man. She wanted that outcome more than anything in the world, but she would do her duty if he decided their marriage could include Celeste.

After some deliberation Lise chose to wear a two-piece suit in a duskier pink than that of Celeste's dress. Beneath the jacket was a pale pink lace camisole. It made the outfit dressier, but not too dressy. Around her neck she wore a strand of pearls. On her feet slingback heels, in a light shade of pink.

For a last touch, she reached for the betrothal ring and slid it on the ring finger of her left hand. She'd only worn it once, at the church. It had been too big. Afterward she'd almost given in to the temptation to throw it at the obnoxious teen when she'd overheard his rude comments outside in the courtyard. Since then it had sat in a satin-lined case for eighteen years, untouched.

She looked in the mirror to apply a last coat of pink frost lipstick. Instead of a special hairdo to accommodate the tiara, she'd opted to wear her hair loose to her shoulders. Her nails had been manicured and polished in a light pearl pink.

The urge to chuck it all for her bush clothes and go find Nic was so strong she could taste it. But she was a mother now, with heavy responsibilities. It was up to Raimondo which way her destiny would play out. Only one thing was certain, and that was her love for Celeste.

Lise walked over to the bed and sat down to play with her for a minute. While she was singing to her, the maid came hurrying into the bedroom. "Your Highness?" She sounded out of breath.

"I know." Lise got up from the bed. "I'm coming. Take good care of my little cherub until I send for you to bring her to me."

"You don't understand. Monsieur Laval from the mission in Geneva is waiting for you in the drawing room with some other people."

She blinked. "Giles is here?"

"*Oui.* He says for you to bring Celeste with you."

"But he didn't even phone me. Why?"

"I don't know." She looked as bewildered as Lise, who suddenly felt sick to the pit of her stomach. She hadn't yet heard back from the palace attorney who'd filed her petition with the Swiss authorities to become a foster mother for the baby. Had Child Services come with Giles to take Celeste?

They couldn't do that!

Maybe they were making one of those impromptu visits to see how she was caring for the baby?

Taking a shuddering breath, she undid the straps of the carrycot and pulled Celeste into her arms. "Come on, sweetheart. We'll show these people how happy you are, how much better you are. No one's going to take you away from me now!"

After giving her a kiss she hurried out of the room and down the ornate hallway to the grand marble staircase. In the foyer below, the glass-paneled doors on the right led to the drawing room. Her brunette maid went ahead of her and opened them for her.

Lise rushed in the room, prepared to use her leverage as a royal princess to deal with these strangers. Instead she saw a sight that almost caused her to faint. Like she was in a fantastic dream, Jean and Marie came rushing toward her, joy written on their faces.

She couldn't believe it. "You're alive!"

"Yes. We were just released! Isn't it a miracle? Oh, Lise—" Marie cried, reaching for her baby. "All this time we had no idea you were the Princess Francette. As far as we're concerned you're an angel from heaven for saving Celeste. How can we ever repay you for what you've done?"

It was Nic they needed to thank. Nic who'd performed the miracle.

Jean was completely engulfed in tears. He embraced his wife and their baby at the same time.

"You're so beautiful, *ma belle*. In just a week your cheeks have filled out."

The two of them were so euphoric over being reunited with their child they didn't know anyone else was in the room. Of course they didn't! Lise couldn't be happier for them, or their baby.

Her thoughts flew to Nic, who'd had the presence of mind to keep Marguerite in the dark.

Over their heads she saw Giles smiling, his eyes suspiciously bright. "Enough pressure was brought to bear from the Swiss government, threatening to withhold important funding, they were able to obtain the Fillouxes' freedom. They just got off the plane and wanted to come here immediately."

Lise understood. She understood everything. But her pain was escalating out of control. Since the raid on the village, Celeste had become like her very own child. With each passing day, and no word of the Fillouxes, Lise had unconsciously imagined herself in the role of Celeste's mother.

She'd made so many plans for the two of them. She couldn't have loved her more if she'd given birth to her. But the Fillouxes were alive and had come to the palace for their baby. Naturally she was over-joyed for them and their happiness. But with their coming, Lise's world had just turned upside down once again.

Without Celeste, Raimondo wouldn't have a reason to call off their marriage. It would go ahead as planned years ago. How could she go through with it when she was so terribly in love with another man? Their union would be a travesty. Yet to break the betrothal would shatter two families, sending a tidal wave of destruction through both principalities.

Giles was eyeing her with concern. "I phoned the palace to inform you we were on our way. But I was told you might not get the message for a while, because you were in an important conference with a visiting head of state and couldn't be disturbed for any reason."

As another groan escaped her throat, her maid came running back into the drawing room. "Your Highness," she whispered, "your parents insist you come to the *petit salon. Now.*"

Lise could hear her father's voice in the message. She really did think she was going to faint. Clutching the back of the nearest chair for support, she said, "Tell them I'll be there as soon as I can."

Help.

CHAPTER TEN

NIC sat in one of the Louis XV chairs of the salon, anxious for this meeting to be over with. For the last hour his parents had been chatting amicably with the King and Queen of Haut-Leman while they waited for the appearance of their daughter.

Unfortunately, the conviviality and excitement were going to change once Nic could get the Princess alone. By the end of their talk she would have given him back the betrothal ring. There was no doubt it would cause a permanent breach between the two families. But better it happened now than after the marriage that was already a disaster in the making.

Tomorrow he would go after Lise and hunt her down until he found her and Celeste. After he'd kissed her into oblivion she wouldn't want to go back to that other man. The three of them would start a new life in San Ravino.

His parents couldn't help but love her and the baby. In time his father might even change the law, so Nic could marry a commoner and still rule one day. Little Celeste was the key. Her addition to the royal household would make them instant grandparents. One of these days she'd be toddling down the halls of the palace. Her sweet little face would win their hearts that had been hungry for grandchildren.

More time went by while they waited. It appeared the Princess had been dreading this moment too. He could hope that, rather than deal with Nic, she'd run off with her lover, but miracles like that didn't happen in real life.

When the doors suddenly opened, he got to his feet—only to see one of the maids in the aperture. "The Princess begs your forgiveness. She had unexpected company and says she'll be with you as soon as she sees them out."

"Unexpected company?" Her mother frowned and stood up. She turned to Nic. "I apologize for my daughter. Please excuse me while I find out what's going on."

"Of course."

Maybe dreams did come true and the Princess had already run away. He'd give the Queen another minute to try to find her daughter, then Nic would pretend concern and get up to go look for her. It would add a touch of poignant authenticity.

Lise gave Celeste one more kiss before Jean and Marie climbed into the back of the limo parked at the east entrance of the palace. Giles turned to hug her. "Stay in touch."

"I promise." After he got in the front seat, she closed the door. The chauffeur started the car and it pulled away, taking Lise's heart with it. While she was waving to them, she heard footsteps behind her.

"Francette Norestier—what on earth are you doing?"

She spun around, unable to hide her face drenched in tears. "Saying goodbye to Celeste and her parents. They were released unharmed and flown from Chakul today."

"How absolutely wonderful!"

"I agree. They came to the palace a few minutes ago to get their baby and take her home to Neuchatel."

Her mother's expression softened. "Oh, darling. After what you and Celeste lived through together, I know how much you've grown to love her." She put her arms around her. "What you need to do is wipe away those tears and come and meet Raimondo. I promise you won't recognize him. He's grown into a very handsome, accomplished man. In time he'll give you your own baby to love."

Lise didn't want another baby. She couldn't go through with this. She couldn't!

"I don't feel well, Maman. Will you please convey my apologies to him and his parents?"

A stillness enveloped her mother. She eyed Lise soberly. "Is that what you really want me to do?"

She knew what her mother was saying: that Lise had been running away for too long. Now it was time for her to face her responsibilities like a grown woman.

"I'm sorry." She wiped the moisture from her face with her hands. She would never be able to go through with a wedding, but it would be unconscionable of her not to meet Raimondo and his family. "I'm ready."

Numb with grief, she walked with her mother down the palace corridor to the main hallway leading to the foyer. Enormous glittering chandeliers lit the way to the *petit salon*. It lay on the other side of the staircase opposite the drawing room.

Almost to the doors, a tall, powerful-looking man emerged from them. Lise hesitated before taking another step because the dark-haired male dressed in a formal suit of midnight-blue looked familiar. Her pulse sped up.

He happened to look around. When he saw her, his body instantly quickened like he'd seen an apparition.

"You—" they both cried at the same time.

Lise trembled uncontrollably. *"You're* Raimondo?" Her voice came out like a squeak. Her heart had jumped to her throat.

He was Prince Raimondo Niccolo Giancarlo di Castellani?

Niccolo.

Nic—

Her brain could only sort out one astounding clue at a time.

"Why did you call yourself *Lise*?"

His voice sounded as unsteady as hers. They were on the same wavelength.

"My grandmother. She was Analise Belard before her marriage to Gregoire Norestier. When the villagers from Chakul had trouble calling me Francette, I adopted her name, then shortened it to make it easier for them to pronounce."

On those hard-muscled legs, he closed the short distance between them. His hands reached for her upper arms while his gaze literally devoured her. "*Francetta.*"

He spoke her name in the Italian way, melting her bones. She heard the shock in his voice.

Shock held her in thrall too. A memory came back to her as she stared into the black eyes she'd once compared to lumps of coal. This time they were on fire for her until she felt like she was burning alive.

A strange sound escaped his lips. "*You* were the VIP." He shook his handsome head as if trying to clear it. She knew the feeling.

"When my pilot said you had to be someone *molta importante*, I told him my father wouldn't have offered the family jet unless it was for another head of state. No wonder Papa sounded so unduly emotional when he told me to be careful. It wasn't like him."

"The jet was as luxurious as my father's," she said in sudden recollection. "I—I thought you'd commandeered some junta leader's jet and were going to take me to a far corner of the earth where no one would ever see me again."

"Except for *me*?" His smoldering black eyes impaled her. "I almost did." The savagery of his tone convinced her he was telling her the truth. "When you told me there was another man in your life, I could have strangled you with your own gorgeous hair," came his fierce confession.

Lise's blue eyes implored him. "Have you figured out yet that Raimondo was the other man? He's been the other man for the whole of my life! I damned him more times than you can possibly imagine."

"You don't know the half of it. My buddy Aldo suggested I get lost in the Afghan mountains so I would never have to deal with my betrothed. I thought about it long and hard, believe me."

"Oh, Nic—"

He cupped the sides of her face with his hands. "It's all starting to compute," he said in a husky voice, "but I can tell something's wrong. This must have to do with Celeste. Is she worse again?"

"No, she's fine," she said in a wobbly voice. "Jean and Marie just left with her."

"Say that again?"

She kissed his lips once more. "Can you believe it? It was a shock to me too. I'll tell you all the details later, but suffice it to say their captors released them. They were flown home today. You've never seen such a happy little family in your life."

Nic rocked her for a long time. "I'm happy for them, but I know how much you loved her. I loved her too."

"Oh, Nic—hold me tight. I'm so in love with you, darling."

His chest rose and fell sharply. "I fell in love with a stranger in the backseat of a car in Africa. No one can tell me differently. I loved your mouth, your eyes, your hair, your body, the scent of you.

"I love you, Francetta. I love your name. I want you in all the ways a man can want a woman. I want to make love to you day and night."

"I want that more than you do—" she cried.

He smoothed the hair away from her temples. "It's going to take us a while to get over losing Celeste, but one day, when the time is right, we'll start our own family."

"She was so precious."

"I happen to know no one will be a better mother than you. With my own eyes and heart I saw the way you took care of her. She could have been yours. Your love for her convinced me you *were* her mother."

"I wanted you to be her father," she admitted.

"We need to get married in the worst way, so I can show you the depth of my love." The second his mouth closed over hers she knew it was a fatal mistake. With their passion ignited once more, they lost all sense of time and place. His hunger was a revelation to her because it matched her own.

"Darling—" She gasped for breath a few minutes later. "We're practically making love standing up."

He chuckled deep in his throat. "I can't stop, even if the eyes of the whole palace are upon us."

"Nic. Our parents— If they see us like this—"

"Right now I don't care." He captured her mouth once more. It sent a voluptuous warmth through her body.

When he let her come up for air again she cried, "Do you have any idea what it was like to be swept away by you, body and soul, only to watch you drive away from the hospital and out of my life? I knew you were going back to your job. The thought of never seeing you again almost killed me." Her voice shook.

He buried his face in her hair. "I'm through with the military. I resigned three days ago. It was the first part of my plan. The second was to get out of my betrothal and come for you. Marry me as soon as possible and I promise to show you the depth of my love twenty-four hours a day."

"I can't wait to find out what that would be like. I don't want to be anywhere else but in your arms."

"To think of the years we've wasted when we could have been together." He pressed his forehead against hers. "We need to get out of here, somewhere I can be alone with you, but first I have a few words to say to my father. Come on."

Grasping her around the waist, he hurried her over to the doors of the *petit salon*. When he opened them, she saw her parents talking to their guests. Her gaze strayed to King Leopoldo and his wife. Both were very attractive people. Lise could see where Nic got his fantastic looks.

He kept his arm tight around her. "Papa? Why in heaven's name didn't you tell me Francetta was the VIP I was sent to rescue?"

By now all four parents had got to their feet.

"When Philippe and I heard the missionaries in those border areas were in danger, we spoke to your commanding officer and he arranged for you to get her out."

Her father smiled at her. "For everyone's protection we thought it best if you both remained incognito."

"Darling…" Her mother spoke up. "Little did we know the dislike you two had for each other as children would turn into something else during your harrowing experience. We're all very thankful for this joyous outcome."

Nic's mother walked over to kiss Lise's cheeks. "When we saw how you two felt about each other at the betrothal, we decided to let you have your freedom. The idea came from a little book of rhymes our son's tutor made him memorize to help him learn English."

"That *Little Bo Peep* ditty had a lot of wisdom," Nic's father piped up. "Something about lost sheep, not knowing where to find them. Leave them alone, it said. In time they'll come home, wagging their tails behind them. You certainly did that!" he teased, in a voice of fatherly affection.

While Lise blushed a deep shade of scarlet, Nic's head flew back and he let out a sound of deep rich laughter that probably filled the whole palace.

His distinguished-looking father came over to kiss her. "I've waited thirty-three years for this moment. Welcome home, my dear."

* * * * *

Expecting the Cascaverado Prince's Baby

MEREDITH WEBBER

Dear Reader,

Before I begin writing any story I muddle about with it in my head, thinking of settings, characters, problems, etc. At this stage of this particular story I took a train trip with some family and friends to a wine-growing area a couple of hundred kilometres from my home. My daughter and another couple had been to Europe only months earlier, driving from France through the Pyrenees to Spain, and so it happened that one balmy evening in the grounds of the Singing Lake Winery, I grabbed these three and set them to brainstorming names and settings for my royal princedom. And so Carlos Eduardo Estefan Deziguel was born and Cascaverado came into being, a medieval princedom based largely on the medieval town of Carcassonne in France.

This is the first time I have written a 'royal' book and I found the process fascinating – here was I building my very own country! The medical part is close to my own heart, as I feel for the innocents caught up in wars in so many countries.

Meredith Webber

Meredith Webber says of herself, "Some years ago, I read an article which suggested that Mills & Boon were looking for new Medical™ romance authors. I had one of those 'I can do that' moments, and gave it a try. What began as a challenge has become an obsession – though I do temper the 'butt on seat' career of writing with dirty but healthy outdoor pursuits, fossicking through the Australian Outback in search of gold or opals. Having had some success in all of these endeavours, I now consider I've found the perfect lifestyle."

**Look out for Meredith Webber's latest novel,
Desert King, Doctor Daddy,
available in March 2010.**

PROLOGUE

CARLOS EDUARDO ESTEFAN DEZIGUEL, surgeon with
an international aid agency and heir to the throne of
far-off Cascaverado, hurried down the fire stairs in
the old hospital in southern Afghanistan, cursing
quietly under his breath. He'd had word of a patient
coming in, and now apparently a group of Australian
Army medical personnel had landed at the hospital.
He was the only person who could speak English
well enough to tell them they weren't needed here.
Well, they *were* needed, certainly, but they shouldn't
be here—couldn't stay—

Unless, of course, they were theatre staff? Could
the Fates be *that* good to him?

The situation—the timing—the patient—the
stairs—

He slipped on the landing of the last flight, and
the temper he prided himself on keeping under control bubbled dangerously close to explosion.

Did explode!

'What's going on?' he demanded of the diminutive colonel who seemed to be in control of the Australians. 'Doesn't your Army know we are under attack here? That we are only doing emergency surgery at the moment and that the hospital is being evacuated? What I need right now is theatre staff, not a gastroenterologist or a physiotherapist!'

Caz was too busy looking around at the decrepit hospital building and trying to quell the excitement of her first deployment as an Army reserve officer to take much notice of the angry conversation going on between the officer in charge of her team and the tall man who had met them in the hospital corridor.

Colonel Meg Wright's words cut into her musings.

'Before she changed direction in her life, Lieutenant Blackman was one of the best theatre sisters in Western General.'

'Then I shall have Blackman, but the rest of you must leave!' the tall man said, adding, 'Immediately!' in a voice that brooked no argument.

Calmly, Meg turned to Caz.

'Blackman, consider yourself co-opted to Dr Carlos, and under his command. I'll take the rest of you back to the helicopter.'

She whisked the rest of the team away, and Caz looked at the stranger in the apple-green theatre pyjamas—really looked. Which was probably a mistake, as something fluttered in her chest. It must

have been his words—'I shall have Blackman'—or
the way Meg had phrased the order—'under his
command'—because, no matter how good-looking a
man might be—and this one was mightily so—she
was so over men that chest flutters were a thing of the
past.

'So, Blackman, come this way.'

The words, slightly accented, curled into Caz's
ears. She followed him along a dilapidated corridor,
noticing his broad shoulders, but at least no longer
able to take in eyes so dark a blue they seemed almost
black—although maybe that impression was caused
by the darker line that rimmed the irises. Unusual
eyes… That had to be why she'd been struck by them.
And by the contrast of those eyes against his black
hair.

'Our patient was in a vehicle which hit an IED—
you know IEDs?'

Carlos glanced over his shoulder as he asked the
question, and was pleased to see the nurse nod,
although she looked pale, as if thinking of impro-
vised explosive devices had upset her.

If thinking about them upset her, seeing what they
did to human beings was going to come as a shock.

'You've done amputation work before?'

He glanced back at her again, aware he should
slow his pace so she could keep up with him, but
wary for some reason he couldn't pinpoint. Not that
there was anything remotely attractive in a slight

young woman in Army desert fatigues—surely the most unflattering of clothing for any woman. But there'd been something about her face when he'd first seen her, something about the clear grey eyes that had met his briefly before moving on, looking around, as if she had no further interest in him whatsoever.

'Here—we go this way.' He held open the door to the fire stairs. 'The elevators are no longer working so we take the stairs, but it's only up four flights. You are fit?'

He held the door open for her and asked the question as she walked into the stairwell.

'I should be able to manage four flights without oxygen.'

The dry retort made him look at her again, but all that was in view was a straight back and a pert bottom, climbing briskly up the steps in front of him. Her hair was hidden under the unattractive cap she wore, but blonde strands were struggling to escape. The colonel's words floated back into his mind—about Blackman having changed direction in her life. It struck him as a funny thing for a commanding officer to say about one of her team, but then they reached the theatre floor and he forgot everything but the sight in front of him. Blackman was already bending over the patient on the stretcher.

'There's no one with him,' she said, eyeing him with disbelief.

'I told your colonel the hospital was being evacuated. We'd been told this patient was coming in. The anaesthetist agreed to stay, but he was the only one. Come, it's this way—the theatre.'

Caz followed him as he wheeled the stretcher along the deserted corridor, then ducked ahead to open the swing doors to a theatre that looked like something out of a nightmare.

'You're seeing it at its worst,' the doctor told her. 'Often we have no electricity, and therefore no lights, so it looks much better today.'

Inwardly shaking her head, Caz found what she needed and changed, returning to the theatre to find the anaesthetist there as well.

Caz stared at the injury—the man had lost his foot above the ankle—appalled by the savageness of it.

'It's what I do,' Dr Carlos said quietly, apparently sensing her reaction with ease. 'Amputations. Not pretty work, and not even profitable, as most people who suffer the loss of a limb can't afford to pay a surgeon to take it off neatly. But in this world of ours it is necessary work.'

He delivered this information with crisp detachment, yet somehow Caz took it as a reproof for the shock she must have shown on seeing the injury.

'I wouldn't be here if I didn't understand that,' she muttered at him, and was pleased to see those dark blue eyes widen slightly. They were all she could see of him above his mask and below his scarf—them and the fine dark eyebrows, which arched slightly as he looked at her.

'Of course,' he said, and then the remarkable eyes softened and fine wrinkles gathered at the corners, so she knew he was smiling behind his mask. 'I get a little obsessive about my work, but that's mainly because so many surgeons take so little care—think so little about the future when they amputate part of a limb.'

'So little care?' Caz echoed, not bothering to hide the incredulity in her voice.

She was cutting away bloodied clothing as she spoke, and trying to prepare a sterile field around the wounded leg, but she glanced up to see how Dr Carlos—could Carlos be a surname?—had reacted to her words.

She suspected he was smiling again.

'That's right,' he said quietly, gently removing debris from the wound. 'When one is finishing an amputation, the life-saving part has been done, but then, if we do things neatly, it will be so much easier to fit a prosthetic device later.'

'Ah,' Caz said, glancing up again, checking out this man who would be thinking of his patient's interests so far ahead—a man who was now totally focussed on his job. She grabbed the trolley of instruments and pulled them closer, passing him a clamp.

'Which side would you like me to work?' she

asked, aware she had to concentrate on the job, not be thinking about the patient's future mobility.

Or the surgeon!

'Opposite. You can take up the slack from there,' he replied. 'And talk to me. I can handle not having a team of doctors and nurses on hand to help out, but the silence—it gets to me, the silence. And Ahmed has little English—I'm sorry, I didn't introduce Ahmed. Ahmed, Blackman—Blackman, Ahmed.'

Caz's stomach tightened. What a way to introduce people. Arrogant surgeons! Wasn't that why she'd got out of theatre nursing?

She turned towards the anaesthetist, hoping he'd see the smile in her eyes, nodding her head and acknowledging the introduction. Ahmed nodded back.

'Ahmed uses words very sparingly,' Dr Carlos continued, 'so, although we can discuss the patient's status, there's no chatter. I miss the chatter.'

Caz set aside her annoyance, considering the noise usually present in orthopaedic surgery. With electric drills and saws, it rivalled that of a carpenter's workshop, so, yes, he *would* notice the quiet. But to talk to this bossy stranger—what was she supposed to talk about?

'Your life,' he said, as if she'd asked the question aloud. 'What brought you here?'

Caz, who was automatically passing him instruments as he needed them, shook her head. What had brought her here? Surely that was a far too long and too pathetic tale to tell.

'Talk!' he ordered. 'You weren't delivered fully formed in a hospital corridor, so who are you and where are you from? Married or single? Anxious family waiting back home? Why would you leave them to do this work?'

Then he repeated, 'What brought you here?' and suddenly Caz found herself talking. At least it took her mind off the patient's horrific injuries.

'I was married,' she began, 'but not now. My father is a policeman and my three brothers are all in the police force, so my mother is used to anxiety.'

'Were married?'

She'd rarely discussed her divorce with anyone, but these circumstances were bizarre, and maybe talking to a stranger—someone she'd never see again—was a good thing.

Free therapy!

'I couldn't have children.'

'Couldn't have?'

'We'd been married six years, trying all the time, then the girlfriend I didn't know my husband had fell pregnant. He knew the infertility problems didn't lie with him, so he divorced me and married her instead.'

She refused to look at the man she was addressing, not wanting to see distaste, or worse, pity in his eyes.

'The bone is taken furthest back,' he said, as if she

hadn't just revealed her most hurtful secret to him, 'because the muscle shrinks and the skin with it, so you don't want the bone protruding later.'

Now Caz did glance up at him, but he was focussed on the job, handing her back the bone saw and asking her to hold the peroneal nerve while he tidied up the muscle around it.

'Keep talking,' he added, so she launched into the next phase of her life: going back to university, joining the Army reserves—

'Rebuilding the self-esteem your husband had destroyed?' he said, taking the nerve clamp from her and tying off the nerve, tucking it back in beside the severed bone.

'Injured, maybe,' Caz retorted. 'Not destroyed. I'm not *that* pathetic!'

Had she snapped too loudly? He looked up, his eyes studying her for a moment before he turned his attention back to his work. But all he said was, 'Good for you.'

Carlos guessed 'destroyed' was closer to the mark, but the woman had got her life back together again, and for that she had to be admired. Ninety-nine percent of his mind was on his work, even while she talked, but that one percent was wondering just what Blackman really looked like—apart from the wide grey eyes.

And the pert bottom!

Even what her first name was.

He could ask, but this was the part of the operation that required the most attention—the least dangerous, but the most important for the patient's long-term well-being.

'You will understand, then,' he said, as he tucked and stitched, 'why I take trouble to make the leg-end just right. A person with an amputation also has self-esteem problems—self-image problems as well. This man is young; he has his whole life ahead of him. It is our job to see that it is a happy and successful life.'

A siren wailed a warning.

'We must go,' the so far silent Ahmed said. 'That is the last call.'

'I can't go, but you can,' Dr Carlos replied. 'I can handle the anaesthetic from here. Take Blackman with you. Find some way to get her back to her team.'

Ahmed hesitated, then said, 'Of course.' He hesitated again before adding, 'I cannot stay, much as I would like to. I must think of my wife and children—of their safety.' He turned to Caz. 'You will come?'

'No, I'll stay,' she said. 'It won't be the first time I've helped with anaesthetic, and this man will need some nursing when Dr Carlos is done.'

'You don't think I could nurse him?' the deep voice said, and then he added, *'You will go!'*

A command, not a suggestion.

Caz just shook her head and continued working.

'You stay, I stay,' she said, and heard him mutter some foreign imprecation under his breath.

'No wonder your husband divorced you,' he added in English. 'Disobedient woman!'

But the final phrase—just two words—was said with more respect than reproof, and it warmed some of the cold places in Caz's heart.

Caz took over the anaesthetist's role, checking on fluid and drug delivery through the makeshift IV equipment, taking the patient's blood pressure and pulse, thinking that this was how things used to be before computer wires and monitors did it all.

'He's stable?' the doctor asked, and Caz assured him the patient was holding on well.

'Good. I'm done here.'

Dr Carlos stepped back from the table and stripped off his gloves, then removed his mask, smiling at Caz for the first time.

Heavens—he was gorgeous!

She'd barely registered this when he came around the table and held out his hand to her.

'Time we introduced ourselves. I am Carlos, and you must have another name besides Blackman.'

Caz pulled off her glove and took his hand.

'Caroline—but I'm called Caz,' she said, ignoring the spark of electricity his touch had generated, sure it was simply the easing of tension in the theatre that had caused it, and nothing more sinister like attraction.

'Caz…hmm. Can I see your smile?' He reached forward and pulled the tie holding Caz's mask, the action feeling far more intimate than the handshake had been, and this time there was no denying the charge that shot through Caz's body.

Tension, she told herself firmly.

She was lovely, in a quiet, understated way.

Carlos was so startled by the thought he immediately sought refuge in work.

'Now that we're introduced, we'd better find dressings and bind our patient's wound,' he said. 'This is important too, for how it is dressed also determines how well we can fit a prosthetic device to his limb.'

'You really are obsessed with prosthetic success,' she said, as she opened cupboards in search of dressings. 'Is there a reason?'

Silence greeted this remark, and when she turned to look at him she caught a glimpse of what looked like sadness in his eyes.

Carlos shut away memories from his childhood and crossed to the cupboard to help her search through the dressings. There was something about this woman that drew him to her. Not pity for her failed relationship—she was well rid of such a man—but something in the stalwart way she'd got on with her life…

He showed her how he wrapped the wound, then together they cleaned the patient and dressed him in theatre pyjamas, which was all they could find in the way of clean clothing.

'So, what do we do now?' she asked.

'We take him downstairs. Hopefully we can find someone to help us, and someone who will know where to take him to join the other evacuated patients.'

'If we can't find anyone to help, I'm sure I can carry one end of the stretcher. He's not that big.'

Carlos looked at the woman, who wasn't all that big herself—in fact, she was a slight, slim woman, though he could see she had curves in all the right places in spite of the shapelessness of theatrewear.

'I hope it doesn't come to that. For all his size, he'll still be heavy. You stay with him—I'll check what's happening.'

In truth, he was pleased to get out of the theatre, away from this woman he didn't know but who was occupying too much of his thoughts. It wasn't that he was short of female companionship—well, not when he was at home—so the attraction he felt towards her was...unusual...

He realised his musings had taken him to the end of the corridor, and he held the handle of the door that led into the stairwell.

It wouldn't turn!

There was another stairwell at the far end of the corridor. He strode towards it. Same thing. They were effectively locked on the theatre floor of the hospital, which was now deserted.

Refusing to believe everyone had departed, he picked up one of the house phones on the wall in the corridor.

Dead!

Back to the first door—could he break the lock? He inspected the heavy fire door and the complicated lock on it, and knew he didn't have the skills required for such a job.

'Can you pick locks?'

He asked the question as he pushed back through the doors into Theatre, and read the surprise on Caroline's face.

'Are we locked in?' she asked, so calmly Carlos felt his respect for her growing.

'We are,' he said, and was surprised to see her smile broaden into a big grin.

'Well, this is an adventure, isn't it?'

'You can't seriously believe that!' he growled, and was sorry when her smile faded and with it the colour from her cheeks.

'I was *trying* to look on the bright side,' she snapped, 'mainly because having hysterics, which is the alternative, wouldn't be very productive. Do you have any idea why this has happened, or how long we might be trapped here?'

'It's a first for me!' Carlos admitted. 'Presumably the fighting was getting very close, but hospitals are usually safe. Neither side wants a destroyed hospital. Why they'd lock the doors I don't know—unless there's some kind of automatic locking system to deny access to all the floors?'

'I suppose that makes sense.'

Carlos sighed. 'Working with aid organisations, there's always something new to catch you out. I've worked in primitive conditions, and under gunfire, but this is the first time I've been left in an evacuated hospital. It might have been okay if we had the run of the whole hospital, but being locked on the theatre floor we might find little in the way of provisions.'

'I'll go and see,' Caz suggested, realising she had to get away from Carlos for a short time, so she could sort out the weird reactions she was having to this situation. Fear, certainly, but surely it couldn't be excitement mixed in with it—that little buzz adventure brought in its train?

'Man the hunter and woman the gatherer,' Carlos teased, smiling at her again so her escape became even more urgent.

She fled into the corridor and walked along it, opening doors as she went, finding very little, and certainly no food. But walking back, she noticed a door flush with the wall and pushed it open, looking into a small room obviously intended as a tearoom for staff. It held a refrigerator—which stopped working as she opened the door. The light overhead went out at the same time, signalling that the power had been turned off.

The refrigerator held some bottles of vividly coloured soft drink, an apple, two oranges, and a tired piece of cheese. On the bench above it was a sack full of some kind of grain, and beside that a small gas burner—the kind that had a little gas canister fitted to it. Camping holidays with her brothers made it immediately recognisable.

'So we won't starve, with grain and the means to cook it,' Carlos said when she told him of her find. 'And there are beds in the post-op room, so we shall be able to sleep. The showers in the theatre changing rooms will be cold, but with the power off the air-conditioning will shut down so we'll be glad of cold showers.'

'What more could any woman want?' Caz said, dredging up a smile for the man who was taking this so philosophically, hoping she was coming across far braver than she felt.

Rescuers will come soon, she told herself, as Carlos fitted a drip stand to the wheeled stretcher so they could move their patient to the recovery room. Just keep pretending things are normal.

'I'll help you lift him onto a bed, then come back and clean up here,' she said—*normal*!

With the patient settled on the bed, Carlos opened the door of what looked like a cupboard in the wall beyond the three post-op beds.

'Aha—an on-call bedroom,' he said. 'If we are not rescued before tonight, you will be able to have some privacy.'

Caz moved towards him, ducking under his arm to peer into the room. Big mistake—she was far too close to this man who was guiding this strange adventure, and it was doing things she didn't want to think about to her body. But it was because of the situation—the tension of it, the uncertainty—that her senses were all on alert and her nerve-endings supersensitive.

'Why me having privacy?' she asked, ducking back away from him. 'I'm the lowly nurse. I stay with the patient—you get the spare bedroom.'

She spoke quickly, trying to mask the strange sensations she was feeling, but Carlos must have heard something in her voice, for he turned and reached for her chin, tilting her head up so she had to meet his eyes.

'That man did really batter you around—emotionally, that is! He was not worthy of you, Caroline, wanting not a wife but a brood mare,' he said softly, and then, to Caz's astonishment, he leaned forward and dropped the lightest of kisses—the brush of butterfly wings, nothing more—on her lips. 'But you are the strong one, remember that,' he added, as calmly as if he hadn't just taken such a liberty.

Although it hadn't felt like a liberty to Caz. It had felt more like a promise of some kind—which was ridiculous, of course. As if this man could promise her anything.

It wasn't really a kiss, Carlos told himself, but he knew he was lying. It had been a kiss, and he'd wanted it to be longer and stronger, but he knew he'd frightened her. Admittedly, it had not frightened him, but it had certainly startled him to feel such a strong urge to press his lips to hers.

'I'll cook the grain,' he announced, thinking if he got out of the room he might be able to think more clearly about his attraction to this woman.

She raised her eyebrows, mocking him as she had earlier, when she'd said he should have the bedroom, and he had to laugh.

'I've been in many places where I'd never have eaten if I hadn't fixed the food myself, so trust me— I can cook grain.'

And he could, Caz admitted later, as she scooped up the strange-tasting concoction he had cooked.

'At least it's filling,' she said.

Their patient was stirring now, and Caz waited by his side, ready to offer him something to drink, perhaps a little grain.

'You need not sit with him,' Carlos said as daylight slipped into dusk. 'Have a shower and go to bed. I'll sleep beside him.'

'You're assuming we won't be rescued today?'

It was a stupid question, considering she could hear the sound of gunfire beyond the hospital's protective walls.

'Maybe tomorrow,' Carlos said, touching her lightly on the arm.

Keeping their patient, Sarwar, diverted from his pain and loss occupied the next day, though Caz found it hard to ignore the sounds of fighting from outside their sanctuary. Carlos obviously sensed her tension from time to time, when the whistling of missiles and the thunder of bullets seemed worst, as he would touch her lightly on the arm, or, if they were sitting by their patient's bed, rest his hand gently on her leg.

Comforting the touches certainly were, but they were confusing as well, for while part of her relaxed, the other part—the part she'd thought she'd shut away for ever—stirred and fluttered and did excited little heart-flips!

Danger-fuelled lust, she told herself.

For a woman who'd never been in a battle situation, she was certainly handling it well, Carlos decided as he watched her cutting up a set of theatre pyjama trousers, making paper people—six of them—then showing Sarwar they were her family: mother, father, three brothers. She indicated through pointing that the smallest one was her.

Sarwar caught on and took her paper people, and the scissors, cutting out two more female people and taking away the brothers.

'You've two sisters? You're the only man?' Caroline mimed and spoke at the same time, and Sarwar nodded.

But was she, too, feeling the attraction between them? Carlos wondered. Would that explain why she avoided being close to him, and pulled away when they accidentally touched?

He studied her, trying to work out whether the attraction was only because they *were* locked away together or whether it was something deeper.

Impossible—he didn't do deeper.

Two days now—and the tension was growing. Until Caz wondered if she could bear it for much longer. Every time Carlos moved it was as if strings connected her to him. Her skin tugged and her nerves twitched and her body began to ache in places she hadn't thought about for years.

'It can be an affair, nothing more,' Carlos said, taking her in his arms when she crept back into the post-op room after showering on the third evening. Their patient was asleep, and through the flimsy material of theatre pyjamas—at least there was a good supply of them, and of paper slippers—she felt the hardness of Carlos's body, his obvious desire. 'You'll return to your life in Australia, and I have so many things to do and only a limited time in which to pursue them all. That is all it can be.'

'It's all I want,' Caz whispered, although she wasn't entirely sure that was true.

And, edging into the small on-call room, they kissed—really kissed—for the first time, their lips melding together as if this was what they were meant for, their bodies so close, soft and hard meshed. And they were as one.

Feeling their way to the bed with their legs, they

were about to strip each other's clothes off when Carlos spoke again.

'Protection! I don't carry it in my theatre pyjamas.'

He tried to make a joke of it, but Caz heard the tension in his voice.

'Six years!' she reminded him lightly. 'If I didn't get pregnant then, how likely is it that I will in one night—or three, or five or however many are left to us?'

She stopped any further discussion with a kiss that deepened as they sank down onto the bed, learning each other's bodies through touch, touching with tenderness as well as excitement, for this was something special and Caz knew Carlos felt it too.

It wouldn't last, it had no future—Caz was well aware of that. But for now it was enough that they had this special time together, time to make memories that would last her through the lonely years ahead when work, not family, would be her focus…

CHAPTER ONE

CAZ tortured herself over the wording of the e-mail, writing and rewriting it, while all the time the image of its recipient was vivid in her mind. Her skin was still feeling his touch, her body thrilling to memories of his lovemaking—lovemaking that had shut out the sound of gunfire and kept her fear at bay—lovemaking that had helped her through what could have been a time of absolute terror.

In the end, she went for a blunt statement of the facts.

To: carlos12@cascanet.com
From: cazb@phyweb.com.au
Hi Carlos,
Me again, hope all is well. Some news this end: unbelievable for me, and I hope not too upsetting for you, but for all my ex's protestations about my infertility it turns out he was wrong. I know you don't need this complication in your life, so I want

to reassure you that, while I very much want this child, I am happy to bring him or her up on my own. My family is very supportive and, as you know, I have enough brothers to provide plenty of male input for him or her. I can adjust my life to fit a small person into it, so rest assured he or she won't be shunted off to childcare at too early an age, and I don't have any money worries—guilt made my ex quite generous. I am telling you not because I want your help, financial or otherwise, but because you have a right to know, and maybe one day you might want to meet him or her. Believe me, he or she will know about you, and I will make sure he or she knows just how important your work is and why you have determined to devote your life to it. The child will know you as a hero—and what kid doesn't want a hero for a dad?

Caroline.

It looked a little bleak on the computer screen, and it was maybe a little wordy, but although she knew he had to know, she'd also wanted to reassure him that she had everything under control.

Under control?

Big joke, when she cried herself to sleep every night. But that was hormonal, she knew that now, and it certainly hadn't been Carlos's fault she'd fallen in love with him.

How could she not have done, when he had been

so kind and caring? He had read her so well. He'd seen when her fears threatened to overcome her, and he'd held her close, reassuring her that her team leader, his aid organisation and Ahmed all knew where they were and eventually, when the fighting stopped, someone would rescue them.

In the end, after six days, it had been Ahmed who had led the rescue team. Six days during which they had tended their patient, with Caz putting her physio as well as her nursing skills to work, massaging his leg to help reduce the swelling, and the two of them laughing and joking with him to keep him cheerful. Without understanding each other's language Carlos in particular had formed a bond with Sarwar that had helped him through his pain and their imprisonment.

But the nights were what Caz mainly thought about—the nights when Sarwar was asleep and she and Carlos made love, sharing bliss and excitement she knew had been heightened by the tense and potentially dangerous situation in which they'd found themselves. And during those nights Carlos had shared his dream—told her of the facility that was almost finished back in the place he came from. Casca-something—presumably some town in Spain—and his plans to bring amputees from all parts of the world to stay there while the best possible prostheses were made and fitted for them, then accommodating them while the recipients were trained in the use of the devices.

He'd spoken with such passion, and Caz had felt the excitement of it in her blood, but he'd never suggested she might like to see it—let alone be part of it, perhaps working as one of the physios he would most certainly need.

'Our love affair is only for now,' he'd told her again and again. 'It is a precious little bubble of time out of life.'

He'd kissed her as he'd said it, softening the blow, although he hadn't known it *was* a blow, for she'd always kissed him back and agreed that that was all it could be, hiding the love that had blossomed under such extraordinary circumstances, knowing he wouldn't want the burden of knowing how she felt.

Her finger now hovered over the 'send' command on the computer, and she wondered for the thousandth time if he really needed to know. After all, there'd been so much disruption to his life lately, with him having to leave Afghanistan and return home following his father's death in a skiing accident.

His e-mail telling her of this had been so matter-of-fact it had been almost curt, yet she'd read the deep pain behind the words and had hurried to reply to him, assuring him of her deepest sympathy and wishing him strength and composure in the time ahead.

E-mails between them had been sporadic from the start—telling each other they'd arrived home safely, then the one about his father's death and her reply. Then only one more from him, thanking her for her concern and assuring her he was still able to give time to his ambitious project even if it wasn't as much as he would like.

The affair—hardly even that, Caz acknowledged to herself, more like a fling—was well and truly over.

Of course he needs to know, she told herself crossly, pushing away the memories. She clicked the command on the keyboard and sent the e-mail winging through cyberspace.

His reply didn't come immediately, and when it did, it filled Caz with such rage it was only thinking of the baby's well-being that calmed her down.

'Am flying out,' it said, with unemotional brevity. 'Will e-mail flight details and arrival time when I have them. Checked where you live, and have arranged genetic testing in closest clinic for when I get there. Have not much time. Carlos.'

Genetic testing! He didn't believe the baby was his! How dared he think she'd lie?

Fortunately the e-mail with his flight arrival details turned up shortly afterwards—obviously sent from an airport somewhere, for he was to arrive the following morning. In sending the flight details, was he expecting her to meet him?

Probably not. But the anger she was feeling meant she wasn't going to wait quietly at home until he contacted her again to explain his behaviour. Genetic testing, indeed! She'd meet him at the airport and tell him exactly what she thought of him, and then he could get right back on a plane to Casca-wherever and be out of her life for good!

But as she stood in the arrivals hall of Brisbane International Airport, hand pressed against her belly lest the jolting of her heart in her chest affect her tiny foetus, she wondered just how to express her anger. She'd never been one to rant and rave—probably one of the reasons her ex, Derrick, had felt free to treat her as a doormat—but she had to do it now; *had* to tell Carlos just how disappointed she was in him.

Then he was there, pushing through doors from Customs, a fat computer case slung across one shoulder. The jolting in her chest stopped, her heart instead doing its familiar little flip-flops of excitement, while the glow in his blue eyes as he came towards her warmed her like a fire on a wintry night. Dressed in charcoal-grey trousers and a soft black polo shirt, the jacket of his suit slung negligently over his shoulder, he looked so different—so darned handsome—she could only stare.

'Caroline…' he said softly, tucking his jacket over his arm and cupping her face in both his hands to look searchingly at her. 'You are well?'

Incensed by her weakness in responding the way she had, she wanted to slap his hands away. But his touch was so gentle, his words so caring, she could do nothing more than mutter, 'I'm pregnant, not ill.'

But was he put off by her terseness? Not for an

instant, because now he was kissing her, and how could she maintain her anger, her disappointment in him, when his gentle kiss of greeting was burning through her blood and her traitorous body was moulding itself to him?

'I must have missed you,' he said, when an aeon or two had passed and the kiss ceased. He sounded ever so slightly confused, which wasn't at all the Carlos Caz remembered.

She looked at him, really looked this time, and saw the lines that grief and strain had drawn on his face—deep heavy lines, and dark circles beneath the beautiful eyes. She lifted her hand now, and drew it down his cheek.

'I was so sorry to hear about your father. It must have been a terrible shock. Your mother? The rest of your family? How are they coping?'

He shook his head, as if the loss was still too raw to talk about, and took her elbow, guiding her towards the door.

'Later,' he said. 'We'll talk of that later. But for now I must explain about the clinic. I hope it will be suitable. It read well on the Internet. You must be eleven weeks, so you can't have amniocentesis, but CVS—Chorionic Villus Sampling—should be okay.'

The conversation, coming so soon after his arrival—after the kiss—stopped Caz right outside the doors.

And brought back the anger that his kiss and the sight of him had cooled.

'Why?' she demanded. 'Why have you arranged this? You seem to accept I'm eleven weeks pregnant, yet you still want a test? Do you think Sarwar might have sired my baby? Or that I went from you to someone else just like that? How could you think that of me? Okay, so we don't know each other well, but I thought we'd shared something special, and now you doubt me.'

Even in her own ears the last bit sounded pathetic, but her anger, never strong, had faded, and what had to be hormonal self-pity was muddling her mind.

Carlos stared at the woman he'd flown so far to be with. Was it jet lag playing tricks on him, or was she angry about something?

'I'm sorry,' he said, reaching out to touch her shoulder, then letting his hand drop as she moved away. 'I don't understand what you're angry about. But then, nor do you understand the need for testing. I'll explain it, and then we need to discuss the implications, but perhaps not here?'

She stared at him, puzzled grey eyes meeting his with such fierce intensity he knew that whatever was upsetting her was important. Then she frowned.

'The need for testing and the implications?' she repeated. 'Are you saying it's not a DNA test for proof of fatherhood you've arranged?'

'DNA? Fatherhood?' He shook his head in disbelief. 'Of course not. Did you think I didn't trust you? Believe you? Oh, my poor Caroline…'

He pulled her into his arms and held her close, sorry he'd given her so much worry, sorry she didn't realise she was the most trustworthy woman he had ever met.

She wouldn't realise, either, the number of times he'd thought about her since they'd parted. Far too often for his peace of mind, considering it had been nothing more than a chance affair.

But now it was about her, not him.

'I blame that man you married for destroying your self-confidence, but I'm to blame too. Yet it was too difficult to put in an e-mail, and besides, it's only right that I'm with you for the test. It's something for both of us to discuss.'

He was rocking her in his arms, smelling the fresh scent of her hair, feeling maybe a hint of swelling in her belly, enjoying the reality of her in his arms, re-membering too much so his body stirred...

'Well, now that's settled, we should move off the pavement,' she said, breaking the spell with com-monsense. 'And, though you've made me feel better about the testing, you're now raising all kinds of fears in my mind.'

He bent his head, but resisted the urge to kiss her again before releasing her.

'Hush,' he said. 'It's probably nothing. I'll tell you about it in the car. Have you a car, or should I hire one?'

Caz smiled at the question, realising he knew as little about her as she did about him—yet here they were, about to be joined in the most fundamental way as parents of a child. A little shiver of prescience travelled like the touch of a feather down her spine.

A cold feather!

'My car's over here. That's all your luggage?' She nodded at the computer bag slung over his shoulder.

'One clean shirt and a couple of changes of underwear, shaver, toothbrush—they all fit in here. I'm used to travelling light.'

But 'one clean shirt' light? It had to mean he wasn't staying—though as disappointment swamped Caz's volatile heart she had to ask herself why he would. Hadn't she told him she could handle this baby on her own? Assured him of her competence? He was here to see her through this genetic testing, for whatever reason, and although the thought of some of the hereditary diseases he might want the unborn child tested for filled her with fear, he didn't seem unduly worried.

'I booked the appointment for this afternoon at one, thinking the flight might be delayed, and I have a reservation at a hotel—the Sebel Suites, it's called. Do you know it?'

Booked a hotel room? Obviously he didn't want to stay with her. And why would he? Business was business. He'd told her all along it was an affair that couldn't last...

'If the appointment is at one, you won't have time

to settle into a hotel room, and if the clinic is near my place it makes more sense for you to come there first. We can have something to eat before we go—although you've probably been eating non-stop on the plane.'

She knew she was blithering on, but seeing him again was causing such havoc in her heart and such sadness in her chest she had to keep talking lest the tangle of her emotions showed.

'I would like to see where you live,' he said, so coolly polite she felt as if she'd been doused with a bucket of cold water. He was obviously feeling none of the desire that had skittered along her nerves, so strong when it touched the deep base of her abdomen it had caused a throbbing ache that no amount of wriggling in her seat would dislodge. Not that she wanted to renew her physical relationship with him. That would be stupidity, and would only make the second parting harder.

And a second parting there would be—and soon. He'd only brought one shirt…

He shouldn't have kissed her at the airport, Carlos realised. It must have been the kiss that had his body aroused. Sitting so close to Caroline in her ridiculously small car was actually painful.

His hand longed to stray, to touch her leg, to brush across her breast, to lift her long, blonde hair from her neck so he could see the pale skin where his kisses had made her squirm with delight.

No, he had to think about the situation. Becoming

a father right now wasn't in his plans—but nor had taking over the throne been. Things happened, fate intervened, and if he looked at it from a purely practical point of view Caroline would make an excellent consort. She was sensible and down-to-earth and didn't panic easily—though the last thing he'd ever expected would have been to marry a woman with whom he'd had a few nights' fling!

Then there was the child. Thinking of the child was enough to kill the last remnants of the arousal he'd been feeling. Though he'd tried to deny it, from the moment he'd received her e-mail the thought of being a father had excited him somehow.

Excited and terrified him—the doubts about his genetic heritage had been enough to make him feel ill with worry.

But that would all be sorted soon.

'Your house—it is close now?'

'Just around the corner.'

Caroline had barely spoken when she pulled into a driveway beside a tiny wooden cottage, the front garden a riot of flowering plants that rambled at will through the small space.

'It's not much, but it's mine,' she said, and when he heard the pride in her voice he had a momentary qualm. All very well to decide he'd marry this woman who carried his child, but what if she didn't want to marry him—didn't want to leave her little cottage?

Of course she would!

But glancing at her and remembering the stalwart way she'd behaved in Afghanistan, hiding the fears he knew she felt, he began to wonder.

'Come on in. Would you like a shower? Something to eat or drink?'

He entered the minuscule hallway and glanced into a brightly furnished sitting room.

'I showered on the flight, but a glass of water would be good.'

Showered on the flight? As the only overseas trip Caz had made had been on an Army transporter, the thought of showers on planes was surprising, but she waved her hand towards the sitting room and headed for the kitchen—pleased to be out of his presence for a while. He might have doused her desire, but her physical responses to the attraction she felt for him still persisted.

She returned to the living room to find him looking very at home in one of her armchairs, although when he spoke his voice betrayed his tension.

'We must talk. I need to explain to you. If I use a pen and paper, it's easier that way.'

Carlos pulled a small leather-bound notebook from his pocket, and took out the slim gold pen that was slipped into a special place in its spine. He nodded his thanks as she pulled a coffee table closer to him and set down a glass of iced water.

'Iced water—can I get you anything else?'

She spoke calmly, yet he sensed her anxiety and could understand it. *He* was anxious, and he knew much more about what lay ahead than she did. Although she also seemed anxious in some other way—as if the very fact of his being here was causing her concern. Something to do with his presence was upsetting her...

Perhaps it was just the test. Yes, that would be upsetting—especially for someone with medical training. She'd be expecting the worst.

'So what's it for, the test?'

His conclusion was verified by her question, and he found himself vaguely disappointed. Why? Would he have preferred to think she was disturbed because of his physical presence—disturbed in the way he was disturbed, seeing her again?

But the question he'd dreaded had now been asked, and he had to forget the confusion his reaction to her was causing and think about her, Caroline, and the pain his confession would cause her.

She had sat down opposite him, and he could read her tension in the stillness of her body, the strain around her eyes.

'It's only a very slim chance—one in six thousand, two hundred and forty-one, in fact—but do you know much about Huntington's Disease?'

The manifestations of attraction that had been lingering in Caz's body fled, and she collapsed back in the armchair, pressing her hand to her belly. Then the implication of what he had asked struck her, and pain for this man she hadn't meant to love had her reaching out across the table to touch his hand.

'You have it? Have the genetic mutation that will lead to full-blown Huntington's somewhere down the track? Oh, Carlos, how dreadful for you. No wonder you're so anxious to get on with your dream while your health is still stable. You talked about limited time, but I never dreamt that disabilities down the track might be what was pushing you.'

Both her hands clasped one of his now, but he couldn't accept her sympathy.

'I'm fine,' he assured her, 'and although my mother is showing the first signs of the disease I didn't inherit her wayward gene. But it runs through the family, and—'

He broke off and came to sit beside her, on the arm of her chair, close enough to touch but not touching, ready in case comfort was needed.

He opened the notebook and began to write a string of letters.

'You've probably had no reason to look at the genetic signposts of Huntington's, but the disease arises from a glitch on chromosome four, where a repeat of patterns—they call them CAG trinucleotide repeats—becomes expanded. Most people have less than twenty-seven of these repeats, but Huntington's patients have over forty of them.'

He was drawing the line of repeats as he spoke, and

Caz understood the basics—although she knew the true genetic picture would be far more complicated.

'People with Huntington's have a fifty percent chance of passing it on to their offspring.'

'But you haven't got it, you said,' she protested. 'You've obviously been tested.'

He touched her face with the back of his fingers, reassuring her, yet warning her there was more to come.

'I'm an anomaly—not totally rare, but certainly not common. Some people in the thirty-seven, thirty-eight and thirty-nine range can also develop the disease, and as it passes from generation to generation the number of repeats tends to get longer. I'm in what they call "high normal", which is twenty-seven to thirty-five repeats. I actually have thirty-two, but with the tendency of the line of repeats to grow longer in each generation there is a chance—a very slim chance, Caroline—that our baby might be affected.'

The fact that he'd said 'our baby' blurred the focus of Caz's mind, and she had to push past the little burst of happiness the words had brought her to concentrate on what he was saying.

And to come to the implications of his words!

'And if the test shows he or she is affected?'

Carlos sighed and knew he had to hold her while they talked—to be close enough to offer physical comfort. Holding her would kindle his own recently suppressed embers of desire, but she deserved the comfort.

He stood up, lifted her from her chair, and sat down with her on his knee. Then, to keep the unwanted desire at bay, he began to explain.

'Ideally I would have been organising the conception of my children through IVF, so the embryos could be tested before they were implanted, but this has happened, and now we must move on. You know the options, don't you?' he said softly. 'If we find our baby has the genetic imprint for Huntington's, do we go ahead with the pregnancy or terminate it? I know it is you who will suffer if we go down the latter route, and that it will be traumatic for you physically and emotionally, but would it be less traumatic to watch your child grow up, knowing that some time in his or her future the twitching and tremors would develop, along with the cognitive disabilities, and eventually he or she would come to an early death?'

He felt her reaction in the tensing of her muscles and held her more tightly, hurrying on so it could all be said and then considered.

'I have stacks of information on the disease you might want to read, but for today it's enough that we have the test. If the foetus happens to test positive then we shall read it together and talk a whole lot more.'

'When you've only brought one shirt?'

CHAPTER TWO

THE bitterness in Caroline's voice shocked Carlos, and he stared at her, trying to work out where it had come from.

'One shirt?' he repeated, when no enlightenment came to mind.

'You're obviously not intending to stay very long, so when are we supposed to discuss it?'

She'd pushed herself off his knee and was pacing the very small living room in her little cottage. It was a comfortable room, but not really big enough for successful pacing, so she was crossing back and forth in front of him like the pendulum on a grandfather clock.

'I can't stay long,' he said, as gently as he could. 'With my father's death, there is so much happening at the moment—a few days was all I could manage.'

He stood up and halted her movement by taking her in his arms, tilting her chin up so she was forced to look at him.

'But I was hoping to take you back with me,

Caroline. We are expecting a child together, and the child will be my heir—we will marry, surely?'

The words echoed in the space inside Caz's head where her brain had once been. They bounced off bone and hit against each other, making them even less intelligible. In the end she put enough of them together to form a question, though it came out very faint and wavery.

'You want us to marry?'

'Of course,' the infuriating stranger in her living room replied. 'Is that not the best option?'

But you don't love me, she wanted to protest— though she knew that would sound pathetic, so she slammed her lips closed on the words and looked into the blue eyes that still so steadfastly held her gaze.

'But marriage isn't in your plans—not yet—you told me that yourself.'

There—that was a better objection, and now she was getting herself back together again her heart could stop skipping around in her chest like a child high on red cordial. Marry Carlos, indeed!

But white doves fluttered in the periphery of her mind, and the scent of orange blossom filled her nostrils—

Pregnancy brain—it had to be that! And Carlos was talking again.

'Lots of things weren't in my plans, Caroline.' He sounded so serious she had to force herself to listen. 'My father's death, for one.'

The anguish in his voice made her hold him again, but in the silence her brain began to work again. Carlos had spoken of having limited time to pursue his dream, and if he wasn't expecting to develop Huntington's Disease, then why…

'Did he have some kind of business that you must now take over?'

'Some kind of business describes it perfectly, and yes—' he said. But before he could explain further his mobile rang. Listening to his end of the conversation, she realised it was the genetic testing clinic.

'They've had a cancellation and can take us earlier—is this all right with you?' he asked.

Caz agreed, in some ways pleased to have the marriage conversation terminated—or at least put off for the moment.

'Have you got the address?' she asked, and he passed her his notebook, opened at a different page from the one he'd been using.

'It's about fifteen minutes away,' she told him, and he relayed this to the person on the other end of the phone.

He slipped the phone back into his pocket and took her hand.

'They'll talk about it with you before they do the tests, but you know the procedures?'

'Chorionic Villus Sampling—yes, I've heard of it. We said fifteen minutes. We have to get moving.'

She tried to tug her hand away, but he held firm.

'And you know, although it's very rare, that there's a risk of miscarriage in any antenatal testing procedure?'

She did know it, but right up to this moment had refused to consider it. However, she wasn't going to let Carlos see her fears, so she forced a smile and tried to make a joke of it.

'Good thing I didn't agree to your proposal, isn't it?' she said. 'Marriage might not be necessary after all.'

Unfortunately her voice cracked at the end of the sentence, and Carlos heard not only the pathos of her attempt at light-heartedness, but her fear. He held her close for a moment.

'You do not have to stand alone any more, Caroline,' he said quietly. 'I will always be there for you, and the marriage offer stands no matter what. I believe we could make a go of marriage, you and I.'

Now she was even more confused—but practicality saved her. She found her car key, her handbag, and her medical records, and led the way outside, pausing only to lock the door behind them.

Was it the uncertainty of what lay ahead that caused them to lapse into silence on the short journey? Although Carlos appeared to be interested in the area through which they passed, looking around him as if fascinated by what he was seeing.

'So many wooden houses—and all of them have their own yards. I can see some blocks of apartments, but do most people live in these separate homes?' he finally asked. And talking about the Queensland way of building—houses on tall stumps to allow cool draughts to flow underneath, people wanting their own little bit of land—kept them going until they reached the clinic.

Where the first task involved completing long and complicated forms!

Caz found filling hers in relatively easy—she'd completed so many recently, having had to find an obstetrician and a radiology practice—so she finished first, and looked across at where Carlos was neatly printing out the information required.

'"Carlos Eduardo Estefan Deziguel"?' she read out from the first line. 'That's your name? Your whole name?'

For the first time it struck her that she'd never even known the surname of the man she'd slept with—let alone that he had a whole string of names.

'Would you have liked it to be longer?' he teased, the blue eyes catching hers while his mobile mouth tilted into a half-smile.

Her heart began its jittering thing again, but she hid her reaction behind meaningless conversation.

'No wonder it's taking you so long to complete the form.'

She looked further down the sheet, thinking how like him the strong, upright black lettering was.

'Apartado de Correo 1? That's your address?'

'You would say post office box—most of Cascaverado is Spanish-speaking.'

'Cascaverado!'

Caz pointed to the word in the address line. 'That is your town? I remembered the Casca-part but kept forgetting the rest of it.'

'It is my country,' Carlos replied, adding, 'Now, hush, or they will want us for the appointment before I am halfway through doing this—I must add the family history, you see, so they understand why we need the test.'

Caz left him in peace, wondering about the country called Cascaverado. She'd never heard of it, but then she knew there were lots of tiny countries in Europe—places like Monaco, but not as well-known—obviously Cascaverado was one of those.

Carlos completed the form and stood up to hand it to the receptionist, then returned and sat beside Caz, once again taking her hand.

'I should have come sooner—known sooner,' he said. 'Filling in the form, I realised how unfair this is on you—we've not discussed what you'd want to do should the test prove positive, or even whether you want to take the test.'

He felt her fingers tighten and try to pull away, but it was important to get it all said.

'It is not too late to pull out—to think some more about it,' he said, watching her face and trying to read her emotions. But the hurt that husband of hers had done her had trained her to school her features. 'I was so surprised, and I've rushed you into this. Life at home is chaotic, so I acted first and thought afterwards.'

She turned towards him, the lovely eyes softening as she looked at him going so soft, in fact, he felt a churning in his belly. He had flung so many shocks at this woman today, yet she was still able to smile at him. Maybe it showed the strength she'd developed after her divorce. Or maybe it had always been there, muted by a dominating husband. And now a different feeling began to steal through him—a feeling that this woman would be perfect as his wife. And not only because he was physically attracted to her—that was a bonus in a marriage of convenience—but because she was able to handle anything that was thrown at her.

And back in Cascaverado there'd be plenty!

A nurse appeared through a side door.

'The doctor will see you now,' she said.

'A moment, please,' Carlos said, and the woman nodded, disappearing, but leaving the door open.

'You haven't answered me,' he said.

She shook her head.

'I can't, Carlos, I honestly can't. I have absolutely no idea how I'm going to react, but yes, even if I'd had more time to think about it, I know I'd want the test. Maybe we'll have to think about termination later, or maybe we won't, but right now we need to know what we're facing.'

She used their still-linked hands to urge him to his feet and led the way towards the door, turning back to smile as she said, 'It can't be worse than bombs and mortar fire!'

He knew the teasing remark was to lighten the moment, but also knew if she was feeling even a quarter of the tension that he was feeling then it was a miracle she'd been able to make the joke.

This was another example of her strength, and combined with a temperament that took most challenges in its stride, it would indeed make her the perfect consort.

The doctor stood to greet them and to introduce his colleague, a genetic counsellor.

'I see from your forms that you're both medical people, which makes explanations a little easier, but that doesn't mean you won't have physical and emotional hurdles to leap both before and after the testing. Firstly, do you understand what's involved in the test?'

Caz answered him, telling him she'd had a friend who'd had CVS for some reason, and she'd looked it up on the Internet to find out more about it.

'And the results?' Carlos asked. 'When can we expect to get them?'

'Normally they take up to fourteen days, although if you wish to pay extra to get them to a specialist laboratory that will rush them through you could know as early as tomorrow.'

Caz turned to Carlos—he was in such a hurry to get home she was sure he'd opt for the fast turn-around—but to her surprise he shook his head.

'Fourteen days gives us time to think about things and discuss all the options, although for your peace of mind, Caroline, would you prefer to know sooner?'

Would she?

She'd certainly sleep better once she knew for sure, and in fourteen days Carlos would be back in his post office box in Cascaverado—there, she'd remembered it—while she...

'You can fly back with me, and we can have the results e-mailed to us,' he said, as if sensing her confusion.

She shook her head.

'No, I'd like the fast turnaround. I'm happy to pay the extra cost.'

'Nonsense,' he said. 'Personally I'd like to know as soon as possible, too, rather than having doubts hanging over our heads.'

He turned to the doctor.

'Fast turnaround, please.'

Caz felt a little of the tension ease from her body, but a lot remained. This wasn't good. If she was tense when they put the needle in anything could happen. She took several deep breaths, only half listening to the conversation going on between Carlos and the counsellor—talk about his family history of Huntington's Disease, who among his forebears had

had it, how it had been misdiagnosed as Parkinson's in his maternal grandfather, and how although he, Carlos, had escaped the problem, he knew the number of repeats could grow with each generation, hence his worry about his own unborn child.

Then somehow the conversation had changed, and he was talking about hereditary diseases in general.

'Unfortunately there was too much inbreeding in the royal families of Europe. Almost everyone was related to England's Queen Victoria, and to one or other of the Spanish kings and the German princes, so hereditary diseases flourished.'

Haemophilia, Caz remembered, although the conversation was still distinctly weird.

But it was when Carlos spoke again that the real shock occurred.

'In our case, though, it wasn't my father's family that brought a hereditary disease, but my mother's. She was distantly related to my father, and, of course, their marriage was arranged. But if they'd known of the time-bomb of Huntington's sitting in her genetic structure I imagine someone else would have been chosen for him.'

Marriage arranged?

Someone else chosen for him?

Okay, so maybe in some places marriages *were* still arranged, but Caz was feeling distinctly uneasy.

'And has anyone else in the royal family—your

royal family—tested positive to Huntington's in the future? Siblings, perhaps?'

The counsellor had obviously been listening more closely than Caz. Had Carlos really been discussing royalty in relation to himself?

His reply gave her the answer, and such a shock that she felt her body tense. A tremor she couldn't control spread through her, so she had to hug herself to control it.

'I'm an only child,' he said. 'So you see, this child will be my heir, and heir to the princedom, whether it is male or female. We do not differentiate—the firstborn succeeds. So you will understand why I am anxious about the testing.'

He was involved in his conversation with the counsellor and the doctor, so failed to see Caz's reaction—but he'd soon catch on if she yelled, 'Heir to what princedom? What the hell are you talking about?' But here? In this office? What would the specialists think of someone pregnant by a man of whom she knew so little?

Princedom?

CHAPTER THREE

CAROLINE wondered if Carlos put his hand on her
arm because he'd sensed her astonishment—not to
mention anger!

'You must be calm and relaxed,' he said quietly,
and before the wrath exploded out of her the counsellor was asking her if they'd considered the options
should the foetus prove positive to Huntington's.

Did they—she in particular—wish to discuss that
now?

'Right now—' by some miracle she managed to
sound quite rational '—all I want is to do the test.'

Then she could get Carlos out of the office and
have it out with him!

It did occur to her to wonder how she, who had
trouble being really angry about things, should be so
overwhelmingly enraged by discovering Carlos was
a royal. But then she was being ushered into a screen-
ing room, helped onto an examination table, and
with Carlos by her side—he'd taken her hand

without so much as a by-your-leave—she felt cold jelly smeared across her belly and then the head of the ultrasound machine tracing across it.

'Look—our baby!' Carlos pointed out, obviously delighted by this first sight of the tiny blob.

'The position is good. You're happy for us to go ahead?'

The surgeon was speaking, but Caz too was staring at their unborn baby, and now fear and anxiety were mixing with her anger. She was doing this test because Carlos had hustled her into it, but could she really, if the test was positive, not allow the tiny dot on the screen to grow and develop into a real person?

She could feel tears on her cheeks, knew Carlos was wiping them away and murmuring to her in his own tongue, soft words that once again curled into her ears. Although now they curled around her heart as well—

'We will talk about it,' he assured her, as if he too now felt an attachment to the child growing inside her. 'We do not make decisions today. Today is just the first stage in finding out.'

The procedure was over in minutes and they left the office, Caz clutching a folder full of information and the phone numbers of numerous people she could talk to about all aspects of the situation should she need more support and guidance in her decision.

'Give me your car keys. I will drive—you are to rest.'

They were halfway across the car park when

Carlos spoke, and Caz had put the possible ramifications of the test far enough behind her for anger to have come to the fore again.

'That's all you have to say?' she demanded. 'Give me the car keys? You have to rest? That's it? No explanation? No apologies?'

Carlos was looking genuinely puzzled.

'Apologies?' he echoed. 'Was I out of order in there?'

'Out of order?' Caz was yelling now—or nearly yelling. 'You were more than out of order! The whole thing was bizarre. As if it's not bad enough to have all this genetic stuff happening, you walk in there and start babbling on about royal families. *What* royal family, Carlos Whoever-you-are? And how come you never happened to mention this to me before? Because I didn't count? Because I was just a little fling while we were stuck together for a few days? Because I wasn't important enough to know stuff like that?'

She paused for breath, but before he could defend himself more grievances surfaced.

'All right, so it *was* just a fling, and we both knew that, but we talked about all kinds of things. I even told you why my mother always washes the clothes on a Tuesday—how pathetic was *that* conversation?—yet somehow it never occurred to you to share information like your being royal with me?'

He was smiling now—not a huge, wide smile,

but there was definitely a smile dancing around his dangerously seductive lips.

How absurd was that? To be noticing seductive lips at this moment!

'I remember your mother washes the clothes on a Tuesday because when your older brothers were little and the family lived in an apartment all the other women washed on a Monday and the lines were full,' he said. 'Am I right?'

Caz glared at him.

'Don't think you'll get Brownie points for remembering such a ridiculous thing. I want to know why, if I was talking such trivia—and we talked about everything under the sun—you never saw fit to mention this royal stuff.'

'Brownie points? What are these?'

Caz was waving away this diversion when a car drove by, and Carlos took her arm to guide her closer to her car.

'I understand you're upset,' he said, looking down into her face, the eyes she saw every night in her dreams studying her with deep concern. 'But you shouldn't be—not now. Now you must be relaxed— and as for the other, I'll explain it all to you.'

Then he smiled again, and dropped the lightest of kisses on her lips. And though anger—or perhaps anxiety—still knotted her stomach, Caz found herself handing over her car keys and allowing herself to be settled into the passenger seat.

He leant across her to fasten her seat belt, then touched his fingers to her cheek, still smiling.

'It's not that easy, you know,' he said, his face still inches from hers. 'To tell someone things like that. What can one say? Oh, by the way—I'm a prince! It sounds ridiculous, no?'

Before she could reply, he'd closed her door and was walking around to the driving seat. He was right, of course. It would have sounded ridiculous. In fact, she'd probably have thought he was joking and ignored it. But right now an even greater worry had surfaced.

'You're going to drive? You know we drive on the left-hand side of the road?'

He patted her hand.

'I learned to drive in England, so I'll manage. You will sit there and give directions, and I will get you safely home.'

Home!

Caz gave directions automatically, but the word 'home' was now hammering in her head. Carlos had talked of this child—*her* child—as his heir. That couldn't happen. She lived here: Brisbane, Queensland, Australia, the World, the Universe, as she used to write on her school notebooks a long time ago. This was her home, and would be her baby's home too.

Carlos pulled the car into the driveway of the little cottage and looked anxiously at Caroline. Although she'd been precise in her directions, he'd known she was giving them on automatic pilot because he'd seen the worries flitting like shadows across her face. *Dios mio*, but she had enough to worry about—that was for sure. The test, the after-effects of the test with the remote possibility of miscarriage, the decision they might have to make…

He took her hand and ran his thumb across the palm.

'We will work it out,' he assured her, and she turned to look at him.

'*Will* we, Carlos?' she demanded. 'Do you *really* believe that? Because from where I'm sitting this situation is getting more and more outrageous, and any possibility of a solution is disappearing further and further into the stratosphere.'

He was about to ask what worried her most—the test results or the decision they might have to make once they had them—when she spoke again, though in such a quiet voice he barely caught the words.

'Perhaps a positive test would be the best result.'

He shook his head, unable to believe he'd heard right, and turned so he could grasp her shoulders.

'You cannot mean that,' he said, but grey eyes awash with tears met his and she nodded.

'Of course it would be,' she muttered gruffly. 'I have a termination. No baby, no problem.'

But the tears now spilling over and rolling down her cheeks gave the lie to her defiant words, and he got out of the car and came around to open the passenger door, bending across her to release the seat belt, then helping her out and drawing her into his arms, holding her close.

'You don't for one moment believe that, so tell me just what problem you feel it would solve.'

She nestled against him, and when she spoke her words were muffled by his shirt.

'This whole heir and royal thing—I mean, how can my baby be your heir when you're there and I'm here and— Oh, Carlos, it's such a mess!'

He guided her to the front door, found the right key on her keyring and led her inside, settling her in a comfortable armchair in her living room.

'You must rest for three days, the doctor said, so I will care for you. I must phone the hotel and tell them I won't be staying there—and buy some more shirts.'

He was thinking out loud, thinking practicalities, because trying to put himself in Caroline's place to work out the source of her distress was proving impossible. But at least he'd made her smile, and something about her sitting there, with tearstains on her cheeks, smiling at him, made his heart pause in its beating. He went and knelt in front of her.

'The "royal thing", as you call it, is no big deal,' he assured her. 'Yes, I had hoped my father would live for many, many more years, leaving me free to pursue my dream, but the building is complete and most of the staff are in place. I have competent management people, and once I've sorted out the absolutely necessary official royal duties I'm sure there'll be plenty of time for me to do hands-on work in the centre.'

He allowed himself a smile.

'After all, my father found plenty of time for skiing and sailing and racing his horses.'

Now she was shaking her head, but she was still smiling, he thought, though only with her eyes.

'Carlos, I know you've a very one-track mind about your dream, but it isn't your royal duties— whatever they might be—that worry me, but where my baby fits in all of this.'

'Our baby,' he corrected, placing his hand against her stomach. 'And it will fit in with both of us—with you and me, its parents.'

'In Casca—?'

She stumbled again over the word.

'Cascaverado. Of course. Where else would my wife and family live?'

It was all too much for Caz. She put her head in her hands and shook it slowly, to and fro. Maybe movement would make some sense of all that was going on. When that didn't work she rested it against the back of the chair, eyes still closed, so she couldn't see the man who knelt at her feet—the man who took so much for granted. He'd all but blown her mind.

'Tea,' she murmured, thinking something as normal as a nice cup of tea might help restore some sanity to the morning. 'Teabags are in a container that says rice. White, no sugar.'

He stood up and left the room—very biddable for a prince!

A *prince*! How could he possibly be a prince?

And how could he possibly assume she could be a princess! Good grief, she had about as much idea of formal etiquette as one of her mother's cats. In fact, the cats probably had more idea. She could hold her own in polite company, certainly, and she didn't think she had any appalling table manners—but royalty?

No, it was impossible—and the sooner Carlos realised it, the better.

He returned—not only with tea, but with biscuits he must have found in the pantry, the whole lot set on a tray she kept beside the refrigerator.

'I haven't asked,' he said as he set the tray down on the coffee table in front of her, 'but have you been well? Have you suffered morning sickness? Nausea at other times? Has it been hard on you?'

She had to smile. This was the Carlos of Afghanistan—always considerate of her welfare, always searching for signs that she might be getting stressed or frightened, always being there for her— a rock of comfort and support.

'I've been disgustingly well,' she said. 'Never better. In fact, my mother says she never suffered during her pregnancies, which is probably why she had four of them.'

'Ah, your mother,' Carlos said, as Caz sipped her tea and wondered how something so normal as sitting in her own living room drinking tea could still be so unreal. 'I must meet your mother—and your father and brothers, too, of course. Your father in particular.'

'Why?'

The question came out far more bluntly than Caz had intended, but for all her assurances that she'd been well throughout her pregnancy thus far, the tea was now curdling in her stomach as she considered the implications of Carlos's statement.

He was smiling at her—more stomach curdling!

'To ask for your hand in marriage, of course, and to discuss the things he will doubtless wish to know about provision for your future.'

Caz shook her head.

'I don't believe this!' she said. 'No one asks the father for his daughter's hand any more—well, not many people do—and my future is my own concern, not my father's.'

She knew she was a bit off track with this argument—that there were far more important things she should be arguing about—but right now she couldn't get a grasp on them.

'I will speak to your father,' Carlos repeated sternly. 'It may be old-fashioned, but it's the right thing to do.'

'And me?' Caz snapped. 'Do I get a look-in here? Are you actually going to ask me to marry you, or are you just assuming, as a prince, that I shall naturally fall at your feet and agree to anything you decree?'

She had a vague idea that maybe parliaments and not royals made decrees, but it was a minor point. Of far more consequence was the fact that Carlos remained totally unfazed by her crossness. In fact, he was smiling.

'Of course I will ask you, but I must ask him first—that's the correct procedure.'

'But if I don't want to marry you, what's the point?'

'Ah!'

He said it softly, but she knew she'd finally caught his attention. He moved towards her, once again kneeling in front of her.

'But why would you not, Caroline?' He sounded genuinely puzzled. 'I realise I will be taking you away from your friends and family, but you can fly back to visit them whenever you wish. As for the two of us— we established liking and respect for each other, didn't we? And we know we can laugh together, and we're good in bed, and we'll have a child in common—is all of this not enough for marriage?'

He stood up now, and lifted her from the chair, sitting down again with her on his knee, doing it so effortlessly that Caz couldn't help but marvel at the strength of the man.

'I know love betrayed you once, and so I do not

ask that of you,' he continued, speaking quietly but letting his lips brush tiny kisses on her temple and cheek in between the words. 'But I would never betray you in that way—never be unfaithful to you. I, too, have seen betrayal, and I am far too fond of you to hurt you in such a way.'

Caz felt the kisses, soft caresses on her skin, and felt his words touch her heart the same way, soft and gentle. But they did nothing to alleviate the ache inside that heart, the ache that she knew now only love would heal. But Carlos was neither asking for nor giving love, he was making that very plain, and though part of her wondered just what else she didn't know about this man—he too had been betrayed?— she knew she had to come to terms with her own pain first.

And learn to conceal her love…

CHAPTER FOUR

THREE days' rest!

How could she rest, with the test results hanging over her head and the decision she might have to make gnawing away at her soul?

How could she rest knowing Carlos was lying in bed just through the wall, in her tiny spare bedroom?

Actually, thinking about the decision was better than thinking about Carlos, so she thought and thought, finally coming to the conclusion that she'd find a termination almost impossible.

How could he sleep, knowing she was lying in bed through the very thin wall that separated the bedrooms? Carlos tossed and turned, remembering the doctor's words—no sex for three days—and wondering if he'd ever make love to Caroline again, the way things were going. Keen as he was to resume the brief but passionate physical relationship they'd had in Afghanistan—his body tightened at the mem-

ory—he knew even without the medical warning
that whisking her back to bed at this stage would be
wrong.

He needed this marriage to be a business relationship, based on their shared child, and commonsense
and respect for each other. It was good that they were
attracted to each other, but he'd seen where strong
attraction could lead and was wary of it.

But thinking of attraction did nothing but excite his
body, so he'd think of the baby instead—his baby!
He'd be a good father—he was certain of that—far
more hands-on than his own father had been. And
although children had been a long way down the track
in his earlier life-plan, now that one was on the way
he found himself thinking it would be nice to have
more.

Or was he thinking that because it would mean
making love with the woman through the wall?

He needed to get this off his mind!

He would think about the baby he'd conceived
instead—and the impending test results…

'A life is a life,' Caz said to him over breakfast the
next morning, whilst wondering whether they would
serve cereal for breakfast in a palace. 'I'm not certain
I would want a termination.'

'Nor would I want you to,' he said, reaching out
to take her hand. 'If my mother's parents had been
forced to make a similar decision then neither she nor

I would be here, and I know, for all she's suffered and is still to suffer, the world would have been a lesser place without her.'

All she's suffered? Caz would have liked to ask him about that, but she'd heard the catch in his voice as he'd talked of his mother so she let it go, concentrating on her cereal instead.

Carlos had insisted she obey the doctor's advice, and now she knew he was in agreement with her as far as the consequences of the test result were concerned, she *did* rest—with her prince, when he was at home, waiting on her hand and foot. Not that he'd been at home all that often, having tracked down her astonished father at work, met her at first suspicious brothers, visited her bemused mother at the small boutique she owned, and apparently, to Caz's fury, organised a whole new wardrobe for her.

It was Derrick all over again—bulldozing ahead, organising her life!

Yet somehow it was different.

Most of the time!

'You're saying my clothes aren't good enough for Cascaverado?' she demanded, when he arrived back at the cottage one evening with a mass of shopping bags.

He smiled at her—which, she realised, was how he usually calmed her increasingly frequent bursts of temper. *She* who'd never had a temper before!

'It is winter over there, very cold, and your mother knows suppliers who could find winter clothes for you in the midst of your hot Australian summer. Caroline, I know this is difficult for you, but the child will be my heir, and he or she should grow up in Cascaverado. So, for now, some Australian designer clothes—but once we are back home there are local designers who will beg to dress you, proud that their beautiful princess is wearing their clothes.'

Caz had been doing all right—calming down under the influence of his smile and his common sense words—until he got to the 'princess' bit.

'I can't be a princess,' she wailed. 'Honestly, Carlos, this whole thing is ridiculous!'

He came and sat beside her, patting her belly as he did so—a little habit that had begun when the test results had come back negative. After sharing her initial relief and joy, he'd patted her belly and spoken to the growing baby inside, telling him or her not to worry, because they would have kept him or her anyway.

But now all his attention was on Caz.

'Princesses are people, just like you and me—well, like you. Human beings—two legs, two arms, a head and all the other bits—though few of them have your natural beauty and your strength of character. And you won't have to do this on your own. My mother will help you, and there are any number of women in the castle who will be only too happy to ease the way as you settle in.'

They'd had the 'castle' conversation before, and, yes, Carlos had admitted, her entire cottage would

probably fit into one of the ballrooms at the castle—
one of the ballrooms!—but Caz still felt a stirring in
her stomach when she heard the word. Instinct told
her that not *all* the women in the castle would be welcoming. Some of them had doubtless thought to
marry Carlos themselves, or had daughters or nieces
they'd considered suitable. To them, having an out-
sider come in would surely be an outrage.

She didn't mention her suspicions to Carlos, who
had brushed away all her previous objections, assuring and reassuring her that all would be well, talking
of the country he so obviously loved, filling her mind
with images of the medieval capital called
Deziguel—his family name.

CHAPTER FIVE

IT WAS exactly as he'd described it. Caz peered out of the window of the plane that had flown them from Paris to see a country that looked like something out of a child's storybook. High, snow-covered mountains, steep-roofed chalets, pine trees showing dark green where the snow had dropped from their branches; tiny towns clustered along the banks of a winding river—and then Deziguel was below them, the thick stone walls that had once been the city's defence adorned with flags; turreted stone buildings crammed side by side up steep, winding streets; a bridge across the river, arched high and covered with a shingled roof—truly a fairytale city.

But she was living out a fairytale, wasn't she? Cinderella, perhaps? And the wonder of it, the make-believe part, thrilled and excited her, even though beneath the excitement and the marvel of it all dark threads of concern tugged at her heart.

It was all happening too quickly, and she suspected that Carlos was deliberately rushing her, so she had too little time to worry—too little time to think. She knew him well enough to know he'd have decided this was in her best interests, for he truly did everything he could to make her happy.

Except loving her, of course. But could princesses really expect love?

She didn't know, but she thought they not only could, but should—though how this particular princess-in-waiting was supposed to win love, she didn't know. There was a part of Carlos that was closed to her. Oh, he could share emotion easily enough, blinking back tears when they'd talked of the options should the tests have proved positive, but love?

'There will be only a few people to meet us—my friends—so it will be unofficial and not too dramatic for you,' Carlos told her as he helped her up from the first-class seat and held the warm coat her mother had somehow been able to find in sub-tropical Brisbane's summer so Caz could slide her arms into it.

The hostess led them off the plane, apparently holding back the other passengers until the couple from first-class—the only passengers in that area—were safely through the tunnel and into the airport proper.

Only that wasn't where they went. A uniformed official greeted Carlos with a sharp salute, then unlocked a door and led them along a passage into a small room where five men and an older woman were waiting.

The men all hugged Carlos, and kissed him on both cheeks, then he went to the woman seated at the far side of the room and bent over to kiss her, taking her hand and talking softly to her, gesturing to Caz to come closer.

'Caroline, this is my mother. Maman, meet my wife-to-be.'

The woman stood up, and Caz noticed how Carlos supported her on one side, though none of the physical signs so typical of Huntington's Disease were in evidence at the moment.

'I am pleased my son has found a wife,' the older woman said, shaking Caz's hand, then pulling her forward to kiss her cheek. 'He tells me you speak a little French, and as that is a better language for me than English, maybe in time we can use it. But while you settle in, I will try my English out on you.'

'Your English sounds far better than my French,' Caz assured her, reading kindness in the woman's eyes—Carlos's eyes! Strong genes... 'Carlos has been trying to teach me a little Spanish, but if I can become proficient in even one of your country's languages, I will be happy.'

'Your country too—and we must settle on our address to each other. I may call you Caroline?'

Caz wanted to offer the diminutive, but as Carlos never used it she nodded her agreement.

'And you will call me Dominique, *n'est-ce pas*?'

'Thank you, Dominique,' Caz said. 'I would be honoured to call you by your name.'

'Honoured, indeed,' Carlos whispered to her as, after introductions to the men in the party, they walked along another passage towards waiting vehicles. 'Very few people get to call my mother by her first name.'

'Then what do they call her?' Caz asked, genuinely puzzled, and wondering if this was some kind of royal protocol that she would have to understand.

'They call her Madame—always have. I called her that myself when I was little, because I thought it was her name, but she explained somewhere along the line, and she's been Maman to me ever since.'

There were a dozen—or maybe a hundred—more questions Caz wanted to ask, but now she was being seated with Dominique in the back of a sleek limousine, with one of Carlos's friends taking the jump seat facing them, while another rode beside the chauffeur. Of Carlos himself there was no sign, and she realised he'd been whisked away in a second vehicle.

Friends or bodyguards? The notion wormed its way into her head, and as the suspicion grew, her stomach churned. This was all getting far too real. She was plunging into a situation about which she knew absolutely nothing, and while she'd been anxious about it—who wouldn't be?—she hadn't, until now, felt any fear.

But bodyguards?

She pressed her hand to her stomach, knowing most of the fear she felt was for the child she carried.

'This is the route the procession will take for your marriage,' Dominique was saying, and Caz pulled herself together enough to take in the scenery outside the car.

The stone in the buildings had mellowed to a rosy yellow colour, so the city seemed to capture sunshine in every lane and alleyway, while the avenue down which they drove was lined with trees, now bare of leaves, the tracery of their branches making patterns against the bluest of blue skies.

Forgetting fear, used to tall, modern towers of glass, Caz gazed in wonder. These old, tightly packed buildings, the arches through which she glimpsed pedestrians hurrying about their business, the cobbled streets—

'It's like a medieval theme park, built to attract tourists,' she said to Dominique, who laughed.

'Not built to attract tourists,' Dominique replied. 'It's real enough, and business goes on here as in any city, but you are right about the tourists. The country relies on them for survival. My husband felt this was enough, but Carlos, as you probably know, has been trying to persuade high-tech companies to make their headquarters here. He believes we should rely on more than tourism. Of course his other project for amputees is not a money-making concern—more a money-taking one.'

She paused, then added, 'Though I doubt it costs him any more than my husband's diversions cost him.'

The bitterness in the woman's cultured voice shocked Caz, and she wondered about Dominique speaking out against her husband in front of the other men in the car. Fortunately, the one called Stefano diverted her attention, pointing out that they were now approaching the castle.

An expletive she rarely used herself but had heard a thousand times in Theatre was the only possible reaction. It really was a castle—a huge, great castle—sitting, as all the best castles no doubt should, on the highest point of a steep hill. Pointy turrets rose towards the sky, battlements marched along the top of the external walls, and what looked very like a drawbridge had been lowered on heavy chains across—yes, a moat.

'Do you keep crocodiles in the moat?' she asked as they crossed the dark water, but while Dominique looked confused Stefano simply frowned at her flippancy.

It was impossible, Caz realised. No way in the world was she ever going to fit into this life! Maybe if she'd had Carlos's love it would have been different—but alone in this great pile of stone? Loving him and not being able to show it because love was the last thing he wanted? She wanted to put her head in her hands and weep—but there was Dominique beside her, sitting so upright, so regal, she might have been a waxwork of the perfect queen.

And she, Caz, was supposed to emulate this woman?

The vehicle had drawn to a halt inside a spacious courtyard and uniformed—or was it liveried?—men were coming to open the car doors. Then, thankfully, Carlos was beside her, taking her hand as she emerged from the car. 'Too much pomp and ceremony for my little Aussie?' he murmured, and smiled at her in such a way she knew she *would* succeed—she *would* fill the role he'd thrust her into. For wasn't that what love was all about? Doing whatever one could for the object of that love? Helping to ease the burdens the loved one carried?

So he mightn't love her back, but did that mean she had to melt into a little puddle of despondency? Weeping, indeed! No way! She'd fought her way back from the destruction to her self-esteem Derrick had caused, and never again would she let herself be put down. She'd not only learn to be a princess, she'd be the best darned princess this country had ever had!

'Definitely not!' she responded, smiling at Carlos to cover the quiver of apprehension her resolve failed to quell. 'Bring it on!'

His answering smile was so warm the quiver disappeared, replaced by the now familiar flicker of desire that raced along her nerves and throbbed deep in her body. Would she ever not feel it?

Worse, would it ever be quenched again? Carlos would have his heir, and any future children, he'd explained, would be conceived through IVF. But on the flight, though he'd talked of separate bedrooms, he'd touched her in a way that suggested the attraction on his part wasn't completely dead...

'Bravo!' he said, breaking into her wayward thoughts and leading her past an array of people she assumed must be staff members who were lined up on both sides of the stairway. They smiled and nodded their heads as she passed. As Dominique was walking behind them, maybe the smiles were for her, but Caz smiled back anyway.

Though it was hard to keep the smile in place when they entered the building itself. She had no idea what the enormous room with its stone floors and wood-panelled walls might be called. Surely it was too grand to be a foyer, or an entrance hall! Elegant stone staircases curved up on either side, guarded by full suits of armour, two to each stairway, so it looked as if metal sentries were on duty at all times.

Heavy, thickly woven and beautifully coloured carpets were strewn across the stone flooring, and huge portraits—no doubt of previous Deziguels— adorned the walls, while high above them the stained-glass windows set into the upper walls threw jewel-coloured light in patches here and there.

Aware she was looking around like a child in fairyland, Caz pulled herself together.

'This all there is?' she said to Carlos, the teasing remark widening his smile.

'Come—we'll do a guided tour later, but for now, Maman has set aside this small sitting room for your personal use. We shall go there and have refreshments, and then I will show you to your room.'

He led her through an arched doorway into a charming room, with comfortable, tapestry-covered armchairs, a coffee table and a small writing desk set over by a window. Caz walked to the window and looked out. She *was* in fairyland, for below her, in a tumble of slate-roofed buildings and a maze of alleys and lanes, lay the city, while to her right the mountains climbed even higher, the pine trees of every fairytale she'd ever read standing straight and tall, the snow-capped peaks above them.

'It's unbelievably beautiful,' she murmured to Carlos, who had come to stand beside her. She shook her head at the unreality of it at the same time.

'As are you,' he whispered. 'The wonder in your eyes, your face, your voice—it is a gift to me.'

Startled to hear such a romantic comment from this man who was usually all practicality, she turned towards him—but a discreet knock was followed by the entrance of a young woman wheeling a cart on which were tea and coffee pots and an assortment of pastries and cakes.

'Madame would like to join you, if that is agreeable,' the young woman said, and Caz was surprised to see Dominique waiting by the door.

'Of course she must join us,' Caz said, adding to Carlos, 'Why wouldn't she?'

'It is your room,' he explained, and then, as his mother came in and Caz sat beside her on the settee, he paced the room, refusing coffee, though he did eat a pastry as he paced.

He was here for her, Caz realised, when he must have so much to do—official things, of course, and in his heart he must be aching to see what was happening at the special centre he had set up for amputees. *That* was his main preoccupation, and she could see it now.

'Go,' she said. 'I'm sure your mother will find someone to show me to my bedroom—but remember that once I've settled in I, too, want to see your centre.'

His smile was her reward, and when he crossed the room and bent to kiss her before departing, the promise in his kiss was an added bonus. He'd explained that they would keep separate bedroom suites even after they were married, although that did not mean they could not share the same bed. And he'd made it clear that for protocol's sake they should keep to their own bedrooms until after their marriage.

This kiss suggested otherwise—or perhaps suggested that arrangements could be made—because now there was no denying the desire Carlos had revealed, nor the answering heat he'd stirred in her body.

'You are lucky,' Dominique said when Carlos had departed. 'It is obvious you stir something in my son—something I failed to stir in his father.'

The statement was so personal Caz was taken aback again, and must have shown it, for Dominique took her hand and squeezed it.

'I apologise, my dear. It was appallingly bad taste to speak to you like that, but for so long I have had no one to whom I could speak openly. Carlos adored his father, which is how things should be, so I can hardly speak ill of the man to him, but he must have known how things were between us—the whole castle knew. Once my father developed Huntington's Disease, and tests showed I too would get it, I never shared my husband's bed again. It was as if the genetic weakness I carried made me abominable in his eyes.'

The expletive Caz rarely used sounded again in her head, and sympathy for this woman who had been so humiliated in front of all the staff at the castle made her put her arm around the upright shoulders and give her mother-in-law-to-be a warm hug.

'That must have been appalling for you. My husband went off with another woman, and I thought that was bad, but to have to go on living here, in such a way, you must have had the strength of Hercules. Was there a female equivalent to Hercules? I don't know—but whatever, you must be so strong, so admirable!'

But even as she comforted Dominique, and listened to her talking about her life in the castle, Caz wondered at the effect his estranged parents must have had on Carlos. Was this why he was afraid to love? Or was it because there'd been no love around him as he grew up that he'd never learned about it?

CHAPTER SIX

A LIGHT tap on the bedroom door drew Caz away from the window of her bedroom. She'd been in Cascaverado less than four hours, and already every window drew her like a magnet. Tearing herself away from the beauty they displayed was becoming increasingly difficult.

'Come in,' she called, thinking the English-speaking Marguerite, who'd been allotted as her special staff member, must be returning to take her to dinner.

But the moment the door opened Caz knew she'd been wrong, for no one but Carlos could produce that tingle of awareness in her skin, the flooding warmth in her veins. For him she'd turn away from the view, and when she did she had to smile, for he was formally dressed in a suit, a snow-white shirt beneath the dark charcoal jacket, a sober-looking tie tucked neatly away.

'So formal—and really handsome,' she teased, unable to *not* smile at him.

'Ah, but not beautiful, like my bride-to-be,' he said, coming towards her to take one hand, then twirling her around so he could see the full effect of the elegant but simple silvery sheath Marguerite had chosen for her to wear.

'Not too formal?' Caz asked, aware of the tremor doubt had created in her voice—although when Carlos was near her she felt far less uncertain.

'Just perfect,' he assured her, then put his forefinger under her chin and tilted it up. 'So perfect, in fact, I am afraid to kiss you.'

She *was* beautiful! Her hair was swept up on top of her head, revealing a long, slender neckline, while her dark eyebrows and lashes drew attention to her extraordinary eyes. In profile, her nose was neat and straight, while her lips curled slightly upward at all times, as if she was about to smile at some amusing thought—a thought he hoped she'd share with him!

Carlos knew he'd kind of been aware of that all along—the quiet beauty of this woman with grey eyes and silvery blonde hair—but tonight her beauty all but took his breath away, and as he touched his lips to hers, tasting lipstick, not Caroline, he felt an unfamiliar strangeness in his chest.

He surely wasn't worried because she was beautiful, was he?

And, if so, why?

She had moved back to the window, asking him questions about some of the buildings she could see in the city below, and as he took in the curve of her body, suggested more than outlined by the silver dress, his body stirred with a primitive urge to make her his, right here and now.

But she *was* his—already pledged to him—the family heirloom ring was in his pocket right now—so again why this internal uneasiness?

'Carlos?'

She'd turned, no doubt wondering why he hadn't answered her, and he shook away the unfamiliar thoughts, dampened down his libido and came to stand beside her, contenting himself with an arm around her waist and the feel of her body by his side.

'Do you want a formal, down-on-one-knee proposal? Or shall I just slip this ring on your finger?' he asked, not answering her question, but producing the ring, looking at it rather than at her.

This marriage was a business arrangement! A marriage to make his heir the legal successor to the throne!

She took it in her hand and examined it, touching the ruby at its centre with a slightly shaky finger.

'That's far too good a thing for me to wear,' she protested, and he had to laugh.

'You really don't get it, do you? It's all still unreal to you. Of course you will wear it. It is a family ring—one of many you will wear—but this one I chose for an engagement ring because it reminds me of you. Rubies promote loving and nurturing, two qualities you have in abundance, and they protect the heart—or so the stories go.'

For some reason Carlos was feeling uncertain again, rushing through his explanation and then prompting her, 'You *will* wear it?'

To protect my heart? Caz thought, slipping the ring on the third finger of her left hand. *It's far too late for that.*

'Yes, Carlos, I will wear it. Thank you,' she whispered, and stood on tiptoe to kiss him on the lips.

A thank-you kiss, nothing more, so she was startled when his arms closed around her, drawing her close, and his lips captured hers, the kiss deepening, becoming a hungry demand to which her body was responding only too willingly.

'What on earth is that?'

Startled back to her senses by the strident noise, Caz pushed away from him as she asked the question.

Carlos groaned and shook his head.

'The dinner bell, would you believe? Hardly a bell—but the days are long gone when servants ran along the passageways ringing hand-bells.'

He was smoothing her hair with his hands, and, looking at his tousled locks, Caz told him to check himself—she'd fix her own hair.

She slipped it out of the simple knot, brushed it, and tied it up again, then renewed the lipstick that had disappeared in the kiss. Carlos stood behind her, using her comb, and as Caz saw the image of the two of them in the mirror, caught sight of the ring on her hand, she knew that it was all only too real. One day, possibly in a pose like this, they'd have their portrait painted, to join the others in the hall downstairs...

But rather than excite her the idea left a bleakness in her heart. Wasn't love more important than a thousand portraits and a hundred castles?

'Come,' he said, dropping a kiss on the bare nape of her neck, distracting her from her straying thoughts. 'Let me take you to dinner.'

And with formal courtesy he took her elbow and guided her out of the room, along a balcony above the great entrance hall and down one of the grand staircases, then through the hall past her little sitting room, past other doors opening into receiving rooms of various kinds, to where big double doors stood open.

Caz halted on the threshold, unable to believe the sight in front of her. A long table seemed to stretch endlessly towards a roaring fire at the far end of the room—a fireplace large enough to roast an ox, she imagined. People who'd been mingling at the end of the room, near the fire, now came forward, taking up places at the table, standing behind their chairs.

'Do we always have to eat here?' Caz whispered, wondering when she and Carlos would ever have time to talk to each other, if not at mealtimes.

'No, this is a semi-formal occasion to welcome

you. We'll eat most often in the breakfast room—it's only half this size.'

Caz hoped he was teasing, but couldn't ask as he was leading her forward, introducing her to people as they passed, taking her to the far end of the table where Dominique stood.

'You will take my place here, Caroline,' she said. 'The gentleman on your right is Carlos's uncle, Eduardo Deziguel, and on your left is my old friend Alberto Salvatore.'

As Caz shook hands with the two men Dominique took her place beside Alberto, while Carlos found a chair about half a mile away from her.

'By rights,' he said, smiling as if he'd guessed her confusion, 'I should be down at the end—the other end is actually the head, and you're at the foot—but unless we all want to shout at each other right through the meal it's easier for me to sit here.'

Later, Caz remembered nothing of the meal, and wondered if it was jet lag or pregnancy that was making her feel so sleepy.

'It is the fire,' Alberto murmured to her, apparently catching the way her eyes kept wanting to close. 'It is beautiful to watch and to warm oneself by, but it drains the energy, and you have come a long way. I will tell Dominique you are weary and she will bring this to a close.'

To Caz's astonishment, although people had barely finished their desserts, Dominique stood up and announced that the women would have coffee in the drawing room and the men could join them later.

As there were only two other women present— one Eduardo's wife and the other a household controller of some kind—they made a little procession of four as they left the room. The men barely blinked, and Caz realised that leaving the men to their brandy was a tradition still alive and well in Cascaverado.

'If you are tired, my dear, I will ring for Marguerite and she will see you into bed,' Dominique said to Caz when they were back in the big hall.

'Thank you—I am tired,' Caz admitted, 'but there's no need to bother Marguerite.'

To her surprise, Dominique patted her cheek.

'Let her help you, my dear. Soon you will be so busy you will be grateful for any help you can get, so learn how to accept it gracefully.'

She pressed a small black button barely visible against the wall, and when a staff member appeared Dominique asked for Marguerite.

Caz found she *was* grateful, for, once undressed, she knew she was too tired to straighten her gown on a hanger or put her shoes away, let alone wash out her stockings.

Marguerite tucked her into bed, asked if she wanted a hot drink, then bustled around the room, returning it to rights before wishing Caz a good night's sleep and disappearing out through the door. Caz opened the book she'd been reading on the flight, but the words blurred in front of her eyes and she was asleep before she'd read a page.

Carlos saw the light beneath the door and tapped gently. When Caroline didn't answer he went in, not surprised to see her sound asleep, the book she'd been reading resting on the coverlet under the fingers of one hand.

Her left hand—the hand that held his ring.

In the light thrown by the bedside lamp the red stone glowed, as if by night it took on a life of its own.

Could rubies really protect the heart? Protect it from what? Surely not love?

And as he stared at his sleeping fiancée he wondered if he should have chosen another stone. He knew Caroline no longer trusted love, but somewhere deep inside him he found himself wanting that emotion from her—wanting her to love him...

Or maybe he was just tired and over-emotional...

He pulled one of the armchairs in the room closer to the bed and sank down in it, needing to think and plan for what lay ahead, yet wanting to be near her as well. Just as her strength and humour during their isolation in Afghanistan had helped him remain strong and confident, so now her presence, even in sleep, would help him sort out his thoughts.

Except it didn't. Sitting here beside her, he was becoming increasingly confused—not about what lay ahead; he could plot that out on a calendar and make time for all he had to do…somehow! But the thoughts that had come into his head earlier, thoughts about Caroline, were harder to pin down or tabulate.

Was it her book falling to the floor that had woken Caz? She didn't know, but once awake she looked around her, glad the bedside lamp was on so she could see her surroundings and not have that dreadful 'where am I?' feeling to contend with. But looking around produced the strangest surprise—Carlos, sound asleep in an armchair by her bed. Not just asleep, but making odd little noises—not exactly snores, but close.

That was what had woken her!

Smiling at the sight of him, though why he was there she had no idea, she reached out and touched his arm.

'Hey,' she said quietly. 'You'll wake up stiff and sore if you sleep there. Get up and go to bed.'

He opened his eyes and echoed the last phrase, then, stripping off his clothes, he climbed into bed beside her.

'Oh, Caroline, if you knew how I have longed for this—to have you in my home, in my bed.'

Caz was so warmed by the sincerity in his voice that she didn't correct him by pointing out it was *her* bed. In fact, technically, if he owned the castle then he probably owned all the beds. Nor did she remind him that until he'd found out she was pregnant there'd been no thought of her coming to his home.

She told herself it was enough that she was here with him, and as his hands worked their now familiar magic on her body she gave in to desire and let her own hands find familiar places on his body, touching and kissing until need burned too deeply to be denied any longer and she slid beneath him, wanting him to take her. Was it nothing more than physical hunger that drove his lovemaking? She had no idea, but very soon the intensity of his possession of her, and her own body's response to that intensity, burnt all thoughts from her mind until they peaked together, then lay, slumped and exhausted, in each other's arms.

Caz shifted under Carlos's weight, but when she tried to move away he held her close.

'No—sleep now, my Caroline,' he said. 'I'll stay with you. To hell with palace protocol!'

My Caroline?

The phrase echoed in Caz's head as she drifted off to sleep, secure in the arms of the man she loved.

If only…

He was gone when she awoke, but when she checked the time she could understand why. She'd slept until after ten! Marguerite must have heard her stirring, for she appeared, asking if Caz would like a cup of tea in bed before she got up for the day.

'The Prince says you must rest after your jour-

ney, so I will bring you breakfast up here, too,'
Marguerite added.

But although her sleep had been interrupted—
very pleasurably—Caz felt awake and alert.

'A pot of tea, not too strong, and a pastry of some
kind,' she told Marguerite. 'That will do me for breakfast. Tell me, where is Carlos? Do you know? Does he
have a secretary or someone who would know if he's
doing official work or has gone to the amputee centre?'

Marguerite smiled.

'I can tell you that. My husband is his—you know
the word valet?'

'I've read of such people,' Caz admitted. 'A kind
of dresser?'

'More a personal staff member who helps with all
kinds of things.' She blushed, and Caz wondered if
'all kinds of things' included waking his master from
the wrong bed and removing his hastily discarded
clothes. But she thought it better not to ask, and
Marguerite was now explaining that while she organised the tea she would find out where he was.

She disappeared, and Caz got out of bed, aware
that somewhere in the bottom of it was a slightly torn
nightdress. Oh, dear—how did people in a castle
filled with staff manage to hide such things?

Or maybe they didn't.

Caz found the nightie, only one strap damaged,
and dropped it into the basket she assumed was the
dirty clothes bin. Then she showered and dressed—

not in her usual jeans, but in black woollen trousers her mother had assured her would take her anywhere, so well cut were they, and a fine black wool pullover with a roll neck and a silvery pattern of leaves across it to relieve the all-black look.

Satisfied she was presentable, she was pulling on black boots when Marguerite reappeared with a tray, and set it at the table in the window alcove.

She frowned at Caz, and Caz sensed Marguerite really would have liked to dress her, but Caz could only take this princess thing so far.

'When I'm going somewhere grand in a ballgown you can help me,' she told Marguerite, who smiled before she replied.

'The Prince said you would be prickly.'

'Prickly? Is that what you think?'

Marguerite shook her head.

'More independent, I would say. I will tell him that is good.'

Caz smiled at her, aware she had an ally in this woman.

'And the Prince himself? Did you find out his plans?'

Marguerite nodded.

'At eleven-thirty he is going to the centre—his official work here will be done—but only for a few hours. At four he must see the Prime Minister. It is about the wedding.'

'I don't want to think about the wedding today,'

Caz told her. 'But eleven-thirty I can do. Can you let someone know I will go with him to the centre.'

'Of course, ma'am,' Marguerite responded, and for the first time Caz realised Marguerite was addressing her formally—probably she had been all along, although Caz had been too bemused and tired to take it in.

Could she ask this woman to call her by her name? Here, in the privacy of her bedroom?

'Does your husband call Carlos sir?' Caz asked, thinking this might be a good way to get around it.

'Of course,' Marguerite responded, then smiled. 'But for you, alone here in a strange country as you are, if you have a small name, a pet name you would prefer I use, then I will be happy to use it—but only in the bedroom suite, you understand?'

Caz beamed at her, so heartened by the woman's understanding that her voice was thick as she replied.

'Call me Caz,' she said.

CHAPTER SEVEN

LOVE doesn't work, Carlos reminded himself as he paced his suite in the early hours of the morning. Not in royal marriages anyway. He had his own parents as an example, and had seen many more so-called love-matches falter—some within a few years of the couple taking their vows. Happy-ever-after might work for some people, but the added pressure of royal duties seemed to drive rifts between people.

Not that the strangeness he was feeling in Caroline's company could *be* love!

However, until he sorted out what it was, the best thing to do would be to avoid all but the most necessary contact with her—to keep his distance.

Having decided this was the answer before he'd even eaten breakfast, Carlos was astonished to find her waiting by his car later in the morning, carrying on a halting conversation in Spanish with one of the chauffeurs who had brought the vehicle from the garages. As Carlos drew closer he saw her hand Alfonso a small note.

He all but growled, although he knew he couldn't possibly be jealous.

'Alfonso has a sister who is backpacking in Australia,' his bride-to-be said cheerfully when she realised he'd joined them. 'I've given him Mum and Dad's address so he can e-mail it to her for when she's in Brisbane.'

Carlos shook his head, realising in an instant that any Cascaveradan youth backpacking through Australia would soon be finding a way to the Blackmans' home. He wondered how they'd handle it.

As easily and as casually as Caroline was handing out the address, that was how, Carlos decided. Her parents would welcome the strangers because they'd bring a glimpse of life in the country where their daughter had settled.

A mental headshake this time.

'And you're here why?' he asked her. 'To wave me off?'

She looked fantastic, slim and elegant in black with a touch of silver, but the boots made the plain outfit downright sexy and he knew he'd been right in deciding to keep his distance from her.

'I'm coming to the centre with you,' she said, her smile lighting up her face. 'Did Marguerite not get a message to you?'

Marguerite definitely had not—although she might have passed it to her husband, who had his own ideas about how Carlos should be treating his fiancée. It was a conspiracy... But now, in front of Alfonso, Carlos could hardly deny her the trip to the centre.

'I'll be busy there,' he warned, opening the car door for her.

'Then someone else can show me around,' she said, refusing to be put off by his abrupt statement.

He walked around the bonnet of the car, glared at Alfonso, who wasn't at fault in any way, then got in and started the engine.

'Do you drive yourself whenever possible?' Caroline asked, and though he was busy guiding the car through the gatehouse and over the drawbridge even her voice was affecting him now.

'For private business like this—my business—whenever possible.' He glanced her way, to see if his cool, practical response had affected her, but she was peering around her, the delight she obviously felt in his city lighting her face.

Beautiful!

Distance!

'Sometimes if I'm going to the city where the parking, as you can imagine, is horrific, Alfonso or one of the other drivers will take me and drop me off.'

Hmm, Caz thought. A different man this morning! Definitely not the passionate lover who couldn't get enough of her in bed last night, nor even the gentle man who'd held her close after their lovemaking, whispering Spanish words she hadn't understood but had sounded, as she'd slipped into sleep, like beautiful music in her ears.

She studied him. His strongly featured face was stern, and his hands were gripping the steering wheel tightly enough to whiten his knuckles—not bone-white, but white enough. Would some conversation relax him?

'What made you so interested in amputees?'

He looked startled, as if he hadn't expected her to speak, then his face grew shadowed, and though he hesitated a little longer eventually, in a low, husky voice that sent shivers down Caz's spine, he began to explain.

'My mother was—still is—interested in many causes, and one of them, when I was young, was the clearing of landmines in war-ravaged European countries. She took me on a visit once, and I met a boy who had the same birthday as I did. He was my age, we shared a birth date, and he had no feet.'

He paused, but Caz knew there was more so she remained silent.

'It seemed impossible to me. I couldn't comprehend that if I'd been him, and he'd been me, it would have been me with no feet.'

Caz reached over and touched his cheek, then dropped her hand to rest it on his thigh, offering the only comfort she felt he'd accept, for the enormity of that experience—the effect on him—was beyond words.

'I decided then I'd so something about it. I'd give him feet. Not only him, but other injured people.'

He turned to Caz and offered up a half smile that told her he was past the agony of the memory and back in the present.

'And you've kept that promise to yourself? Not many people do that, Carlos. You are very special.'

He shrugged away her praise.

'Not many people have the assets and contacts to see that it gets done, but when you are passionate about something other people see and feel that passion, and they want to be part of it. That's how I've got the centre built, and how I know I can continue to fund it in the future.'

Caz could hear the passion now, and understood it—understood also how frustrated he must feel.

'It upsets you, having so little time to give to the centre?'

He glanced her way, then turned his attention back to the road.

'Of course,' he said, and the words were blunt enough to discourage further questions. But in the end it was he who expanded on them. 'I thought I'd have another—well, ten years at least. My father was in his early sixties, and as healthy a man as you could imagine.'

Skiing, sailing, horse-riding—he would have been fit, Caz thought. And that thought led to another.

'But if he found time for all the activities he loved, can't you use that time for the centre?'

His lips thinned, and he sighed as he glanced her way again.

'He got away with far too much,' he said, turning his attention back to the road. 'Mainly because my mother carried a lot of the load of official duties.'

Caz's head spun. Would Carlos expect that of her? Should she offer? But in that case what would she become? A stand-in for him at official occasions and—?

She remembered an occasion back in Afghanistan, when he'd talked about his belief that marriages would be better if they were business arrangements. Then the description Carlos himself had used about her, describing Derrick's expectations—brood mare— flicked back into her mind. A coldness she'd never felt before crept through her body, icing the blood in her veins and stiffening her muscles.

Relax, she told herself, her hand finding her belly and pressing it, so the emotional coldness wouldn't affect the tiny person growing inside her. This was all supposition.

Wasn't it?

And did it even matter when she knew he didn't love her?

'Oh!'

They had pulled up in front of a very modern

building, all steel and glass, set in spacious parkland that had thickets of trees here and there, a wandering stream and smooth lawns. The parkland isolated the building from the old brick and stone buildings of the city, yet something about the lines of it was not out of keeping with the medieval uniqueness of Deziguel.

'It's beautiful,' she said, aware she was still staring as Carlos helped her out of the car.

And now, for the first time this morning, he smiled at her, unable to hide the pride he obviously felt in his centre.

'And more beautiful inside because of what it can achieve,' he said, walking beside her towards the front entrance, not touching her or holding her hand—but that might be because they were in public, and protocol demanded circumspection.

Or it might be because of the coldness she had sensed in him from the moment they'd met at the car…

He had to get away from her. Carlos knew that with a certainty bone-deep. Her smile of delight when she'd seen the building, the happiness in her eyes as she'd praised it, had nearly undone his resolution to keep his distance from her.

Fortunately one of his division managers was coming towards them—a young American woman who had heard about the centre and e-mailed him, begging him to let her work there.

'This is Justine,' he said, introducing her to Caroline. 'She'll be happy to show you around.'

Justine looked slightly taken aback, but she rallied, telling Caroline she'd be delighted to give her the guided tour.

'This is the file we were going to discuss,' she said, handing Carlos a plastic folder. 'And there's a message from the aid organisation—they think they've found Sarwar.'

'Our Sarwar?' Caroline said, turning towards Carlos. 'You've been looking for him?'

The happiness on her face nearly undid him once again—especially as his mind went back to the days they'd spent together, talking through gesture and mime with their only patient, trying to distract him from the despair he must have been feeling, not only at having lost his foot, but being trapped in a situation that might not have a good ending.

'Of course our Sarwar,' he told her, unable to not return her smile. 'Didn't I promise him a new foot?'

He spoke briefly to Justine about other business, then strode away, calling back something in Spanish.

'He says I'm to see you into a taxi later, as he might be delayed,' Justine translated, and explained that she'd learned Spanish in school.

But once Caz reached the children's section of the centre she knew she wouldn't be leaving for quite some time to come. There were only four children in residence, and their parents were also provided with accommodation—although there were enough carers to look after them if the parents couldn't come. One of the children had lost her legs and one hand through meningococcal disease, but the other three—two boys of about ten and a girl of seven— were the victims of landmines.

'They're all from different countries, speak different languages, yet they are able to communicate somehow—just look at them.'

And Caz did look, watching the interaction as the children played together, the older ones assisting the smaller ones in strapping on their prostheses, which seemed to be the object of this morning's exercise.

'We want them to be as independent as possible,' Justine explained, 'so even the little ones are encouraged to learn to fit the devices themselves. It's harder with hands, of course, because they need a shoulder harness. The muscles of the shoulder are used to work most prosthetic hand devices.'

Caz got down on the floor beside one little girl, Melanie, and watched as the nurse in charge fitted first a soft sleeve and then the device onto Melanie's lower arm. The little girl was obviously fascinated by her new hand, touching it and patting it.

The time flew by, and Caz was still playing with Melanie—although she'd helped one of the boys taking off and putting on his new legs, and steadied another one as he'd practised running—when she heard a familiar voice.

Felt the familiar tingle.

Brood mare! she reminded herself. She was a brood mare and an official hostess—a business arrangement—so she mustn't get too carried away.

And if Carlos was involved in doing such good as he was, with these children and the adults on the other side of the building, then wouldn't her life be worthwhile if she did what she could to free him for his work here?

He was still talking to someone behind her, so she had plenty of time to mull over this new concept of her future marriage, and then suddenly he was squatting beside her, talking to Melanie and admiring the new hand she held up for his inspection.

'As for you,' he said, touching Caz lightly on the shoulder. 'I thought I left orders for you to be put into a cab. Do you know it's close to three? You should be looking after yourself. Have you had lunch?'

The touch on her shoulder had sent the now familiar ripples of desire through her body, but she fought them, knowing she had a lot of thinking to do before she gave in to the desire he could generate so easily.

'Of course I've had lunch,' she said. 'I had it with the children.'

Then she turned to look at him, really look at him, her eyes meeting his.

'I will do what I can to spare you official duties,'

she said, 'but I want to be part of this as well. Especially part of the children's area. I won't just be a cipher, nor a—'

She hadn't meant to say the words—she'd really wanted to give some thought to the situation first—but they came out anyway.

'—a brood mare.'

His eyes narrowed, then she saw that he'd remembered the description he'd used of her before, and what looked like pain crossed his face.

'I would never dream of thinking of you that way,' he said, standing up and putting out a hand to help her to her feet. 'I have to go. I've a meeting I can't avoid at the palace, so I'll take you home.'

Home?

Could a castle ever be a home?

It could if the people who dwelt in it made it one, Caz decided as she kissed all the children goodbye, but she wasn't sure one person on her own could do it.

Nor was she certain she wanted to. Having heard the bitterness in Dominique's voice when she'd spoken of her husband, Caz knew she didn't want to go down that path…

'Tell me about Melanie's hand.'

The question was so abrupt Carlos suspected it was the last thing Caroline had been considering. In fact, given the stormy look that had been on her face, and the accusation she'd levelled at him earlier, he rather thought she'd asked about the child to stop herself thinking about whatever it was that was bothering her.

But answering the question was certainly easier than considering the things troubling either of them—her place in his life, and his continued desire to be near this woman, and the dangers inherent in his feeling this way.

'We felt—her parents and the other specialists in consultation—that while a hand that looks like a hand is not as useful to her as a claw device might be, at her age, starting school, a realistic-looking hand might be better for her confidence. She's had her legs fitted for some time, and is adept in using them, and with long pants as part of the school uniform she won't stand out from the other children.'

'Are they still cruel, do you think? Children?' Caroline asked, turning towards him and frowning slightly. 'I was thinking with all the access they have to television, with things like the Special Olympics highlighted, they might be more accepting of differences.'

'I don't know the answer to that,' Carlos confessed, 'but I imagine, just as any child with something different about them must come in for some teasing, so too would a little girl with prosthetic legs and hand.'

'I wonder about a video explaining how prostheses work—or perhaps, better still, a cartoon of some kind, with a hero or heroine with bionic legs. Would producing something like that and showing it in schools, or even on public television, both raise awareness and take away any stigma attached to prostheses?'

Now he had to smile at her.

'Great minds think alike—isn't that one of your English sayings? I already have a production company looking at developing such a thing. I believe we need a cartoon character who will be heroic, but at the same time real enough for children to empathise with him. Not being able to remember where he left his second leg—little things like that to make children laugh but also help them to understand that even heroes have problems.'

'Do they ever!' Caz replied, smiling back at him. 'I've always been worried about how Superman managed to get out of his suit in a telephone box— I mean, there's barely space enough to turn around— and then what happened to his clothes? Did he just leave his suit there? How many suits did he have?'

Carlos laughed, and for the first time today Caz felt herself relaxing. No, that wasn't right. She'd been relaxed when she'd been with the children, but this was the first time she'd relaxed in Carlos's presence. For some reason the loving man from the previous night had withdrawn, and only now was she catching a glimpse of him again.

A brief glimpse, that was, for already the laugh was nothing more than an echo in her mind and he was frowning again.

'I would never think of you as a brood mare,' he declared again. 'You *must* know that, Caroline!'

'Why must I?' she asked, knowing the answer she wanted was so simple.

Because I love you. That was all she wanted him to say.

But all she got was silence for what seemed like for ever, and then he said, 'Because I have far too much respect for you, for your skills and intelligence and courage, and your ability to cope. You are by far and away the most outstanding woman I have ever known—you are very special, Caroline, and exceedingly special to me.'

Would 'exceedingly special' do?

Carlos obviously thought so, for he had offered the words with great sincerity, but although they'd warmed some of the cold places in Caz's body, they hadn't touched her heart.

Did it matter?

She knew it did—but what could she do about it? She was carrying his child, the heir to the throne of Cascaverado, so somehow she had to work out a strategy for the life ahead of her—and her child.

Carlos turned onto the avenue that led up to the castle. Ahead of him he could see the place he thought of as home, but even earlier, when he'd used the word to Caroline, he'd wondered if that was what it was. It was where he'd grown up, and he knew and loved every brick and stone in the place, yet a home…?

During his years as an aid worker he'd seen families in many countries, refugees living in make-shift shelters with filth all around them, yet in many of those shelters he'd felt the concept of 'home' and known it bore little relationship to his own upbringing. He'd felt it again at the Blackmans'. Caroline's parents and brothers had welcomed him to their family, with wives and grandchildren buzzing around and a sense of loving chaos enveloping them all.

Did growing up in a castle, with staff all around, preclude any chance of feeling that kind of homeliness? Or had it been growing up with estranged parents? Somehow knowing from a young age of his mother's unhappiness? And guessing, early on, that it stemmed from his father, from love that wasn't returned?

Love that was frequently betrayed...

That was the danger with emotions—with love in particular—and his mother's pain was why he'd always been determined to stay free of such a debilitating and often transient sentiment. Even with his mother he'd been careful not to show too much, while for his father his feelings had been more admiration and respect—at least in the beginning.

As a young boy he had worshipped the tall man in his splendid uniform who rode and skied and shot so well, and he'd yearned to be like him. It was only in his late teens that he'd started to realise how self-focussed his father was, and begun to wonder if he really was the hero his childhood self had painted him.

'We can make it a home,' he said as he pulled up in the courtyard at the bottom of the wide flight of steps. 'You and I. Our child deserves that.'

Caz stared at him, wondering just how their thoughts had become so entangled that he'd answered the question she'd been asking herself.

'Not only can, but must,' she said, tucking all thoughts of love to the far corner of her mind and telling her heart it would survive without it. After all, they had great respect and admiration for each other, and he was fond of her—she was sure of that. Plus the—

Her mind faltered on the word 'lovemaking', and then bluntly substituted 'sex'. If she was going to cut sentimentality from her life, she could start there.

CHAPTER EIGHT

BUT would it work? The thought haunted her as she made her way back to her suite of rooms, where Marguerite chided her for being so long away.

'You had forgotten our most popular designer was coming, with ideas for your wedding gown? He could not stay, but he has left some pictures and samples of material he thinks would be suitable. But before you look at them you should rest—you are pale, and the altitude, the baby, they all take a toll.'

Caz was only too happy to lie down on the bed and rest, but although she felt drained and weary, sleep wouldn't come. It was all very well to tell herself a marriage without love would work, but to be contemplating a *wedding—another* wedding— no, she couldn't fool herself into being either happy or excited about that.

How could she don a gown and smile and laugh for photographers and guests, knowing it was all nothing more than a stage-managed performance?

She clambered off the bed and rang for Marguerite.

'What time is Carlos seeing the Prime Minister?' she demanded.

Marguerite glanced at her watch.

'Now—well, within a few minutes.'

'And it's to discuss the wedding?'

Marguerite looked puzzled, but she nodded.

'I must see him first. How can I contact him?'

Marguerite lifted the phone and pressed some buttons, spoke to someone, then handed the receiver to Caz.

'We have to talk,' she said. 'Now—before your meeting! Can we get out of the building—can we walk somewhere?'

Carlos obviously heard the desperation in her voice. He instantly agreed, telling her he'd meet her at her suite in a couple of minutes, then speaking in Spanish to someone as he put down the phone.

'You'll need a coat—it's cold outside,' Marguerite said, finding a thick jacket and wrapping it around Caz's shoulders.

A sharp rap on the door announced Carlos's arrival, and Caz slipped out to meet him in the corridor.

'Come,' he said, and his anger was audible in that single word. Not that she could blame him—he must feel she was behaving irrationally.

Which she probably was—but she had to try and explain to him.

He led her along the corridor, away from the grand staircase, then out through a door right at the end, which, to her surprise, led across a small bridge and onto a path that wound through the pine trees towards the top of the mountain behind the castle.

They walked in silence for a few minutes, then, when the path led through a little glade where a wooden seat provided a place to sit and admire the view below, Carlos halted.

'You say we need to talk?'

He looked so stern Caz's courage faltered, but she knew she had to at least try to put her views into words.

'It's the wedding,' she said. 'It's such a sham. For a start I'm pregnant, and waltzing down the aisle in virginal white. I've been married before, and done all that—and then there's love, Carlos. I know it isn't part of our marriage, but without love isn't the whole wedding deal just a farce? I realise you need to be married to the mother of your child for form's sake, but do we need all the kerfuffle of a big wedding? Your father's just died—isn't that reason enough that we have a quiet wedding? We could even tell people we got married in Australia and just do it quietly somewhere to make it legal…'

Her voice trailed away, and although Carlos could see that she was desperately unhappy he couldn't help but voice his reaction to her words—a reaction that was hot and angry, and somehow made worse when she'd talked of love.

Or the lack of it!

'I'm the leader of this country, the royal ruler, and you want me lying about some pretend marriage that didn't take place? Why? Because you don't want to put on a white dress and pretend for a day that you might have some feelings for me? You did it for Derrick—oh, but then of course you were in *love*! Yes, we *could* get married quietly— but my country has recently lost its much-loved ruler, and I am on trial still. How will I be? Will they learn to love me? Starting off by denying them a wedding—an opportunity for a large percentage of the population to make money out of the tourists a royal wedding will attract—would hardly be a winning action.'

She was staring at him, pale and still, and all he wanted to do was take her in his arms and hold her close, or make love to her until her cheeks were flushed and her eyes shining again.

'So we're doing it for the country—it's a duty— that's what you're saying?'

He nodded his head, immeasurably hurt by her words yet unable to pinpoint why.

'And the white dress, the cathedral, the procession, the whole deal is more or less inescapable?'

Carlos felt the sigh that seemed to rise up from his toes.

'I wouldn't force you to do it, Caroline. I would never force you to do anything you don't wish to do.

So if you really don't want to go through a formal wedding ceremony then we can get married quietly, here at the castle.'

She walked on up the path and he followed, wondering if he'd ever get to know what she was thinking—well, not what she was thinking all the time, but would he ever understand even her thought processes? This had certainly come at him like an unexpected clap of thunder. Just where would the lightning strike next?

She stopped a little farther on and took off a glove to pick up a tiny bud of a pinecone, out too early so it had fallen from its branch. She twisted it in her fingers, then sniffed the strong scent.

'I don't have to *pretend* to have some feeling for you, Carlos,' she said, looking at the pinecone, not at him. 'And I can go through with the white wedding and all the rest of it—but not without you knowing how I feel. I know you don't want my love, and having talked a little to your mother I can understand why love's an emotion you don't trust, but I can't go on pretending I don't feel anything for you.'

She looked up at him then, her eyes bright with unshed tears, and added, 'I love you, okay?'

Then she headed past him, back down the path towards the castle.

'I've got wedding dresses to look at, and you've got an appointment with the Prime Minister.'

Carlos watched her go, too stunned by her admission—no, her declaration—to do anything but stand, as rooted to the spot as one of the pine trees that towered above him.

She loved him?

Was that really what she'd said?

And what did it mean?

To him?

To them?

He had no idea!

The sharp trill of the mobile in his pocket reminded him he had delayed his appointment long enough, but he couldn't get his feet moving down the track, his mind too busy with things he'd been avoiding thinking about for a long time.

Love.

Oh, he loved his mother—he was sure of that—and he'd definitely admired his father as only a child could have loved him: unconditionally. But he'd found childish love a very unrewarding experience, very one-sided, cosseted away from his parents as he'd been, brought up by nannies, tutors and staff members, then sent off to boarding school in England when he was ten.

Love hadn't seemed to bring anything but pain in its wake, so he'd learned not to make too much of it.

And he'd certainly refused to factor it into any adult relationship he might have. Friendship, fondness, fidelity—these things he'd brought to his previous relationships with women—but in his thinking the word *love* was overused, used too easily, too loosely, and so it had lost its currency, along with the emotion it was meant to convey.

Yet he knew, for sure, that Caroline had not used the word in this way—nor had she used it as a weapon, although he'd known women who had. No, she'd simply stated a fact, let him know something she felt he needed to know—told him that *her* love, at least, was no pretence.

Which left him where?

Apart from late for a meeting with his Prime Minister—

He started back down the track, hoping to catch a glimpse of Caroline before she disappeared into the castle, but she was well and truly gone.

Love!

The word beat out beneath his feet as he hurried down the path, echoed off the walls as he walked up the corridor and down the stairway to the small receiving room where he knew the country's top official was waiting.

No, he had to put it right out of his head.

As if he didn't have enough to worry about now.

He'd had no idea of the complexity of the duties he was expected to perform as Prince of Cascaverado, nor even much idea of where the government and the royal family crossed over in the governance of the principality.

So much to learn and so little time—because it

was now, when the centre was still in its infancy, that it, too, needed his attention.

Though at first determined to seek refuge in her rooms, the thought of fabric samples and pictures of wedding gowns had Caz turning away from the castle and taking another path that led across the face of the mountain, towards another patch of pine trees. There in the scented stillness, with old snow crunching beneath her feet, she felt a kind of peace steal through her.

She hadn't intended to tell Carlos of her love, but somehow it had come out, and now, in retrospect, she found she didn't regret it. Knowing he didn't love her, she'd probably embarrassed him, but she didn't want him thinking she was pretending love as she went ahead with this tourism-driven wedding.

She understood now that it was important for the country and for the people of Cascaverado, and as the child she carried would one day be the ruler of those people she must play her part, so the child would be loved and cherished by his or her people right from the start.

The child!

She crossed her arms over her belly and held on tightly. Wasn't he or she the most important part of the equation? Wasn't it for their child that she and Carlos were marrying?

For all that Carlos avoided mention of the word,

their child *would* know love, of that she was determined, and she'd seen enough of Carlos's caring, tender side to know he would make a loving father.

Wasn't that enough for her?

It would have to be!

She drew in deep breaths of the cold air and walked on, until a break in the trees showed her the city spread below her. Moss and algae darkened the slate tiles on some of the buildings, and this late in the afternoon the stone was no longer golden, but grey and bleak, yet still the sight of the old city filled her with wonder and excitement, and she patted the tiny baby in her belly and talked to it about this place that bore its name.

'Deziguel!' she whispered quietly, not wanting to disturb the stillness of the pine forest. 'Soon it will be my name as well,' she reminded herself, and, having come to terms with love and names and weddings, she turned back towards the castle, for it was getting dark and the chill evening air was penetrating her warm jacket.

CHAPTER NINE

SHE loved him!

How could Carlos face a sensible discussion about wedding plans when Caroline had just dropped this bombshell on him?

Hadn't he lived for years tormented by the damage his mother's love for his father had done to her?

Hadn't love been the last thing he'd wanted in a marriage?

Dios! One of the reasons he'd felt so certain this marriage would work was because he'd been sure that Caroline would never love again—that she'd accept it as a business arrangement.

So, moving on, getting past all that—did it matter?

He was striding down the corridor, then down the grand staircase, picturing her as a bride coming down these same steps, and the churning in his gut didn't feel like disappointment that she loved him, but more like—

'*Maldita sea!*' he cursed out loud, then looked around to see if anyone might have heard him.

Could it be love that was confusing him? Love that was knotting his guts and causing a heavy tension in his chest?

Hardly likely! He didn't do love!

Love caused pain.

Love muddled things and, like all emotions, it could cloud a man's thoughts and blur the edges of common sense.

He reached the bottom of the steps and turned towards the receiving room where, hopefully, the Prime Minister was still awaiting him. But with his mind still following the disasters love could strew in a person's path he collided with one of the suits of armour, apologising absentmindedly as he straightened the helmet before continuing on his way.

Fortunately the Prime Minister had the plans all laid out: the route the coaches would take to the cathedral, the seating plans, the return trip to the palace for the reception taking a different route so more people would see the happy couple. He also had a list of dignitaries who would be present, and another list of citizens chosen for the volunteer work they did in the community—something Caroline had suggested to her dresser, who had passed it up along the channels to reach him late yesterday.

Carlos knew he shouldn't be surprised. It was exactly the kind of thing Caroline *would* think of—and including ordinary citizens in the celebrations was a stroke of brilliance.

He was mentally congratulating himself yet again on his choice of wife when the memory of her confession returned, and with it all the physical manifestations the thought of love was now producing in his body.

At this rate he might not make the wedding, so cramped-up he'd be!

Somehow he concluded the meeting, approving all the arrangements, but pointing out that they'd have to have closed carriages on hand, as they could hardly ride in the open ones if it was raining, but the Prime Minister waved away his suggestion.

'It will not rain on your wedding,' he decreed, as if he'd already made a pact of some kind with the weather gods. 'It will be a joyous occasion for the whole country to share.'

Carlos wished he felt as confident, but with so much to be done in the two weeks before the great day he knew he had to put all his doubts aside and concentrate on the increase in his official duties— with any spare time he could wangle to be spent at the centre.

Which, of course, would keep him out of Caroline's way, and if he wasn't seeing her, except at dinner from time to time, he would surely be safe from all thoughts of love…

Caz met with the designer the following morning, apologising profusely for missing their appointment and then apologising again, revealing that a parcel from her mother had arrived unexpectedly—a parcel containing her mother's carefully preserved wedding dress.

'So, you see, I must wear it,' she told the man.

'Of course,' he agreed. 'Put it on. I will see it on you and make any alterations that might be needed.'

Marguerite was waiting in Caz's suite when she led the designer in, asking him to wait in the little sitting room while she dressed.

'Ah, but it is beautiful,' the designer admitted, although Caz wondered if the elaborate beading that crossed the top of the strapless dress and then trailed down across her waist and splayed out over the skirt might be a bit too—showy…

'But it's strapless? Isn't it too bare?'

Bare? She felt naked in it, having always been more comfortable in stylish but unrevealing evening dress. Her first wedding dress had been a pale pink suit—chosen, of course, by Derrick, who had claimed they needed money more than they needed a wedding dress…

'You have beautiful skin, so slightly tanned, and the ivory looks brilliant on you,' the designer decreed. 'But I will take it and have my best seamstress re-sew some of the beading that is coming loose here and there—and maybe we could add just a small train. You are, after all, a *royal* bride.'

His emphasis on the 'royal' part made Caz feel slightly ill, but she agreed that he could take it. She turned away, thinking to remove the dress, and hopefully her shaken nerves with it, but the designer held her back.

'We have not discussed a veil. Your mother did not send hers?'

Caz shrugged, and it was Marguerite who explained the dress had been the only thing in the parcel. The designer then produced a length of fine white tulle and played with it, tucking it here and there in Caz's hair until he was satisfied.

'I shall speak to the Prince,' he decreed, 'but you must wear your hair up in the simple style I have seen in the newspaper photographs of you. We will fit the veil accordingly.'

He departed, taking the dress and leaving a very shaken Caz behind.

'It's all too real,' she said to Marguerite.

'Of course it is,' that practical woman replied. 'And pre-wedding nerves are natural.'

Not these ones, Caz longed to say, but to no one would she admit her anguish about agreeing to a loveless marriage. Instead she checked the daily calendar of engagements set out on the little table by the window, and saw there was a formal dinner planned for that evening.

At least she'd see Carlos there, even if they wouldn't have any private time together. Though maybe later…

But later never happened—not that night nor any night that followed. Having now acquired a social secretary, as well as a dresser, Caz made her way through day after day of official functions, meeting royalty from across Europe as guests began to arrive for the wedding.

The only bright light on her horizon was the impending arrival of her own family. But even they were swept up into wedding hysteria—well, her mother was, deciding the flowers Caz was to carry didn't go with the dress and changing them, then huddling with Dominique over family jewel boxes, deciding which of the priceless heirloom pieces would best suit the gown.

'The gown, not her daughter!' Caz muttered to herself when she heard this, but she knew how excited her mother was, and didn't wish to spoil that excitement in any way.

In the meantime, her father seemed to have taken up residence at the local police headquarters, explaining to Caz that he was useless at wedding arrangements but always anxious to learn how other services operated. Her brothers, with their wives and children, were travelling around Europe before they came to Cascaverado, taking advantage of being so far from home to see more of other cultures and countries.

So she worked her way through the days before her wedding, meeting people, keeping appointments, resting when she could. Her reward most evenings was a touch of Carlos's hand when they met before dinner, or a quiet, 'How are you?' when they crossed paths at yet another civic reception.

She assured him, always, that she was well, and smiled more brightly when he was around—although every time she saw him she began to wonder whether this wedding wasn't proving a bigger strain on him than it was on her, for he had dark shadows under his eyes and lines of strain in his face. The longing to hold him—and be held by him—grew so strong that at times she wondered just how shocked the castle staff would be if she made a midnight sortie to his suite.

But unwilling to embarrass him in any way, or add to whatever was tormenting him, she played her part: the bride-to-be, the perfect consort!

He *had* to talk to her!

Yet, waking on his wedding day, Carlos knew he'd left it too late. He might not be totally au fait with wedding protocol, but he knew it was bad luck for the bride to see the groom on the day of the wedding—before, that was, they met in church.

And bad luck was the last thing he would wish on Caroline, who was handling the whole circus with such aplomb he knew for sure he'd made the perfect choice.

Except that he hadn't made the choice—it had been thrust on him—and now this perfect choice, this perfect woman, for if such a thing existed it must be she—was going into her wedding, embarking on what should be the happiest day of her life, without knowing how he felt about her.

Perhaps she'd be too busy to be worrying about love.

He shook his head. Love was so much part of Caroline she'd never be too busy to not be thinking of it, considering it—nurturing it, even…

Carlos rolled out of bed, calling to his valet to get him the archbishop on the phone.

'Maybe it's a change to the ceremony that *should* be made,' he was arguing, minutes later. 'Maybe it's something that should become compulsory and possibly save marriages from divorce further down the track.'

The archbishop sounded most unimpressed, but he agreed to alter the order of service just slightly—although he warned Carlos that it would be too late to change the printed orders that would be given to the guests.

Refusing to accept defeat at this stage, Carlos sent his valet off to speak to the printers, knowing the man who'd been with him since he was a child could achieve miracles, should a miracle be needed. Then, with things sorted as best he could, the Prince ate a hearty breakfast before sitting down to ponder exactly what he needed to say, and attempting to condense it into the three minutes the archbishop had agreed upon.

* * *

It was beyond fairytale stuff, Caz decided, and into total unreality. Yet here she was, walking down the long aisle of the Cascaverado cathedral on her father's arm. The big man who supported her was resplendent in his dress uniform, and her brothers, as she passed them, looked equally at home among this crowd of royalty, with her sisters-in-law elegantly clad and beaming with pride as she passed by them.

Behind her Jane, her best friend from schooldays, was her sole attendant, Caz having refused to lead a parade of strangers down the aisle. And way up there at the altar Caz could see the back of Carlos's head. When would he turn to look at his bride?

Would he turn at all? Or would his training and his adherence to protocol keep him facing forward until her father placed her hand in that of her husband-to-be?

He didn't turn, not until she stood beside him, and then he took her hand from her father and tugged slightly. The three officials conducting the ceremony—one in French, one in Spanish and one in English—then all spoke, more or less together. Caz's ear picked out the English voice.

'The groom has requested a slight change to the usual order of service. He believes marriage is a contract between two people, and although he is delighted to share this special time with so many well-wishers he has asked for some private time with his bride. So the bride and groom will now withdraw for a few minutes, while Cascaverado's own internationally known tenor will entertain you.'

Caz's mind went blank, although the continued tugging on her hand forced her forward, following Carlos she knew not where.

'Where' turned out to be a small alcove to one side of the nave, and here Carlos offered her a chair.

'That's if you can actually sit down in that beautiful dress,' he added, his voice so tight with tension the little joke fell flat.

'What is it?' Caz demanded, lifting the short veil the designer had insisted she wear over her face.

'It's love,' he blurted out. 'I woke up this morning and felt like you did a couple of weeks ago. I knew I couldn't go through a farce of a wedding. I knew you had to know.'

A coldness she'd never felt before crept through Caz's body. He loved someone else? He had some arrangement he had to confess?

But he was talking again, and she forced herself to listen.

'I could not go through our wedding with you believing it was a farce, without you knowing just how much I love you, Caroline. I love you from the very depth of my being—love you in ways I never dreamed possible—as if somehow you have become the very best part of me, without which I'd be nothing.'

He took her hands in his and looked into her eyes.

'I think I probably fell in love with you back in

Afghanistan, back when you refused to leave the theatre with Ahmed, simply saying you would stay, and then steadfastly refusing to give in to the fear that I knew crept into your heart and paralysed your mind from time to time.'

He paused, gripping her hands as if they were his lifeline, while Caz tried desperately to make sense of what he was saying.

He loved her?

'My problem was I'd refused for so long to acknowledge love as anything other than a source of pain that I didn't recognise it when it happened to me. And when it did I tried to deny it, to pretend it was something else—a protective instinct—that made me want to be with you all the time, to touch you, hear your voice, listen to your laugh.'

Another pause, but Caz was warmer now, and her hands gripped his as tightly as his gripped hers.

'Then you confronted me and told me you wouldn't go through a wedding that was a farce pretending that you didn't love me—pretending it was nothing but a business arrangement.'

He looked deep into her eyes.

'Caroline, you took my breath away that day, and I've barely caught it since. You made no demands of me, simply pledged your love, and that unselfishness, so typical of all that is good in you, brought me to my senses. But still I couldn't say it. Until today.'

Blue eyes confirmed the emotion behind his

words when the phrase she'd so longed to hear from this man was finally spoken.

'I love you, Caroline,' he said. 'And when we pledge our lives to each other out there, very shortly, you will know I mean every word I say.'

Somewhere beyond the alcove came the glorious sound of a man's voice singing, Caz was sure, of love. Carlos brushed his lips very lightly across hers—an echo of that first kiss he'd given her—then adjusted her veil across her face once more and led her back to their positions in front of the altar of the cathedral.

Was it obvious from her face, even veiled, that something momentous had occurred? Caz didn't know. She only knew that everyone in that beautiful church was smiling at her—smiles that wished her well—wished both of them well—and with all her doubts and fears resolved, and the man she loved by her side, she repeated the age-old vows, secure in the knowledge that this marriage was for ever.

EPILOGUE

'OH, LET me do it!'

Caz's mother took the incredibly fine silk and lace garment and fitted it over the baby's head, sliding his little arms into the sleeves and pulling the long trailing gown down over his chubby body.

'There, my little Eddie! My, but you're handsome.'

'Oh, Mum, don't let anyone hear you calling him Eddie. I know you call Dad that, but this little guy's Eduardo—very proper!'

Her mother laughed.

'He'll get Eddie from me and all his cousins when he comes to Australia for his holidays, so he might as well get used to it.'

Marguerite and Eduardo's nanny were standing by, with Marguerite holding the heirloom bonnet and booties that went with the christening gown. Both women were flushed and excited to be part of the big day. But the person Caz longed to see was Eduardo's father, who had left early this morning to check on something at the amputee centre and wasn't yet back.

Could she really be this happy? she wondered, as her mother, Marguerite and the nanny bore Eduardo from the room, wanting to show him off to the entire palace staff before he was taken to the cathedral for his christening.

Caz crossed to the window, looking out at the view that never failed to delight her.

And felt Carlos enter the room behind her!

She turned and held up her hands in mock surprise.

'Oh, so splendidly turned out, my prince! You'll steal your son's thunder!'

He *did* look handsome in his dark blue dress uniform, with a scarlet sash slashing diagonally across the jacket held in place by a sparkling cluster of stones—not diamonds, surely?

'If anyone would do that, it is you,' he said quietly, coming towards her and then lifting his hands to show her a similar sash held between them. 'Especially once I put this on you and pin it in place.'

He slipped the sash across her head so it ran from one shoulder to her waist, then pinned it in place with another sparkling ornament.

'You are now a member of the Order of Cascaverado, my princess,' he told her, dropping a featherlight kiss on her lips. 'The decree was passed in parliament yesterday, in gratitude for the work you have done since becoming my consort.'

Caz blinked away some tears, then sniffed—a not very princessy thing to do, but Carlos was ready with a handkerchief, and he dried her eyes, kissed her again, then took her hand to lead her out of the room.

'We'll be late—and although it's okay for the bride to be late for her wedding, it would be very bad form for parents to be late for their child's christening.'

He looked around.

'I assume we do still have a son somewhere?'

Caz laughed.

'He's being shown off in all his finery to the entire staff—we'll probably find him in the kitchen.'

Eduardo was downstairs in the Great Hall, with two doting grandmothers fussing over him while Caz's father held him proudly in his arms. With the infant restored to his parents, they were all shuffled into open carriages and driven behind matched horses into the city, where crowds outside the cathedral waited to meet their new Prince. Carlos held him in his arms, turning this way and that while people cheered and shouted.

At the front of the cathedral the carriage stopped, and the footman opened the door and let down the steps. But as Caz was about to step out Carlos stopped her with a light touch on her arm.

'Have I ever thanked you?' he asked.

She turned to him and smiled.

'Only every day,' she reminded him.

'And told you that I love you?'

'That too—every day,' she assured him, and then she stepped out of the carriage, turned to take Eduardo, and waited for her husband, who put his arm around her waist and walked with her into the cathedral, exultant music sounding around them as Cascaverado celebrated its new Prince.

* * * * *

Too Ordinary for
the Duke?

MELISSA JAMES

Melissa James is a mother of three, living in a beach suburb in New South Wales, Australia. A former nurse, waitress, shop assistant, perfume and chocolate demonstrator – among other things – she believes in taking on new jobs for the fun experience. She'll try anything at least once, to see what it feels like – a fact that scares her family on regular occasions. She fell into writing by accident, when her husband brought home an article stating how much a famous romance author earned, and she thought, *I can do that!* She can be found most mornings walking and swimming at her local beach with her husband or every afternoon running around to her kids' sporting hobbies, while dreaming of flying, scuba diving, belaying down a cave or over a cliff – anywhere her characters are at the time!

Look for an exciting new novel from Melissa James, *One Small Miracle*, available in Mills & Boon® Romance in April 2010.

CHAPTER ONE

Summer Palace, Orakidis City, Hellenia

The Wedding of Her Royal Highness Princess Giulia to His Grace Tobias, Grand Duke of Malascos

THIS day—this past year, in fact—was enough to make a girl believe in fairy tales. Was she, Mari Mitsialos, a bridesmaid at a royal wedding? Was she *really* cousin to a king and a princess royal?

Life took weird turns sometimes…but what a *good* weird this was! Both her cousins, living in the backblocks of Sydney a year ago, were ecstatically married to the people of their dreams—but Charlie was a *king,* and Lia was a princess royal!

What did that make her? Kind of a halfway to royalty, halfway past nowhere person—and she couldn't decide which was better.

Mari smiled when Toby, or the new Grand Duke as he was known in the family, dipped Lia in the

Viennese Waltz they'd chosen for their wedding dance. The devoted love she'd always suspected Toby felt for Lia fairly blazed from those summer-blue eyes. And as for Lia, she could barely leave her husband's side long enough to "do the pretty-polite", as Charlie called it, with all the nobles and royalty of Europe who attended her wedding.

It was still so strange to even be here, let alone be the cousin and bridesmaid of a princess royal—but even her dreamer's heart couldn't fool her. Mari had been born on the ordinary side of the family—the Greek side. Aunty Katina had been a girl from the mountains outside Athens who had boarded a boat for Australia forty years ago, and met Uncle Arthur at a Greek party in Marrickville, Sydney.

She and Uncle Arthur had died in a car crash, never knowing their titles, never knowing Uncle Arthur had, through the destruction of the royal Marandis line of Hellenia, become the heir to a kingdom. Charlie and Lia hadn't known their true identities until a year ago. Great-Uncle Kyri and Great-Aunt Giulia had never told a soul about their big secret: Uncle Kyri had been a Grand Duke, who'd disappeared from royal life to marry the royal nanny.

But oh, how Great-Uncle Kyri had organised his grandchildren's lives—even from beyond the grave! He'd taught them the language, customs and culture of Hellenia—even the royal dances—and instilled in them a deep sense of duty, so that when they'd found out their true identities and Hellenia's need, they'd barely hesitated before making the hard decision to stay for ever and rebuild the shattered nation.

In his will, Great-Uncle Kyri had left Toby, Charlie's best friend and Great-Uncle Kyri's adopted son, a duchy and two hundred and fifty million euros—and, more importantly, he had given Lia the man she loved, and Toby the bride of his heart.

Mari sighed in her brother Stavros's arms as they danced beside the bride and groom. If she'd been born on the *other* side of the family, on Uncle Arthur's side, what would she be? To be so close to a life most people could only dream of entering, yet locked behind the permanent barrier of her birth, felt—weird.

Weird described it to a T…but even she, the family dreamer, had no idea if she'd want to be royal. She'd seen both sides of life here, through the eyes of the media and adoring fans who couldn't buy enough magazines about the new royals, and she honestly didn't know if she could take a life filled with intrusions—

"I'd like to dance with your sister, if I may."

A beautifully cultured yet imperious voice broke into Mari's reverie, and she realised the bridal waltz was done; people were changing partners.

She didn't need to look around to know who was speaking. She knew the voice of His Royal Highness

Prince Mikhail of the small Euro-Asian border kingdom of Chalnikan too well. She'd met him five months before, when he had been Charlie's groomsman, and she'd been hearing his voice regularly since she'd returned to Hellenia to become Lia's bridesmaid. She'd had his gifts, his notes, heard his calls— and all the messages were variations on the same theme. *Come and live with me and be my lover.*

How romantic it all sounded…a prince focussing his attentions on her, an ordinary girl…and maybe she'd find it romantic if only he'd meant *come and be my bride*—not *come to my bed for as long as I find you convenient.*

Question: how could most young girls' fantasy— having the undivided romantic attentions of a handsome young prince—turn into a nightmare?

Answer: if the said prince was an unlikeable, arrogant snob who'd tried to charm Jazmine and Lia, both princesses royal at the time, into marriage. But with Mari he'd only wanted a little fun during his seven days off the parental leash—in her bed.

And how could Stavros, the most protective of brothers, who'd chased away more men than she could count since she'd turned fourteen, now step back with that look of silent awe?

"What am I supposed to say? He's a *prince,* Mari," Stavros had protested when she'd asked him to protect her.

As she allowed His Spoiled Highness to take her

in his arms, her parents beamed. In their eyes, if Charlie could marry a princess and Lia could *become* one, there was no reason a prince of the blood couldn't fall in love with Mari.

"Weren't you crowned Princess of the Festival four times running?" her dad had demanded the first time she'd tried to tell her parents that Mikhail's intentions could never be honourable to her, a commoner.

"Princess of a Greek festival in Marrickville isn't quite the title a real prince looks for in a wife, Dad," Mari had sighed. "And the voting was rigged. Uncle Harry was the president, and Petros's dad was on the board, too."

The entire family knew Stavros's best friend Petros still held a torch for Mari. He'd proposed every year at the Festival since Mari's first win. Her parents had encouraged her to think about it.

At least until Mikhail came along. Even her mother seemed to have waved aside the lifelong belief that marrying a non-Greek was tantamount to heresy the moment she'd looked into Mikhail's melting caramel eyes—or, more strictly, the moment she'd learned his title.

"What was Princess Mary of Denmark before Prince Frederik met her? A girl just like you! The world has changed. You are cousin to a *king*, Mari. Didn't Great-Uncle Kyri teach you the language, customs and manners, just as he did Charlie and Lia?"

"You are worthy of a king…or a future king," her father had said, ending the conversation with the firm tone that told Mari argument was futile.

"You look beautiful, Mari," Mikhail whispered in her ear, holding her a few inches too close for propriety. "Your dress shimmers over your lovely body until you look like a star."

"Thank you, Your Highness," she replied with repellent demureness. As he pulled her against him, she froze so he had as little benefit as possible from the closeness.

"Still so cold?" he asked, with a mixture of the sulky boy and plaintive charmer she couldn't find attractive. "Haven't I given you enough gifts, spent enough time convincing you of my intentions towards you—only you, my sweet star?"

Intentions of what? she almost retorted, but what was the use? He'd only launch into enthusiastic rhetoric about how life would be for a royal lover: fame, wealth and a jet-setting lifestyle while it lasted, and a nice house in the place of her choosing when he ended it.

The look in those thick-lashed caramel eyes wasn't caring; it was predatory. Though Mikhail was handsome, rich and royal, he didn't like *her*; he enjoyed the chase, and the thrill of the win.

Though she'd told him at least ten times already, she said again, "I love my life in Sydney—and I'd rather be the bride of a common man than a royal mistress." Mari said it with pride. She wasn't asking him to marry her—God forbid! Mikhail's wilful arrogance, spoiled tantrums and treating of the lower orders as if they were disposable had turned her off within two days of meeting him, and now all she felt was a weary revulsion.

Mikhail made a sound of indulgent contempt. "Of course you would. All women want to be a bride. Perhaps if you were titled, like your cousin…" He shrugged elegantly. "Face it, Mari, nobody but your parents expects you to be a virgin when you marry." His eyes gleamed with predatory intent as his hand moved with intimate heat over her back, sliding down towards the curve of her bottom. "Being loved first by a prince will only enhance your chances of finding the right kind of man. Come to me, Mari," he whispered in a voice like chocolate cream, layered with an exotic accent many women would find impossible to resist. "Your life will be blessed from your time with me."

Mari looked at Mikhail and wondered why he still bothered. Even if Jazmine and Lia hadn't told her—strictly on the QT, of course—about the way Mikhail treated any woman he didn't consider his equal in station, and even if Charlie hadn't also warned her that Mikhail refused to acknowledge any of his less important former lovers when they tried to pull the influence card, the simple truth was she didn't *feel* anything for Mikhail, and that ended that.

"No," she said, quiet but firm. "It's not going to happen, Your Highness. Please try to find a more... agreeable woman."

Mikhail's face darkened. He'd taken her other rejections as a prelude, a challenge—but tonight this had to be her final answer. "You're lying, Mari. I've seen the look in your eyes, heard the hesitation in your voice every time you've put me off."

Mari stared at him in wonder. Only a man as self-assured as Mikhail could see her firm *no* just moments before as a "putting off". What would it take to convince him?

After a struggle with his self-control, he went on with dark intimacy, "I can assure you that the King has no objections to my—"

Charlie didn't object? That wasn't what he'd told her...

The name made her turn her head. Charlie and Jazmine danced not far away, and she caught her cousin's wife's eye with a pleading glance.

Jazmine, who'd become the new Queen of Hellenia shortly after her marriage, whispered in her husband's ear. Within seconds Charlie was saying, genially, "Mikhail, my friend, I know a wedding isn't the best time for it, but your father called me this morning. He wishes us to speak on a matter of—" He glanced at Mari, and said apologetically, "Sorry, my beloved cousin, but it's a matter of national security, and some delicacy."

Filled with relief, Mari kissed Charlie's cheek. "Of course. I'll go speak with Jazmine."

Even a prince had protocol to which he must bow. Commoner though he'd been all his life, Charlie was now a station above Mikhail; Hellenia had importance to his family in matters of state and trade in Europe. Mikhail forced a smile to his face. "Lead the way, Your Majesty," he said formally, refusing to call him Charlie.

But perhaps Charlie hadn't yet invited him to such friendly intimacy. For all his careless ways and Aussie upbringing, Charlie had walls and barriers of his own.

As Charlie led Mikhail out of the state banqueting room, Mari knew her freedom wouldn't last long. She had five to ten minutes to escape before Mikhail or her family stopped her. She tossed Jazmine a grateful glance; the Queen winked at her, and tilted her head towards the royal exit. Mari's eyes widened as Jazmine beckoned with a hand.

As she reached her, the Queen slipped her arm through Mari's and led her to the royal exit. Once there she whispered, "Out through there, turn right and right again, and you'll find a royal limousine waiting for you. Your things are packed and ready." Jazmine pushed an envelope stamped with the royal insignia into Mari's hand. "This note tells the driver—he's waiting outside for you—to take you to the pier. Charlie's arranged our smaller yacht for you to sail on for a few days—until Mikhail is safely under the parental thumb again."

"What?" she gasped, too stunned to be polite.

"We might be new at the job, but we keep an eye on things," Jazmine said softly, "and this situation has become rather delicate. I've known Mikhail too many years. There's no way he'll give up until you give him what he wants—or worse, he ends up creating a rupture between Hellenia and Chalnikan. It's been difficult to keep him under control every time he's come here before, but with Lia and me, our positions prevented him from going too far. Even Grandfather refused to think of him as a potential husband for either of us, prince of the blood though he is. I was hoping you could convince him it was useless, but obviously that isn't going to happen."

Mari found herself blushing again, but she was glad Jazmine hadn't referred to her parents' humiliating approval and interference.

Jazmine pressed her hand. "We hoped we could help you go quietly after the reception, to save everyone embarrassment, but it seems he'll make a scene if he doesn't have his way. He's not used to losing."

Mari had to hold back the tears—and the urge to hug a queen. "Thank you so much, Jazmine...you and Charlie both."

Jazmine smiled. "Thank Lia too, when you can. Mikhail offered her an open marriage after she gave him a few sons. He said she could play around with Toby all she wanted after he had his heirs, and he'd have his women."

Mari smiled and nodded. "Hug her for me, and say I'll call her from home when she and Toby are back."

Jazmine nodded. "Now, go—before he sees where you went. We've told the servants to tell Mikhail nothing of your whereabouts, and the palace gates are to close after you, but he can still order them to open if he sees you. And don't worry about your family," she added as Mari hesitated. "Charlie has it all covered—and he can be quite charming when he wants to."

Without another word, Mari bolted through the doors the liveried servant had opened for her. She slipped off the high, black, strappy heels that probably cost more than a month's wages at home, and kept running. She turned right at the end of the hall, and right again, smiling at the servants in on the secret and whispering her thanks. From experience she knew that she got a lot further with people with a smile than an order. Great-Uncle Kyri always told her she could catch more flies with honey than vinegar.

She burst out into the cool night air with a sigh of relief—the car was there, just where Jazmine had said it would be, and there was a man leaning against the hood with a glass in his hand. Mari ran to the car and jerked the door open before he could move to open it for her. "Take me to the royal pier, please— as fast as you can."

After a moment, the man said, in a tone of amusement, "Of course, my lady." He hopped into the driver's side. "The keys are in the ignition. Everything's in place."

"The King and Queen ordered the car to be ready for me," Mari replied, trying hard to be pleasant while she was literally squirming. "The palace gates will open when we reach them." She flicked a glance at the doors she'd left. Were they about to open? "I'd appreciate it if you'd lock the doors," she said, mindful not to be imperious or cold. "Please," she added again, turning to the rearview mirror to smile at the man. "Please, I really need to leave *now*."

After a bare second of hesitation the man started the engine, gunned it, and let it go. Then they were at the gates, which opened smoothly for them. Mari sat twitching in the back seat, tossing constant glances over her shoulder—

Nothing yet, thank heaven, but he could come at any second. Charlie's gentle, hands-off approach with Mikhail told her how delicate this situation was. It looked as if things might get ugly if she refused him again. Who'd ever have thought ordinary Mari Mitsialos could become entangled in international relations? But this was a kind of importance she'd give anything to not know! "Faster, oh, please go faster," she pleaded, worst-case scenarios running riot through her head.

A smothered sound like a laugh met her desper-

ate plea, but the limo moved through the gates. As
Jazmine had stated they would, they swung closed
behind the limo.

Flashes popped as the paparazzi assumed it was
the bride and groom. She cringed away from the
lights, covering her face; then they were through the
thronged crowds. The boom gates and road spikes
placed at the end of the private road, for royal safety
in case of war, did the job on their pursuit, stopping
the cars and bursting the tyres of the motorbikes.
There'd be an official apology later, and talk of ac-
cidents, no doubt—and in the meantime the royal
limo headed at breakneck speed for the royal pier.

CHAPTER TWO

As HE drove for the royal pier, the note from the King and Queen of Hellenia lying open by his side, Lysander Marsalis wondered when would be the best time to tell her that he wasn't really a chauffeur, but a duke, with distant ties to the royal family…

The eleventh Duke of Persolis since his brother's retirement to a monastery a year ago, and a royal diplomat for the past decade, Sander was the current minder of the spoiled Royal Highness from whom the King's cousin was currently bolting. He'd been sanctioned by both the King and Queen to discreetly take the girl out of a situation fraught with a hundred potential landmines in the way of international diplomacy.

At the very least he was going to lose his position in Chalnikan for acting against Mikhail's interests—but having been given the orders by both Mikhail's father and Charlie, what else could he do?

"Can't we go any faster…please?"

A grin tugged at reluctant lips. The *please*, like all

the others, had been so obviously tacked on as an afterthought. "Not without being arrested, miss:"

"Oh." She slumped in her seat. "I'm sorry. I wouldn't want to get you in trouble."

The grin vanished. The girl...Mari...really was worried—and yet she took the time to be concerned about his position as well. She was a nice young woman, far too sweet and innocent for an infamous playboy prince only after some fun. "Not much longer, miss. In perhaps ten minutes we'll arrive safely."

Relief rose in her face like the morning sun, until all of her seemed to glow. "Oh, *thank* you. I must seem like a drama queen, but I *really* need to get away."

In the space of ten minutes Sander had begun to feel as if he was living on a roller coaster. This girl really lived on her emotions. "Was the wedding so bad, miss?"

She rolled her eyes. "You have *no* idea."

He strongly suspected the title "drama queen" wasn't entirely incorrect. Mari Mitsialos, with her mercurial and vivid emotions rushing across her face like movie panels, was a refreshing change from the languid debutantes and elegantly bored nobles' daughters paraded in royal company every year. Every thought and feeling showed on her face, like sunshine bursting through clouds. She was just...cute.

It was obvious she wasn't born to privilege. In high-society circles one never snapped at underlings;

one merely conveyed the impression that disobedience to the slightest whim wasn't an option. But Mari had a cute little wobble in her voice that gave her away. *Please, I need you to do what I want, because I'm so scared you won't, and I'll have no idea what to do then...* With a little training, she could be—

"It's all right, miss, no one's following us," Sander said in a soothing tone as he saw her twist around to stare through the rear window for at least the twelfth time.

"Ooooh...that's good. *Thank* you." The girl leaned back against the plush, butter-soft leather, and smiled into the rear vision mirror at him. "Honestly, you have *no* idea what it was like in there."

The smile lit her face—in fact, it lit the entire car with inner sunshine. Despite her apparent addiction to italicising a word in almost every sentence, Mari Mitsialos was pretty, with long dark curls and sleepy eyes similar to her cousin the Princess Giulia—but when she smiled she was...well, *dazzling.*

That smile was lethal. Not that she had dimples or perfect teeth—he couldn't put his finger on what it was. But whatever it was Mari had, she had it in spades. The *It* factor.

He'd known that from the day of Charlie and Jazmine's wedding. Seeing her dancing at the reception, he'd known Mari was unusual. From a shadowed corner he'd watched her laugh and smile and charm every man between fifteen and ninety-five into adoration without even trying. She was…well, lovable.

All of which meant he'd kept a serious distance. Mari was a nice girl, not one for a few nights' fun or discreet liaisons in designated places. And she was the King's cousin.

He had to remember to keep his face stolid, like a servant, as he answered. "I'd have thought a royal wedding with this new royal family would be a lovely affair, miss. You've been to both weddings, if I remember rightly?"

He put a tiny hint of question into the observation, leaving the way free for her to talk if she wanted to. It was obvious she was bursting to say something, to relieve the pressure somehow. Unfortunately her immediate family seemed oblivious to Mikhail's true intent, and pushed her into his arms at every opportunity. Poor girl… He'd noticed—

Don't think about it, Sander. He had to keep the King and Queen of Hellenia on side. He needed to come out of this madcap experience with some kind of credibility, and that meant a strictly *hands-off* policy.

"Yes, I was at both weddings. I'm first cousin to both Charlie, um, King Kyriacos, and Lia, I mean Princess Giulia," she replied, with a quiet touch of pride that made Sander squelch another smile. Well, why shouldn't she be proud? From obscurity to the cousin of royalty was a leap in status most people could only dream of.

"The King, the Prince and Princess have brought a breath of fresh air to the nation," he offered, to see what she'd say next.

"Yes—and it was needed, from what I can see." Though she spoke without rancour, he felt a touch of defensiveness. She probably thought he was one of the old King's supporters, wanting to keep the almost medieval status quo.

"Their knowledge of the common people seems to have reinvigorated the country. They've done a lot already in putting Lord Orakis at odds with the people," he said.

"He can never return after the arson investigation. That was down to Toby—the new Prince. Toby's one of the original good guys. He saved Lia's life, years ago—and he risked his life in that burning building to prove Orakis's guilt. He did that to save Lia. He would do anything to make Lia happy— *anything*."

Ah, there it was again, the tiny, wistful note. Sander knew then why Mikhail's chase had been fruitless from the start. The extreme romance of the two royal weddings in the Hellenican royal family had infected many a woman around the world, but to be the cousin of the new royalty in love…well, why shouldn't she hold out for real love and a wedding?

"They seem very happy in the pictures I've seen, miss."

"They've always loved each other. The whole family have been waiting for them to get together for years." The yearning grew in her voice, misted her milk-chocolate eyes, and her smile was...well, *luminous*—

Beep!

At the indignant honking behind, Sander pulled himself together and looked at the road ahead with fixed determination. He'd known the deal when he took on the position of the Prince's Private Secretary. The King planned on abdicating as soon as Mikhail proved himself worthy. It was Sander's job to get him to that destination on an express train. Taking Mari on a yacht was saving Mikhail from the worst *faux pas* he could make. It was *not* for personal pleasure, no matter how much he derived from merely looking at her.

He was on an excellent wicket with this job, and Charlie and Jazmine had offered him the ripe plum of being Hellenican Representative to the UN if he handled it right. No way was he about to risk his career, no matter how pretty or tempting Mari Mitsialos happened to be.

"Sorry about that, miss," he said woodenly, and, after answering her reassurances with dogged politeness and no curiosity, he kept his gaze ahead with absolute determination.

* * *

Boy, they really have gorgeous chauffeurs here...

Despite his sudden Pinocchio face, Mari couldn't help staring in the rear vision mirror at him. His eyes were almost as green as those she'd seen in the stained-glass windows at the church today, and they *danced*. His dimples seemed grooved from the deepest part of his skin, warming a mouth full and carved from Michelangelo's imagination. Warm honey-brown skin, strong features, a voice of smooth, dark temptation, and an accent that was half-Mediterranean and half-Oxford—oh, what wasn't to like? A Greek god sat in front of her, seemingly risen from the sea on Neptune's trident. Oooh, to see him rise from the water, droplets of Mediterranean-Aegean running down his body...

"KING'S COUSIN RUNS OFF WITH CHAUF-FEUR!"

After all Charlie and Lia had done for her family, both before and after their elevation to royalty, could she make a mockery of the new Marandis Royal Family by feeding the paparazzi machine for months on end? No, family came first. Charlie and Lia needed them all to behave with strict propriety. Running away with gorgeous chauffeurs was absolutely in the realms of fantasy.

And he could be married for all you know, with five kids. And even if he was single, and you did know his name, he hasn't once even smiled at you.

She turned her gaze out of the window, to where the aquamarine Aegean sparkled all along the coast road. Why was it that the men she found irresistible never looked at her, and all the nice guys she found so boring hung around in droves?

Yet when she'd been confronted with the kind of man she'd always dreamed of attracting, she'd discovered the difference between dream and reality—and she'd realised what a big, old-fashioned, one hundred percent hypocrite she was! What she wanted was a good man to fall to his knees with a big fat diamond, his family lined up behind him in adoring approval of her.

But hey, it hurt nobody to dream, right? And if that daydream face had shifted subtly, so it now had deep-grooved dimples, eyes that sparkled like the ocean in sunlight and a smile that made her heart flutter, what did it matter?

"What do they *all* matter? Line up, fantasy number four hundred and thirty-seven," she muttered in disgust—and then realised she'd said it aloud. She peered at the driver's face again, and blushed when those dancing-in-the-waves eyes met hers, his deliciously masculine mouth quivering to hold in a smile. "Sorry," she said, with a rueful sigh. What was the point in being embarrassed? "I know—talking to myself is a bad habit."

"It's said all the world's geniuses talk to themselves," the driver said gravely enough, his eyes still twinkling.

"Thanks, but you don't believe I'm in their number any more than I do." She shrugged and laughed, her hands lifting in mock-surrender. "But I haven't hurt anyone yet."

"I'm glad of that, miss," he replied, with such fervour she laughed again.

"My name's Mari," she offered, putting out her hand, hoping to hear his name in return.

After a visible hesitation, he said, "I'm Lysander, miss."

Though feeling the sting of the untaken hand, Mari felt her brow lift. "So you're named for the famed general and friend of Cyrus, the conquering prince of Persia. Your parents gave you a lot to live up to," she said, grinning.

Lysander's mouth twitched again—then the wooden demeanour returned as he pulled off the road and rolled up smoothly to a guarded gate.

The guard stepped out of the small guardhouse, frowning at Lysander. Lysander produced the Queen's letter, and after a moment the man nodded and returned inside.

The car moved through the gate, and it closed behind them. The yacht Jazmine had called *small* was enormous, at least two hundred feet—which begged the question: what size was the *big* yacht? — and, judging by the appointments on the outside, absolutely oozed luxury. It bobbed in the calm waters before her in a silent siren call. *Come and play...*

Playing wasn't on the agenda. All she needed to

do was to get on board safely, spend a few days there until Mikhail left Hellenia, then she could return to her safe, anonymous life.

"Hurry, oh, please hurry," she murmured, feeling urgency grab hold of her.

In answer, Lysander murmured quiet words into an intercom-style phone—and she saw the gang-plank move and a larger one take its place a level down. It was wide enough for a car…and a dark, gaping hole had opened high up in the yacht.

Lysander drove into the yacht's hull, and blessed cool darkness filled the car, like a benediction of safety.

"Thank you, Lysander," she breathed as the hole closed up behind them and she heard the engines start up. "Please, let's take off—push off—whatever it is boats do."

She heard a choked-off sound as he opened his door and came around to open hers. In the darkness, his face glowed in the subdued lighting of the limo—and she saw he was laughing. It didn't matter if his lips were under total control, his dimples danced, just as his eyes did—and the combination fascinated her. "Aye, aye, Miss Mari. I'll go to the Captain right away and convey your orders to him."

She felt intense relief fill her. "So you're coming with me?" And she was *not* thinking of having his company for the next few days—just the fact that she wouldn't be alone.

His eyes darkened as the laughter died. "The

Queen's letter makes it perfectly clear—I'm to look after you." The slight bow of his head was touched with respect and filled with irony. "So until my orders change, Miss Mitsialos, your wish is my command."

CHAPTER THREE

SANDER wasn't sure he liked that speculative, wistful gleam in Mari's milk-chocolate eyes. He felt like the genie must have when telling Aladdin he had three wishes…and, judging by the way she kept looking at him, brimming and overflowing with innocent fascination, he couldn't help but know what one wish would be.

He hadn't seen a woman look at him with such honest admiration and shy appraisal since he'd become Duke. Yes, women had found him attractive since he'd shot up past the six-foot mark when he was fifteen, but the way Mari blushed when she looked and smiled at him, and when she looked away, and the light in those sweet, dreaming eyes…

But the only kind of women he'd bothered with over the past ten years played the game, and it was glaringly obvious Mari was a straight-shooter, a nice girl to take home to Mother…if only Mother didn't expect her to have a heralded pedigree.

He forced himself to remain expressionless as he handed her out of the limo. "Would you come up on deck for a few moments while I give orders to the Captain, miss? Then I'll see you to the Stateroom."

The dreaming fantasy in her eyes vanished as if he'd smacked her. "The…? Isn't that the room reserved for royalty?"

Amused by her wide-eyed near-shock, he nodded. "That's right, miss."

Expecting her to breathe a few words of ecstatic agreement, he was taken aback when she said, "But that belongs to Charlie and Jazmine."

Touched by her anxiety to do the right thing, when most of the women he knew would probably have shoved him to the ground in their race to sleep in the King's bed, he showed her Jazmine's note. He hoped she didn't notice that he was carefully covering the *"Dear Sander"* at the start of the royal instructions with his thumb. "The Queen's instructions are clear, miss. You're family to royalty now. Whenever you stay with them, you'll live as they do."

Mari read the note, eyes still wide, but then she shook her head. "It's so nice of Jazmine to offer, but I'll be more than happy in one of the guestrooms. Just so long as we push off soon," she added with an endearing nervous nibble at her lip and a glance around the darkened cargo hold, as if expecting Mikhail to pop out of a shadowy corner any second.

Knowing that tone well—his mother spoke just

like that when she was determined to have her way—
Sander didn't bother arguing as he lifted her bags out
of the trunk. He'd just put her bags in the Stateroom,
and let her awe and pride do the rest. "Ready?" He
was surprised to find he was enjoying the novel experience of playing employee to a commoner.

She nodded. "Definitely. The sooner the better."
She headed for the lit door marked Exit in a form of
Koi Greek rare outside of Hellenia, but close enough
to read.

He only realised then that Mari had been speaking Hellenican Greek the whole time—and so had
he. It had been that easy with her, so natural he
hadn't noticed.

Alarm bells went off in his head. What was it
about Mari that drew princes and dukes to her like
compasses to the north, when she wasn't even
trying?

An hour later, Mari stood on the deck of the yacht,
watching the harbour recede from view. Her sigh
was heartfelt when she saw no yacht or chopper
racing to catch them.

A soft tingling at her neck told her Lysander was
nearby, watching her.

How she knew, she had no idea. He had that effect
on her; all the denial in the world wouldn't change
it. She found him—well, gorgeous. It didn't mean
anything would happen.

She turned with a smile that felt forced on her lips. "Beautiful, isn't it?" She waved around at the harbour, at the beaches and cliffs of the coast, and the yachts and little fishing vessels bobbing in the water.

He watched her with the same forced politeness he'd had on his face for hours. His gaze remained on her face, not sweeping over her changed attire: cargo shorts and a pretty just-on-the-shoulder rose-pink jersey shirt, tied in at the waist, flip-flops on her feet. "I've always thought this part of the world fairly stunning," he agreed, adding with belated subservience, "miss."

Absurdly disappointed that her best casual summer outfit hadn't brought the boy out of Pinocchio, she turned back. "Have you travelled much?"

"A little, miss."

"Have you been to Sydney?" she went on doggedly, determined to find some common ground with her only companion for the next few days—and she'd only been to Sydney and Greece until now.

"Once. I've been to Sydney, to Canberra, and on a day-trip to the Blue Mountains. Its beauty is very different to here."

A tiny smile curved her mouth. "It's wilder," she agreed, "especially in the national parks and the beaches. Here, everything feels—civilised."

"Tamed, you mean?"

Her head tilted as she thought about it. "It seems that way, I suppose. But it feels like a sham. Like the calm before a storm. You feel the sense of all the things that have happened here, all the history and wars, and you know it's just a breath away from happening again."

"That's very perceptive of you," he added, with a half-surprised inflection. "Life has been like that here for a long time." Which was why Charlie and Jazmine's more relaxed rule was like summer wine on an overheated day, and why almost everyone loved them already.

She shrugged. "My cousins have to have people to talk to sometimes. Being what they are now is pretty overwhelming. In a year they've had to learn so much, change completely, and understand their new world while making life-altering decisions. It helps to speak to people who love them, who'll keep their confidence—and who know them from the time when they used to be just like us."

Lysander joined her at the rail at last; but the tingling didn't abate, and she had to control the urge to move away. It wasn't his fault that she couldn't—that she wanted—

"Do they miss their old lives?" he asked, in such an ordinary voice that she felt another spurt of guilt. Lost in the confusion his nearness engendered, she hesitated a moment too long, and he went on quietly, "I understand, miss. You don't know me."

"The Queen trusts you," she said, wishing *she* had reason to trust him. Just because she was attracted to him it didn't mean she could spill royal secrets. "How would you feel if you suddenly found out your whole life had been a lie, that the person you loved best in the world wasn't what you thought he was? Great-Uncle Kyri gave them a safe rug all their lives, and then pulled it out from under them after he died."

He turned his head and looked at her with those *alive* eyes of his, and again she had the feeling she'd surprised him—like with her decision not to sleep in the Stateroom. "Most people would probably toss their old lives without thought to become a king and a princess, and inherit all they have."

Her mouth pursed into a half-smile. "I don't agree with that. Most people put family first—at least all the people I know. Our family's always worked hard for what we have, but how does money or position replace the bonds of love and family?"

"Is that how you feel?"

The question had a curious feel to it, as if beneath the stolid demeanour he wanted to know the answer—to know something about her.

What was it about this man that caught her off guard?

"Yes," she said eventually, thinking of Prince Mikhail, of Charlie and Lia's struggle to get everything right. "I don't think life in the public eye is for me—and I'm definitely not made for it, either," she added with a glimmering smile.

"And the power? Is the thought of rising in the world—the glamour, the titles—appealing to you?" he asked, and she had the curious belief he was pressing her, really wanting to know how she felt about it.

She tried to think of something clever and subtle to say, but she just didn't have that in her nature. "I can't answer for Charlie and Lia, but I don't think any amount of power or wealth could make up for living under a microscope." Indeed, that sense of always being watched was the thing that had convinced her that the reality of Charlie and Lia's new life was far from the dream she'd imagined when she'd first heard the news through the international media. The fact that their courtships, their royal training had all been conducted under such intense scrutiny—well, all she knew was *she* couldn't have taken it. "I like my privacy—the right to fail at something without the whole world knowing about it."

Lysander was very still. His hands gripped the rail. "You don't think you would—?" Whatever he'd been about to ask, he obviously thought better of it, for then he said, in a lighter tone, "I guess for those of us who haven't lived with it, it would be rather a culture shock."

"You could say that," she agreed fervently, remembering the first time the cameras had flashed in her face and a clamour of voices had yelled, "How does it feel to be cousin to royalty?"

"I suppose the reality of joining the Beautiful People isn't what most dream it would be," he said, with a thoughtful lilt at the end, like a question.

She shrugged. "Probably being born to it might make a difference. I wouldn't know." She turned her face again, smiling at him to lighten the intensity she felt in him.

He didn't smile back, barely even glanced at her. After a moment, he said, "Neither of us will ever know, miss." The words held that same hidden sense of thoughts held back.

There it was again—that "miss", like an intrusion into what was a semi-intimate conversation for such new acquaintances. And his word-choice and his accent—were all royal chauffeurs so well-educated?

"Do you think you could call me Mari, since we're going to be shipmates for the next few days?" she asked, with a wistful note that made her squirm with embarrassment.

"It's best to keep things as they are, miss," he replied, without missing a beat.

Mari felt herself freeze. "All right." She spoke from a cool distance. If he wanted to remain the chilly chauffeur, let him have his way. "Feel free to do whatever it is chauffeurs do on board yachts. I'll take a walk on deck before dinner." She waved him off, needing distance from him. If these were the rules, she'd play by them. The faster she could dismiss his smiling face from her ledger of unattainable fantasies, the better.

He ducked his head in a small bow that smacked as much of irony as it did respect. "Enjoy your walk, miss."

And then he was gone.

During the next half-hour, before she needed to change for dinner, Mari discovered the meaning of the grand term *solitary splendour*—and she also discovered she didn't like it a bit.

And it was all Lysander's fault.

He'd hurt her feelings.

From his table in the secondary dining room, where he'd elected to dine, Sander watched her eating alone in state in the royal dining room. Pretty and fresh in a floral print dress, with her curls falling from a loose clip at her nape, she looked small and lonely. She was barely eating, even though the food was superb. She kept her face averted from where he sat, trying to catch her eye, to make her smile as she had this afternoon, and he knew her eyes shimmered with tears she was trying to control.

Guilt ate at him. Gregarious and impulsive by nature, Mari was a sweet extrovert who needed company and friendship to make her shine. Protocol dictated that he was the only one she could talk to here. The King's cousins couldn't make friends with the staff on the yacht in case it embarrassed the royal family. He'd known that all along. Yet when she'd offered her friendship he'd played the wooden chauffeur, blocking her off. He'd put distance between them because he knew she was attracted to him...because she was dangerous to his peace of mind.

She'd offered friendship without reservation, and he'd left her humiliated and alone because he wanted her even more than Mikhail did—had done since he'd first seen her. Her birth held him back—more because she was Charlie's cousin than because she wasn't good enough. She had the power to destroy him without even trying—and he could only ruin her.

But none of this absurd situation was her fault. She couldn't help being...well, lovable...and it was no fault of hers that she was totally ill-equipped for his life.

He had to make this right. He'd lower himself to a position where she could retaliate...or, if he was really lucky, forgive him. Eventually.

Taking his plate, he walked through the sliding glass doors to where she sat, and took the place opposite her. She whirled around to look at him, her eyes wide, startled—and, yes, shimmering with tears unshed.

Though she didn't exactly seem welcoming, she was so *pretty* he gritted his teeth before he forced a smile. *It's not her fault she could break my career and cause international rifts between nations, with potential repercussions for one small, unimportant duchy on the edge of Hellenia.*

"I'm sorry I said what I did this afternoon," he

said, in true sincerity. "Can we start over? I'm Lysander—but my friends call me Sander." He put out a hand.

After a visible hesitation, she nodded and took his hand in hers. "Hello. I'm Mari."

She withdrew her hand the moment he slackened his hold. Looking down, she applied herself to food that by now had to be even colder and less appetising than his.

"Pleased to meet you, Mari," he said warmly, angling for her smile.

A brief, beautiful blaze of light hit Sander in the solar plexus as she smiled at him, but then it vanished. She sat opposite him at the table, only inches away, yet she appeared distant, like a shooting star flown out of reach.

"You too."

He noticed she didn't use his name. Disappointment streaked through him, but he knew she was only playing the game by the rules he'd set for them.

"You know you can send the plate back and ask for fresh?" he commented, when her face took on a stoic expression as she chewed her food.

She shook her head. "I've worked as a chef's assistant in a Thai restaurant," she said, showing him her working-class background without shame or embarrassment. "I won't give this chef extra work because I didn't eat when the food was hot."

"Did you eat too much at the wedding?" he asked, smiling.

Slowly, as if drawn, her eyes lifted from their determined gaze on her plate, and she looked at his mouth. A hard thrill ran through him at the half-shy wonder—then she looked in his eyes. Her brows drew together and she shrugged.

A spurt of irritation shot through him. "How much you ate today is hardly a state secret."

Her hands fluttered up and fell back to her lap. "I don't know who you are," she said simply. The words carried a double meaning that a trained diplomat couldn't miss…and he was in the danger zone. If she knew—

Still he couldn't keep his mouth closed. "You think I'm the media in disguise?" he asked, to get her to talk.

She shrugged again. "The Queen trusts you, so she must have had you security-cleared. If you're media you're in deep cover. And the way you speak—well, you sound like Prince William, or someone like that."

Sander felt his heart pounding too fast. It was coming, and he couldn't stop it. "You sound like a thriller writer," he teased, to divert her from the logical conclusion.

"You're not just a chauffeur, are you?"

There it was—the question he'd been expecting for hours and half-dreaded. He had instructions from the King and Queen, and he wondered at his curious reluctance as he said, "No, I'm not. I'm in the Royal Hellenican Diplomatic Corps."

She nodded, as if expecting that. "I thought it might be something like that. Only titled men and women can enter the Corps in Hellenia."

He kept the sigh inside. There went any chance to be anonymous, to just enjoy each other's company for a few days, man to woman, without titles and wealth getting in the way. "I'm the brother of the tenth Duke of Persolis. I was Lord Limontis."

"You *were* Lord Limontis?" she asked, too languidly for him to call it jumping on the past tense, yet she hadn't wasted time.

"My brother abdicated last year to become a monk," he said, refusing to look at her. It was strange—such an intimate conversation, yet neither one looking at the other.

After a couple of moments in which neither of them moved, she spoke. "So, then, since you're no longer Lord Limontis—does that make you the eleventh Duke?"

An even longer moment before he answered. "Yes."

Mari pushed her plate away. Her gaze was on the exquisite candelabra to his right. "If you're a diplomat, you must have been assigned to help me. You know exactly what's been going on."

She sounded so tense. A small corner of pity touched him. "Yes."

"My thanks are unnecessary, since you were doing your job...but I do thank you, Your Grace. And your decision to maintain distance from me makes perfect sense." Her chair scraped back, and she stood. Her face averted, she lifted a hand in negation as he jumped to his feet with instinctive good manners. "Please enjoy your meal. I'm tired. Good night."

"Please, Mari, it wasn't like that. Won't you listen for a few minutes?" he asked in low, pleading tones he'd long ago learned melted the hardest of feminine hearts.

But Mari shook her head yet again, her frown deeper, as if he'd offended her. "It's been quite a long day for me, Your Grace, so if you'll excuse me—?"

The distance between them was growing by the nanosecond—and when it was Mari creating the abyss, he really didn't like it. "Please don't call me by that title. I told you—my name's Sander. 'Your Grace' reminds me of my father, or my brother," he added, trying to make her relax in his company. "I wasn't brought up to be the Duke. I was the spare heir who fell into the title when Konstantinos's lifelong love of the Church led him to a monastery."

Slow-burning eyes looked into his then. "Would you have told me that—or asked me to call you by name—if I wasn't cousin to a king? Would you be so friendly to a commoner from Sydney?"

The question made him flush. "We'd never have met if you weren't cousin to a king," he said, and it sounded more pompous than he'd meant it to be.

"Exactly."

Strange, but when he looked at her he saw only acceptance of his snobbery. "Mari—"

"I think you're right," she said very softly. "It's best if we maintain distance."

Sander's mind scrabbled through options as he tried to work out how the situation had unravelled so fast. Where had all his tact gone—all the effortless charm, the light-handed control of all matters—that led kings and princes to trust his judgement?

The trouble was he wasn't used to dealing with people other than high-maintenance hyperactive politicians or languid members of born aristocracy. Mari belonged to neither class, and she was her own woman with her own set of values and a deep core of strength.

"I should have known things would end this way tonight when you moved your bags out of the Stateroom," he muttered.

"Twice," was her only comment, and his gaze flew to her like metal particles to a magnet when he heard the gentle laugh.

He raised his brows. She'd also refused the services of the maid, much to that lady's intense disappointment. "You moved your entire wardrobe back to the guestroom?"

She lifted a shoulder and grinned. "Only the clothes that were already mine—and it's only a walk across the hall."

"And down about sixty feet," he retorted, enjoying the banter.

"I told you it wasn't my place to be there." When he didn't answer, her grin grew. "You're not alone in underestimating me, Your Grace. You'll soon understand that when I say something, I mean it. My parents always say I'm too stubborn for my own good." Her voice held sweet empathy turned against herself in bubbling mirth, and he had to gulp down a physical longing to move closer to her, to drink in that happiness by osmosis. "Um, Your Grace…" she added, a much-later afterthought, spoken in impish fun, as he'd done by calling her "miss" today, and he found himself laughing with her.

"Why do I get the feeling you're going to be harder work than—than any king or queen I've served?" he finished smoothly, almost saying *Prince Mikhail.*

"Perhaps, but in a totally different way than you'd be used to." Her voice was like champagne, filled with floating bubbles.

"I work for your cousins, too," he reminded her, but he knew his face gave away his laughter. He might have a good poker face, but people always said his eyes were like Pinocchio's nose—always betraying him.

Did they show how much he ached to touch her,

to feel her skin and drink in the sunshine she seemed to carry around in her pocket? Were his eyes telling her that his thoughts were every bit as lustful as Mikhail's, yet somehow far more…personal, yearning?

"If you're the Duke, why are you still working as a diplomat? Don't you have a dukedom to run or something?"

The question took him by surprise, and he answered without thought. "A duchy—yes, I do. In another year or so I'll retire from my work and do my duty by my people."

"Returning to lay down the law and make them all obey?" She laughed.

"Not quite. I'll return to Persolis from my post, marry a suitably well-bred young lady, produce heirs and let my mother retire at last," he drawled, a little offended by her assumption that he'd rule with a fist of iron. He was a *diplomat*. He knew how to make people do as he wanted while allowing them to think it was all their own idea.

All people, that was, except this mercurial young woman, with her original ideas and unshakable stubbornness. Had he met his Nemesis—his Daughter of Night?

"Yes, I'm sure all the well-bred girls will be lining up for the opportunity, Your Grace."

Startled anew, Sander frowned at her—then he realised what he'd said, the unintentional insult in retaliation for her little joke. He cursed his unaccountable lack of tact and his empty mind, not knowing what to say next.

Was there a handbook on how to treat an ordinary young woman with higher moral standards than the Prince he worked for?

A slight swish of air whispered by his cheek, and Sander knew that while he'd been lost in thought Mari had left the room without a sound.

CHAPTER FOUR

"ONE fantasy is now fulfilled," Mari sighed as she stood on deck the next morning, the wind in her hair and the sunshine kissing her skin.

"What's that?"

She controlled her jumpy reaction to Lysander's closeness. "This has been a dream of mine since I was a girl." Keeping her gaze on the surreal beauty *off* the yacht, she waved around at the intense aqua of the water, dotted with islands straight from her childhood bedtime stories. "All my life I've day-dreamed about *this*." She patted the rail and sighed. "I mean, who doesn't dream of being on a yacht in the Aegean Sea, island-hopping and seeing the play-ground of the old gods?"

"Every time I come here I feel the same. Like it's a dream." He leaned beside her at the rail. A glorious male scent, reminiscent of ocean and deep forest and…Lysander…wafted to her. She breathed it in, and a vision of his face filled her head.

How ridiculous was it that she was mooning over a man who was standing right beside her, a man working at being close to her? But the inches separating them were like the abyss off Santorini's cliffs—deadly dangerous to the unskilled…

"I think I'll be homesick for here when I go back—though Australia's always been home," she said softly, watching an albatross soaring over them with minimal effort.

"You're not tempted to stay?"

The question held that odd intensity again—and suddenly she knew what he was hiding: he was attracted to her, too. A thrill ran through her, but she had to hold it in. "I can't afford to be." She frowned at the island they were passing, so beautiful with its whitewashed stone houses and steep cobbled roads. "This is Charlie and Lia's life. I don't belong here. It's borrowed time for me—a fantasy world only few can live in every day."

"Charlie and Jazmine are very family-orientated. You'd be welcome."

"Don't you see that's exactly why I couldn't stay?" Was her voice wobbling with the yearning to take the hand of temptation being held out to her? Right now she didn't know which tempted her most: the country, the family or the luscious man beside her—a creation from the imagination of the gods, with an unspoken empathy that…that— "They already have too many people taking advantage of their closeness to the commoner King and Princess."

"Do you mean the plane sent for the firemen to come over? Sending the royal jet to bring family for the wedding? I doubt anyone believes they took advantage."

Mari slanted him a look filled with irony. "You're born to this life, Your Grace. You go home to a palace probably not far removed from the Summer Palace. You were born in Persolis, which is part of Hellenia. It's easy to leave knowing you'll go back. You have no idea how the temptation to never leave grabs hold of me here." She laid a hand over her heart. "This land—in hours it felt like part of who I am, as if I belong here. But I don't."

"Actually, I was born in Paris," he said quietly, "but I know what you mean. I do take it for granted now. But ten years ago, when I joined the Diplomatic Corps, Hellenia was at war with itself. I was glad to be posted elsewhere and leave the high-pressure decisions to my father, and then my brother." Low, he added, "Then Father died, Konstantinos renounced his position to become a monk—and I became Duke."

All he hadn't said played in her mind like a re-run of the last scene of *Casablanca*: the impossible decision facing a young man who'd never seen the choice coming. A new, reluctant duke in a nation with divided loyalties, and a royal family imploding.

No wonder Sander had decided to remain a diplomat when he'd become Duke.

"I'm sorry." She laid a hand over his for a moment, her eyes shimmering with pity for a man born to more wealth and privilege than she'd ever have. "It must have been so hard. Is— Was your duchy...damaged?"

"Yes." He spoke in a strange blend of remoteness and warmth, as if an internal war raged in him and he couldn't decide how to feel. "My brother left as the war ended, and I inherited a duchy in a shambles. I stayed on in the Corps in order to create ties to nations that could help us in the long term."

Feeling intense curiosity and sympathy mingled, she asked, "Then who—?"

"My mother agreed to handle my duties for a year or so while I finish my tenure and—and learn the minutiae of being Duke. My brother and I talk for an hour at night. His abbot allows him that much speaking for the good of the nation," he added with a wryness she couldn't describe. "If I can combine both duties for a few years, perhaps rise to Ambassador, it can only do my people good."

Mari understood far more than he'd said. She'd been the one Charlie and Lia had talked to when she'd arrived for both royal weddings. She'd heard stories of the hardship as well as privilege. "I saw the effect on Charlie when he lost his parents and Great-Uncle Kyri. It would have been just the same for him if he'd been here, if he'd been King." Wanting to give him comfort, she smiled at him and squeezed the hand she still held. "Love and grief are the same in any class of humanity—hard decisions, too."

"Except that our decisions affect more people than our families alone." He turned to her with that dark intensity that fascinated her. His eyes could dance or create a tempest in the ocean, as they did now. "Your great-uncle's decision sent our nation into over twenty years of war, and still he never came back, nor told his family who he was."

Mari couldn't answer that. It was too hard to reconcile the loving, giving old man she'd known with the one who'd created a war and done nothing to end it. "And your decision to remain a diplomat—who else does *that* affect?"

Lysander's face darkened still more. "I'd say the same amount of people that my brother's decision to enter a monastery did—no, one less, because his decision surely changed *my* life."

She tilted her head, studying him. The unplumbed depths of this man fascinated her. For a duke, a man with wealth and privilege, he seemed so—alone. "Your decision has obviously affected your mother."

He turned on her, stepping an inch too close in his passionate denial. "You think what Konstantinos did didn't affect her? I wasn't *trained* to be the Duke. I was the spare—the one destined for the Navy, the Air Force or the priesthood. Everyone says Konstantinos's decision was a noble one. I was supposed to step in and act like I was always meant to be the Duke. But I wasn't born for it. My brother never asked me how I felt about it until he was safely installed in his peaceful life inside the monastery."

Her breathing shifted; she willed her heart to slow its racing at the masculine heat only inches from her. *How can anyone find this man a disappointment?* her mind screamed. Standing this close to him, she certainly couldn't find a single fault. "Maybe he was afraid to ask, because then he'd have felt too guilty to go where he knew he belonged."

Slowly the storm clouds faded in his eyes; he stared at her and shook his head, but didn't speak.

"Maybe he had more faith in you than you do in yourself," she added gently. "Maybe he knew in his heart he wasn't meant to be the Duke, but you were."

His frown intensified, but it wasn't frightening. "He always loved the Church—the rituals and the chanting." A smile glimmered. "It only ever put me to sleep."

She gave him a lilting smile. "So we do have something in common—a lack of interest in the Church. My parents think I'm the next best thing to a heathen because I crash when they start droning in the old Greek."

His whole face came alive as he threw back his head and laughed. "Droning—I love it. I always start yawning within seconds."

Mari stared at his smiling mouth, fascinated beyond decency, aching to move closer, to touch her fingers to the living beauty of his face, the warmth of his skin. "And don't talk to me about the incense. Our church was small, but they used enough sandal-wood for a cathedral."

His grin was the splitting-face variety of a man who'd found a soul mate at last. "I always felt the urge to bring a breathing apparatus."

She laughed, wondering if he felt a tenth of the violent need to touch that she did. She'd never become so enthralled with a man so fast before. He was like—dangerous magic.

"Are your parents disappointed in you now?" he asked, racking up the conversation another notch in intimacy.

She sighed and nodded. "They think Mikhail will marry me because of Charlie. Why shouldn't their daughter become a princess?" Her eyes met his, and she immediately wished they hadn't, because the mixture of mirth and empathy was—compelling. "I don't know if your parents have the same need to brag about their children as mine do, but in their minds I'm denying them the opportunity to have a royal daughter. They seem to think I deserve it."

Lysander's gaze softened as he looked down at her. "Well, why wouldn't they? All families want the best for their children, and with your cousins having become royal it must seem within the bounds of reality. And you're beautiful, with strong morals like Charlie, Lia and Toby. And, as we've said, they've been a breath of fresh air to the country."

"Well, I don't like Mikhail," she almost snapped, the sense of being hunted filling her again. "He's selfish and arrogant, and no title makes that appealing to me."

"You weren't tempted by his wealth or power?" he asked, sounding totally unoffended by her anger—more curious, if anything.

She shrugged. "I've learned the past year that there are other, more valuable things. What's the point of wealth if you don't have love, family or self-respect?"

He kept his eyes on her face, and seemed to take a half-step closer before he halted. "I think you're a very wise as well as a lovely woman, Mari Mitsialos," he said quietly.

Blushing, she turned away. "What's so wise about knowing the one basic fact of life?"

A quizzical look touched those amazing eyes of his. "You don't think much of yourself, do you?"

She was lost in the feeling his closeness and his smile engendered in her body, and the question confused her. "Why would I?" she asked. "I'm just an average woman. My only claim to fame is through a couple of suddenly royal cousins."

He chuckled. "'Suddenly royal'—you have an interesting turn of phrase, Mari."

She felt a little shiver run through her as he said her name on its own for the first time. Intimate and beautiful and *dangerous*...

As if he'd seen her internal reaction, he took a step closer, his eyes lighting with a candle of open desire. "The Captain told me to ask you if you'd like to stop at Santorini, which is a really beautiful place, with loads of things to do, or move on to a less populated island. He said we could sail around, finding places to swim until we reach Patmos—" his eyes twinkled again "—which I suspect is his personal favourite, since he was born there."

She gulped against the yearning threatening to send her into total stupidity. *He's not a chauffeur; he's not married...* "Ah, and here I was thinking he must be a Bible fan," she croaked. "Isn't that where some books of the Bible were written?"

Lysander's brows lifted, as if she'd surprised him again. "I know St John was imprisoned there. There are some tours you can take, if you're interested in Bible history."

She chuckled. "And have my parents think I'm ready to return to the fold?"

"Drone...drone..." he chanted, deadpan. When she stopped laughing, he said, "So, what is your choice for the day? The yacht is at your disposal."

She looked at him with a hopeful, wistful feeling. "I know it's touristy and all that, but I'd really like to see Santorini. They say it could be the real Atlantis..."

He smiled down at her. "Then Santorini it is. Would you like some company?"

Wistfulness grew in her. "Yes, please—if you don't mind. I might get lost, or not know how to bargain for things." And just because she wanted him beside her—and the least of his attraction was his title. She'd been just as fascinated when she'd thought him a chauffeur. Even now she knew who he was she couldn't go back, couldn't think of him as a duke, couldn't distance herself. She couldn't stay away...

One day. How had she become so enthralled by him in a single day?

As if he understood her inner dilemma, Lysander sobered. "I think you could probably bargain your way into whatever you want by just smiling."

Mari caught her breath. As if they were in a go-cart on a steep hill, she saw the inevitable crash before them—but they were going to do it anyway, going to take the ride and endure the fall.

She was already on that go-cart, already falling. And she couldn't make herself care.

"I'll tell the Captain to head for the dock, then," Lysander said abruptly, and walked off, his clean stride seeming somehow hunted.

That evening

"Oh, my goodness, how wonderful was that?" Mari walked along the pier to the yacht beside a loaded-down Lysander, who was carrying her bags for her. "I can't decide which was best—the markets, the tomato balls and couscous, or the volcano." She gave a delicious shiver. "To think half the island just disappeared in an hour…a minute…"

Lysander smiled down at her, those dancing eyes shining in the light of the setting sun. He looked five years younger than this morning—his load lightened, just a man having fun. "I would have thought you liked the swimming best."

She shook out her still-damp hair, falling in a corkscrew mess around her shoulders. "Well, wasn't it wonderful? I know Australia's famous for its beaches, but the water's never like that—so gloriously warm, but not hot—except in the North, and then you have to watch for crocodiles. I felt like I was floating around in a warm salt bath."

"Yes." His tone—so amused without laughing at her—sent another delicious shiver through her. "The local men seemed to enjoy watching you…um… floating, as well."

She blushed and shrugged. She couldn't refute it, since at least a dozen had tried to charm her, both in the water and then offering their help in walking up the rocky sand. "I wasn't trying to—oh! You don't think they knew who my cousins are, do you?"

His face softened. "No, Mari, I think they saw a pretty woman enjoying life, and they wanted to enjoy it with you. I know I did."

She couldn't look at him as she said huskily, "Then why didn't you swim with me?"

He didn't speak, because they both knew the answer; and suddenly she felt a lump in her throat. "Stupid question. I need a shower to wash out all the salt before dinner. Thanks for carrying my bags." Without meeting his eyes, she held out her hands; he put her bags into them. "See you at dinner."

"Mari?"

About to run, she turned her head, but didn't look at him. "Yes?" Curse the huskiness in her voice! Did everything in her have to scream *I've got a crush on you*?

His voice sounded so gentle. "It wouldn't have been wise for me to swim with you."

She gulped. "I know. It's all right. I wasn't expecting—" Oh, what a fool she was making of herself!

"Will we go swimming tomorrow? It's supposed to be a beautiful day, and the Captain knows some coves that are private on the way to Patmos, at Naxos or Icaria."

The pity buried inside the offer made her burn inside with shame. He knew how she felt about him— falling faster than a bungee-jumper off a bridge—and he *pitied* her. "Someone might see us and put the wrong connotations on it. You can't risk your career for me. We should stick to tourist things. It's less— personal."

"What if I want to get personal with you, Mari?" he asked, as husky as she. "What if I no longer care about the consequences?"

Her cheeks aflame, she whispered, "One of us has to care." *For your sake.* And she found that was her real reason; he was a duke, and there wouldn't be any consequences in their having a relationship for her.

But he could lose his career.

She all but fled inside to her cabin before he could look at her, touch her—or say a single word to change her mind.

Did she dare do it?

Blue dress: safety—little black dress: joy—green dress: protection—lavender silk...*bliss*...

"What are you carrying on about? For all you know, he doesn't feel anything but politeness and diplomatic duty for you," she muttered. "He hasn't shown one single sign of interest. Wear something sensible and don't make a total idiot of yourself—again!"

The sun had slowly dropped in the sky and, clad only in her underwear, fresh from her shower, she was choosing dresses at random and tossing them aside. She owned all of three sexy dresses, kept carefully from her parents' view, and about ten safe, pretty, schoolmarm dresses that screamed, *Take me home to meet Mother.*

The trouble was she wanted to be sexy *and* be taken home to meet Mother—but the truth stared her in the face every day, with every word from his beautiful, cultured mouth: Lysander could never take her home. The way she saw it, she had two choices. She could follow her heart and her body's pleadings, wear one of her three hidden dresses and, if she could seduce him, become Lysander's lover for as long as she could hold him. Or she could play it safe, do the right thing for everyone else, and lose—

Lose what? That was the question, really. She'd known within a couple of days that Lysander was everything she'd ever dreamed of, but in her dreams she'd seen a man who loved her for life, not for a few days or weeks. Prince or duke, it made no difference for a girl like her. Lysander was as unattainable as Mikhail. She only wished he was as easy to reject and forget.

But still that lovely, silky, low-cut and high-slit lavender dress was in her hands…and then over her head…

Then she'd piled her hair up, letting it fall in tendrils over her neck and shoulders…soft make-up was on her face, and she'd sprayed that gorgeous perfume that made her think of black-hearted roses. And those naughty silver heels her mother had said made her look like a bad girl that she'd never been able to bring herself to return or wear…

Heart pounding and stomach churning, she left the room nine times and came back nine times, pacing the room and talking herself alternately into and out of it all. Brave chance or stupid risk? If only she knew. All she *did* know was that if she didn't try, didn't touch him, she'd regret it for life.

With that thought, finally she screwed her eyes shut and opened the door a tenth time, walked through it and closed it behind her.

Sander choked on his wine the moment she walked into the dining suite. Was it the Fates conspiring against him? He'd talked himself into and out of a tuxedo, into and out of soft, romantic music and candlelight...the staff didn't know if they were coming or going. Finally "out" had won, common sense had prevailed, and he'd begun to tell himself it was the right and noble thing—for Hellenia, for Persolis and for Mari. Definitely the right thing for everyone concerned to not even think of seducing her.

But then she'd come in wearing *that* dress.

Soft, swishing silk with thigh-high slits and cut low, revealing creamy cleavage. The honey-satin skin of her throat and neck was revealed by the curls piled high and tumbling down; a scent like sweet sin enveloped him in moments.

And that smile, so naughty and yet as adorably unsure as the look in her eyes, was his downfall. Duke he was, diplomat he might be, but beneath it all he was just a man...

He only knew he was on his feet, walking to her when he lifted one of those soft, sweet-scented hands to his mouth and felt her quiver. Masculine heat and triumph flared through every pore and cell when he saw the look in her eyes. He pulled her to him, a question in his eyes and heart, and she answered with that dazzling, vivid smile. And that scent, reminiscent of full-blown roses on hot summer nights, filled his head as her core body temperature grew with her arousal.

She wanted him so badly she wasn't even trying to deny it.

She'd come here tonight hoping or expecting—he didn't know or care. The pounding of his blood made hope expectation, and expectation imperative. He tried to speak, but couldn't find words. There was only here and now: a lifetime waiting for a single moment.

"I don't think we're going to talk about droning in church, are we?" she whispered as he lowered his mouth to her, her eyes shimmering.

He choked on laughter, thinking of all the most poetic words to give her, but his mind failed him and he said simply, "No, we're not." And still smiling, he drew her right against him and kissed her.

He'd never known he could smile as he kissed a woman, but Mari did that to him. For years he'd wandered the world, equating success with happiness, learning how to do everything right and please everyone. Then this smiling bundle of feminine joy had come into his life—everything he shouldn't want and couldn't have. In a day she'd shown him how empty his smiles had been, how shallow his heart had been until she'd filled him with her sunshine and her passionate commitments, her high principles and her giving nature, so crystal-clear and so wonderfully impulsive. Everything he shouldn't want and couldn't have was standing in his arms, in one dazzling package of so-called ordinary woman.

Dimly he heard music as they kissed—the steward must have seen them, and that should have worried him, but didn't. Slowly he moved to the music, she followed, and still they kissed as he moved her out from the glass-enclosed room to the deck beneath summer stars.

Mari made a soft noise and wound a hand into his hair, tender and intimate, and something inside him exploded. Other women had touched him there, but somehow none of them had affected him the way Mari did. She touched him and he felt so *happy* inside… More, he had to have more—and he lifted her up against him and made her part of him, body and heart.

Impossible to ignore, unable to deny, he was *gone*—for the first time since he'd had a crush on a princess, fifteen years ago. What was it about Mari? She was blunt, outspoken and no prettier than twenty women he knew—but her joy in living, her sparkling sense of adventure, drew him time after time. And her caring, her strong moral sense of right and wrong, her fear of hurting others, her vivid passion for—

Him. He'd only seen a shy kind of embarrassment with the men who had flocked around her this afternoon, but for him she smiled, blushed, and the yearning in her eyes came alive…just as he came alive with her, and had done from the first moment he'd seen her.

This was why he'd avoided her from the start. Losing his position with Mikhail had been a convenient excuse. When he was close to her he forgot everything but his need to be with her. Mari held the power to make him toss aside consequences and not care a bit. She was like liquid sunshine, and he wanted more and more…

He wanted too much, too fast. Mari had said clearly that she was going home in a few days. She loved it here, but she belonged in Australia. If she complicated his life, he could take the consequences—but he'd ruin her chances of ever going back to safe anonymity. Would she hate him for that?

"Lysander, Lysander," she mumbled between kisses. Her hands were tangled in his hair. So much passion, such vivid, innocent need for him—

And if she couldn't stop, he was completely addicted to the shots of bubbling happiness she injected with a smile, with a touch, with the way she said his name. And her kisses—

Consequences go hang. This was here and now. She was in his arms, and she was staying there as long as he could keep her.

CHAPTER FIVE

Three days later

"AT THE risk of sounding like a complete tourist—
what a fantastic place," Mari sighed as they moved
back onto the yacht. "The tour was really excellent."

"It certainly was informative," Sander agreed,
with a fatalistic feeling inside. If his mother heard of
his Bible tour in Patmos, he'd never hear the end of
it.

So why was he smiling?

The answer was right in front of him, her curvy
backside swaying as she ran up the gangplank. Mari
made him smile just by being near him. Her enthusiasm for life was infectious, and it made him feel
glad to be here—just glad to be alive.

"Couldn't you just *imagine* St John sitting in the
cave, seeing all those visions?" she asked, flushed
and starry-eyed as she flopped down on a deck
lounger. "The guide described it so you *knew* how

he must have felt. Coming here makes it all real, doesn't it?"

Actually, Sander would have been totally bored but for the constant entertainment of Mari's wide-eyed wonder as they toured the island. And her italics, instead of annoying him, kept him amused. Mari's dramatics were as natural to her as breathing, and endearing because they weren't designed to draw attention to her. She just said what was on her mind, and she was as passionate about others' interests as her own.

On that note, he said, "The donkeys were real, at any rate, and very grateful to you."

Mari's chin lifted. "It's a disgrace the way that master treated them. None of the other masters were cruel—their donkeys were well cared for. Somebody should do something about him, like those animal liberation groups."

"You did something," he replied, holding in a smile, thinking of her cold refusal to ride on a too-thin donkey with scars on its back. She'd walked all the way up to the caves…and one pleading look from those pretty eyes had had him climbing off his donkey as well. A few sad glances at the state of the donkeys other tourists rode on had had some of their riders joining in the silent protest.

"Maybe you'll do better business if you learn to take care of your donkeys," she had told the indignant master. "Take a lesson from the other masters."

"A private protest isn't enough," she said now. "Are we online on the yacht? I'd like to find a website—"

"You can't save the world, Mari," he said gently.

"Don't say that!" Her eyes flashed. "It's an excuse to do nothing! If everyone cared enough to right one wrong, just one, how much would the world improve?"

She was right. Most of the women he'd been with cared only for their next beauty treatment, or being the first to wear a new dress or hairdo or sunglasses and set a fashion. "So you're righting the wrongs of donkeys?" he teased, wanting to see her passion continue—with him. Their kisses were getting more intense by the hour, and he was more and more enchanted by her. They both knew it couldn't last; he'd eventually find his Duchess and have heirs, and she'd find a man to walk her down the aisle—

He had to blank out the thought, for the face he saw was his own—and the face of his Duchess was Mari's.

"At least I care for something more than my own wants and fears," she flashed. "Do you? Do you care enough for your people to give up what you love and do your best for them?"

With a few pithy words she'd cut through the layers of his self-delusion to the ugly core truth. Though his diplomatic work and ties would help Persolis, that wasn't why he'd stayed on in the Corps. He hadn't planned to be Duke, had never wanted it.

He liked his life as it was. He didn't want to change it, didn't want to right anyone's wrongs on a deeper level than he did now. And when the promised time came to take over and let his mother retire, would he continue making excuses?

Not now. Not now he saw himself for the man he was—and didn't like it. He *did* care for his land, his people—and it was time to stop running away.

"I'm sorry, that was out of line," she mumbled, as he seemed still lost in his thoughts. "It's none of my business what you do, Lysander. It's between you and your mother."

"And my people." He fixed his gaze on her, loving the honest remorse in her pretty face. Loving her *caring*. Just—*loving*. Wanting her to feel proud of him, he gave her similar honesty. "I'm going back, Mari. Even if I don't feel qualified, I'm going back."

Her smile, so tentative, grew until a light like sunrise filled her eyes. "Start small and work your way up, Dad always says. He began by picking up rubbish on the beaches. Now, twenty years later, he earns a good living in recycling with his 'clean green' business. He even consults with members of the Australian Government on safe rubbish storage practices."

"Impressive," he murmured, wanting to kiss her so badly it was pain. But—hadn't he met a green representative on unsafe rubbish practices last time he was in Persolis? He remembered signing something to make changes to an edict of his father's, so that residents near the dump were exposed to less hazardous waste…

Suddenly intrigued, he asked, "What does he do with rubbish that's so unique the government consults him on it?"

"He's invented a kind of environmental blanket for naturally-degradable rubbish, and is working on a radiation-reducing container for toxic waste." Grinning, Mari rose from the deck lounger. "Dad's passion for a cleaner environment is too serious a conversation on a stomach only filled with ice cream. See you at dinner."

She ran lightly along the deck, her curly ponytail floating behind her. She had a little tripping step; he always thought she'd fall flat on her face at any moment. Sander had been appreciating her unusual way of moving for days. He'd finally worked it out, after watching her constantly: she had a slight tendency toward pigeon toes she was forcing outward, and it made her awkward. Graceful she was not.

And yet though this couldn't possibly last beyond the few days they were on the yacht, he couldn't stop smiling. And wishing. And wanting.

The worst of it was the more he had of her, the more he wanted—a lifetime of *more*—and duty was flapping out through the window on the wings of an albatross, slow and relentless.

Slow? He'd known her all of five days, and for the

past four days all he'd been able to think of was touching her again, and the joy of having that gorgeous smile beaming up at him as she laid her sweet little hands on him. When they'd swum off Naxos he'd been in pain, trying to keep his hands and body to himself; but she hadn't had such scruples. She'd started a splashing contest as an excuse to get closer, and wrapped silky-wet arms around his neck.

"I know," she'd breathed, as an attack of unwanted conscience had taken him over and he'd tried to hold off. "This is all we can have, Lysander. It's just a holiday romance—so let's enjoy our holiday."

The tender acceptance in her words had made him hate himself, but he hadn't held back. Sweet, salty kisses in the warm ocean with a woman he liked, respected as well as desired—a memory to keep when he had to do his duty and marry the right woman.

He'd made dozens of memories since then: dancing beneath the stars at night; eating from her fork at lunch at Naxos; her soft moans when they touched; the feel of her against him when they kissed, her body always straining to be closer.

They had to get back to Hellenia, and fast. He couldn't hold out much longer—and not just against making love to her. Every day, every hour, he was falling in deeper. He was barely sleeping, filled with the need to get off the bed, walk about forty feet, pull her into his arms and tell her, *Let's do what your*

great-uncle did—run away and forget the conse-
quences. It won't start a war this time...

He groaned to himself. How could she say yes,
given her family history and her love for her cousins?
But it didn't stop the stupid hope that she'd put him
first... That she'd marry him and give him a lifetime
of her caring, her scruples and her joy in living, in
touching him. He couldn't lie to himself: he loved
Mari, but he couldn't make love to her. He couldn't
bring himself to hurt her, knowing he had to walk
away. All he could hope for was more wonderful
kisses...and that he'd remember her and their time
together with a smile when he did his duty.

"Your Grace, Her Majesty the Queen is on the
phone for you," the steward informed him respect-
fully.

"Perfect timing," he murmured beneath his
breath. Racked with guilt, filled with hidden resent-
ment against the future and the duty he had to embrace, Sander walked to the bridge to speak to
Jazmine.

"Tonight's the night," Mari said softly to herself as
she pulled the little black dress from its hanger.

They were out of time; they docked back at
Orakidis Harbour tomorrow.

Lysander's scruples made him even more wonderful to her—she knew he was holding back on making
love for her sake—but if this time was all they could

have…if this night was their last…she wanted to have a night to remember.

Tonight, all she hadn't been able to bear with Mikhail would become all she could dream of. Tonight she'd give everything to Lysander. One night with the man she was head over heels in love with would be worth the price she paid later.

How she'd fallen in love so fast, after a lifetime of never loving any other man she'd met, she had no idea. Perhaps it was holiday love—maybe it could never last for them—but right now she didn't care. She only asked for tonight.

Deliberately she wore no shoes, no jewellery, and left her hair down, mussed with mousse, as if she'd just risen from bed. She wore no make-up but shimmering lipgloss. The dress, with its spaghetti straps and flaring short skirt, gave the message she needed.

This time there was no agonised indecision. She walked straight out of her room and up the stairs to the dining hall—and caught her breath. Lysander waited for her in a magnificent tuxedo, with a deep red rose in his hand, and that smile. "Mari *mou*," he said softly—*My Mari*.

Wanting nothing more than to run into his arms, she couldn't ruin the moment. She walked slowly to him, her whole body alight with joy and need. "Lysander…" she breathed.

"We're not going to talk about safe garbage practices tonight," he murmured as he put the rose in her hand.

Even as she lifted the rose to her face, she choked on laughter. "No, we're not." And she slid her arms around his neck. "Make love to me."

His eyes took fire, but still they searched hers. "Are you sure?"

"I know we can only have tonight." She smiled bravely up at him, a mass of yearning and sad acceptance twining in her heart. "Tomorrow we pretend it didn't happen, for everyone's sake—you'll keep your position, and I'll go home. But tonight is ours."

"No. Either way, I'm going home too. You were right—it's time for me to take my place in Persolis." A tender hand caressed her cheek; his eyes were filled with desire, with *caring*, and she felt her heart splinter. "I don't want just one night with you, Mari. I want you to know that if it were up to me we'd have so much more."

She closed her eyes in joy and agony. One of them had to keep their head. *For Lysander's sake, and for his people.* "Change will come to Hellenia slowly. There's no convenient duchy for me, to make me acceptable. I can't be like Great-Uncle Kyri and Great-Aunt Giulia, and toss aside the consequences to others. So let's have tonight."

Lysander kissed her once, twice, and melting honey filled her body, sweet yearning and hot need. "You're so lovely, so strong and caring—you'd fight

for what's right. You'd make a magnificent duchess…" he whispered in her ear, and she felt the *if only*
hovering in the air between them.

Moved, lost, she had to struggle against saying
something stupid. "Take me to bed."

He lifted her in his arms. "I feel so happy when
I'm touching you."

That was it—she'd waited for so long for this kind
of happiness, for the dream to come. But this could
only be a holiday romance. They were worlds apart;
only the here and now existed for them. "Me too."

"I tried to stop this," he mumbled hoarsely between kisses. "But how do I resist a woman who's
perfect for me in every way, or tell my heart to stop
feeling like this? In a world where I rarely know
what to believe, I believe in you, Mari."

"Lysander," she whispered against his mouth,
angling her face so it fitted his perfectly. She felt so
wonderful in his arms… He murmured endearments
in his native tongue, and her heart became his—but
she gave it in silence, for his sake.

"This is inevitable," he whispered. "*We're* inevitable. We're right. Tell me you feel it, Mari. I
know you do."

Oh, she did, but at this moment, when dream
could become reality, the strong streak of practicality in her overtook her fantasies and stepped
gently on them. "I want to make love," she said in
reply, because there was nothing else to say.

Instead of taking her to bed, he put her back on her feet and cupped her face in his hands. "You don't believe in us?"

Hating to hurt him, she hesitated a moment too long, and his hands dropped from her face. She felt the words hovering on his tongue—then he stepped back; the emotion in his eyes dimmed, and he said, smooth and oh, so cool, "Dinner will be getting cold."

Mari's smile faltered; the stars dimmed in her eyes and she nodded. "I understand, Your Grace." Her voice was thick. "I'm not very hungry. Good night."

And with her acceptance, when his words had been designed to make her fight for him, Sander panicked. "No, Mari." He strode to her—she was already walking out through the door—and snatched her close and kissed her, but she didn't respond. "Stay," he commanded roughly. "I'll *make* you believe in us."

She shook her head and stepped back out of his arms. "I should never have started this. Like Prince Mikhail, you can't offer me anything better, and I can't humiliate my family."

There lay their conflict in a nutshell. She'd said everything he wanted to ignore when he'd spoken of fate. "This *isn't* like Mikhail. I *respect* you. I want more than a few weeks in bed." More like the next five decades—but he wouldn't say that until he was sure his feelings for her would last. He needed to feel enough to base a lifetime on—for all the wrong reasons as well as the right ones.

"You can't have it." Her voice wobbled with sadness, but she spoke with the conviction of knowing she was right. "Charlie has changed the law for future kings and queens. Great-Uncle Kyri had a Grand Duchy to hand Toby in order for him to get his miracle. But even a duke isn't powerful enough to change the way things are in Persolis. Uncle Kyri started a civil war after disappearing with a commoner—and he had a title and power. I have nothing." She stepped back. "I think we should remain separate until we reach Orakidis Harbour tomorrow."

She was probably right, but angry at her fatalism, he snapped, "Why did you come here dressed like that if you won't take the next step and accept the consequences?"

She shook her head. "I thought I was courageous. I thought I could be your lover for tonight and be happy with the memories. But I'm afraid of hurting Charlie and Jazmine, Lia and Toby—not to mention my parents. I don't care if I'm a hypocrite. I'm traditional. I want an old-fashioned wedding with both families there and being happy for us."

Her voice trembled, her eyes shimmered, and he wanted to see her cry even less than she wanted to be weak in front of him. "Go," he said wearily. He didn't know what the future held, but he was hurt that Mari wasn't willing to risk everything for him. "I'll order a tray to your room, and the yacht to return to dock by morning. We're not far from Hellenia."

She turned away and left the room in a soft swish of black silk. She looked like a dream of lost beauty, a sweet ghost floating through the doors, leaving his life.

And it was only as she walked away that he knew he couldn't bear to think of a day, an hour without her. He'd do whatever it took to hold her—even face the wrath of princes and kings.

All he had to do was convince her.

CHAPTER SIX

THERE was a right royal welcoming committee waiting for them when they entered Orakidis Harbour the next morning.

Mari's heart sank when she saw the *big* royal yacht—at least twice the size of the magnificent one she now loved so much—sailing up beside them, with no less than three royal personages on deck: Charlie, Jazmine and Mikhail. All three of them were dressed casually, but looked grim. Charlie and Jazmine smiled at them as the yacht drew alongside, but Mikhail's handsome face was set in impenetrable lines. Though the sun was shining, and the sky was clear, Mari saw storm clouds ahead. She sidled up to Lysander; her hand crept into his. "Prince Mikhail wouldn't be here unless…"

He nodded, his face smoothing out to diplomatic neutrality. "I'll deal with this." He squeezed her hand briefly before he stepped away. "We've done nothing, feel nothing we need to be ashamed of, Mari. Hold onto that when Mikhail starts."

Knowing what she now knew, after ten minutes' research that first night, she knew what a sacrifice he was offering for her sake. "All right—thank you."

Then three more people emerged from the enormous double doors leading inside the royal yacht... and she groaned inside. "My parents, and my brother... Dad's likely to insist on a wedding. I'm sorry—so sorry..."

Lysander sent her an oblique smile. "I don't think marrying you would be my worst nightmare, Mari. I'd survive the ordeal of a shotgun wedding...even if your brother's pretty big and intense-looking. He didn't bring a shotgun with him from Australia, did he?"

Unbelievably, Mari heard laughter escape her lips. Envisaging a lifetime of diplomatic disasters leavened by laughter wasn't so hard at all right then—if Lysander was the one sharing with her the drama and the intimate jokes for two. "Of course he didn't—and if he has one now he's probably still aiming it at Mikhail."

"That's a relief. Leave it to me," he murmured with an infinitesimal wink.

She smiled and nodded, almost without movement. They moved towards the gangplank now connecting the two royal yachts.

* * *

Sander had felt the axe hovering over his head ever since Mari had discovered he wasn't a chauffeur, but like an idiot, he'd chosen to ignore it—to live the half-lie another day, another minute. Unable to stand seeing the admiration, the joy in his company fade from those lovely eyes, he hadn't been able to make himself do it.

And he was about to pay for it. Mikhail would make certain of that. So far he'd kept silent as those in precedence spoke—Charlie hugging her and Jazmine asking about her time away—but, his face taut and his eyes hard, Sander knew Mikhail was just biding his time.

"Can you do something about those poor donkeys?" Mari was asking Charlie, her gaze pleading. If she'd looked at him like that Sander would have agreed to standing on his head. He was totally besotted—and counting the seconds until he lost her. He'd planned on winning. If Mikhail hadn't come…

Charlie looked torn. "It's not my country, Mari— but I can try to work it into a speech somewhere," he added hastily, as his cousin's eyes shimmered.

Mari threw her arms around the King of Hellenia. "You're the best cousin in the world—and I would have said it even if you weren't a king," she added with impish generosity.

Charlie chuckled and lightly buffed her chin. "I know, Mariela. You've been saying it since I chased the dog off that bedraggled old cat you loved when you were six."

"And I've always meant it." She buried her face in Charlie's neck.

Sander watched, fascinated. The dynamics of an ordinary family wasn't something that had come his way. Seeing the common man inside the King of Hellenia made him respect Charlie more. He didn't pretend to be something he wasn't, and the innate strength of his background and family ties made him a monarch people could relate to and trust.

Sander saw the same half-hungry fascination in Mikhail's eyes, and the amused contempt he used to cover his true emotion. He realised Mikhail did care for Mari, but had no idea how to be honest with her, or how to play any part but the prince. His inner helplessness at failing to win her had made him just as angry at himself as at Mari, Charlie and Jazmine—

Mari smiled at him from her cousin's shoulder, sharing her joy with Sander over the hopeful salvation of those poor donkeys.

Drumroll, please…the guillotine blade was in place…

"So, are you going to marry my daughter after compromising her in this public fashion?" Mari's father demanded of Sander in a mild yet inflexible tone. "The press knows where you've both been— and alone."

"Stop it, Dad," Mari murmured, her tone as imperative as it was anguished. "Nothing happened."

"You were alone with a single man for days, touring the islands—and at night," her father replied, in a parental *this ends the argument* tone. "I *will* protect your reputation, Mariela—and the reputation of our family," he added, flicking a glance at Charlie.

In answer, Mari looked to where Mikhail stood, furious and silent. The irony in her expression couldn't be clearer.

"They were hardly alone, Uncle Taki," Charlie protested, just as mildly, his voice filled with respect for his uncle. "Jazmine and I made certain Mari was protected at all times."

"But not from the spotlight of the media," Mari's father retorted. "Charlie, you know by now that not even a king can stop rumour and speculation. There was enough about Prince Mikhail's *honourable* intentions."

The slightest hint of irony in the stressed word made Sander want to smile. So that was where Mari got her flair for drama from—and it seemed Mikhail had shown his true intentions during the past few days.

"Nobody knows what His Grace's intentions are towards our girl."

With a sense of fatalism, Sander recognised

Mari's father's ambition for his daughter to become a duchess—but, over that, a hard thrill was running through him that had nothing to do with his duty. Thanks to her father, he now had a chance. He might not win her fairly, but he'd win her. Mari would be his—she'd be his wife, his love. His doubts fled. The simple truth was he'd never be happy without her.

"You're right to ask, sir," he said, with the same quiet respect with which Charlie had spoken. "I care deeply for Mari, as she knows. It would be an honour and a privilege if you would allow me to ask for your daughter's hand in marriage."

Taki Mitsialos beamed at him, and moved forward to shake his hand. "Good boy, good boy," he said heartily, pumping Sander's hand. "Charlie told me you were well brought up, but you never know with the upper classes if they are sincere or playing games, thinking we commoners are expendable." A flicked glance at Mikhail showed Sander that they'd definitely discovered the Prince's true intentions some time in the past few days. "Our girl will be a duchess!"

"No, Dad, I won't."

The inflexible tone, exactly like her father's, made everyone turn to Mari. She stood small and alone, a step away from her royal cousin, her face pale and her hands clenched. "Thank you for asking, Your Grace, but the answer is no. You've done nothing to necessitate marriage. I won't have anyone believing you did. I won't trap a good man into marriage."

Mikhail's face changed subtly at her calm declaration. From barely concealed fury to hunter. Sander saw the plans crossing Mikhail's mind.

In that moment Sander knew his diplomatic career was at an end. But he'd toss aside all consequences if it meant Mari would be safe from Mikhail's predatory clutches.

"It's no trap," he said, over the protesting voices of her family. "I want to marry you, Mari. You know that. I told you last night how I feel." And he smiled at her—the unfair smile that made her desire him.

Mari stared at him, her mouth open, and moistened her lower lip with her tongue. He saw the pulse beating hard in her throat. "No, you don't. Please stop lying for my sake, Your Grace. There's no need to protect me. I'm flying home—today, if that's all right?" She turned to Charlie and Jazmine, her gaze pleading. "I want to go home and forget any of this happened." Her clear-eyed gaze, first at Mikhail and then at Lysander, told him how serious she was.

But he wasn't going down without a fight.

Amid the loud protests of her parents and her brother, and the cautious silence of the others, Sander knew this would be the fight of his life. "Mari, if we could talk privately, I think I could convince you of just how much I want you to be my wife," he said. And his smile grew.

Her eyes widened a little; a delectable flush filled her throat and her breathing quickened. He felt that hard thrill chasing along his nerve-endings—she wanted him so much she couldn't hide it, even in front of Mikhail—but then she backed away, a hand lifted in denial.

"Really, there's no need for it, Y-Your Grace. You have your life, I have mine, and the two aren't compatible. You can't become a commoner, and I don't want to be a duchess. We've had a lovely few days— and I hope we can remain friends—but we hardly know each other. We only met six days ago. The very thought of marriage is ridiculous."

Her father and mother burst into indignant speech; Stavros made a helpless gesture at Charlie. The young King's face reflected a weary fatalism: his family was ignorant of the intense pressure of international politics. The threat of an Orakis coup if the new Marandis dynasty showed too much nepotism was real. He couldn't press for more law changes for their sakes, or even for Mari—his favourite cousin.

Jazmine, her face calm, moved to hold Mari's hand. "I propose we stop here. Obviously we've come here with expectations that aren't reflecting the truth, and we're only distressing Mari. Aunt Maria, why don't we take Mari somewhere quiet to talk?"

"Thank you, Your Majesty, but this isn't a matter for you or the King," Sander said, with a mixture of respect and inflexibility. "This is between Mari and me, without interference."

A look of surprise crossed Jazmine's face. "You're right, Sander. I beg your pardon—Mari as well." With a soft kiss to Mari's cheek, she moved aside.

Sander kept his gaze wholly on Mari. "This doesn't belong to anyone but us, Mari—not your parents, not kings or princes—just us."

Mari blinked, her pretty face covered in confusion that he was still even here, let alone still trying to win her.

He took her hand in his. "I understand what you're saying, and why—but you can't deny there's something between us, no matter how short a time we've known each other." He saw the blush creep up her cheeks, and with a smile he held out a hand to her. "Will you please give me an hour, Mari?"

He saw it, saw her eyes soften and her sweet mouth give that tiny half-pout that meant she was thinking…she was tempted…she was giving in…

"Loath as I am to interrupt this magical moment between lovers, I have appointments to keep—and I have a few words to say. You're fired, Sander. I don't keep disloyal employees—and don't bother asking for a reference. Your time in Chalnikan—and with the Diplomatic Corps, if I have anything to say about it—is done."

Sander held the groan inside. Mikhail was going

down swinging. He still wanted Mari—and, more, he didn't want Sander to win. Now Mari knew it all. He moved to take her hand, to force an hour in private, to explain—

But Mari, her face amused, had turned to Mikhail. "If that was meant as a revelation, Your Highness, you're a few days too late. I've known for days that Lysander worked for you—or, more accurately, for your father the King. And not only does it not bother me, your firing him for following the orders of your father, as well as his king and queen, doesn't make your proposition to me more attractive. Once and for all, Your Highness, I will *never* want you."

Mari's family gasped at her bluntness; Jazmine and Charlie kept their faces impassive, as did Sander—though it was the hardest thing he'd ever had to do when he was dying to swing her into his arms and kiss her senseless—but all gazes swung to the young, spoiled Prince who'd never had to take no for an answer from a woman, and never in public.

Mikhail's cheeks whitened, but after a moment he sneered. "I withdrew that particular offer days ago, Miss Mitsialos. I care nothing for what you do, or who you choose to sleep with. I came only to fire a disloyal employee."

"Liar," she said calmly, smiling at him as his cheeks changed from pale to mottled dark red with fury at a term no one had ever dared throw at him before. "Your face gives away everything you think and feel. You know, looking at yourself honestly—and accepting defeat now and then—will make you a better king when your time comes, Mikhail. You should take lessons from my cousin. He puts others before himself. That's what a good king does."

Without a word, Mikhail turned and strode down the gangplank to the other yacht.

"Well, that's a relief. Back to family," Charlie said—but his face changed in moments when his wife gave a tiny shake of her head. "Um…right. Uncle Taki, Aunt Maria, Stavros—I think we should leave Mari and Lysander alone to talk."

The family vanished before either of them could speak.

"Traitors," he heard Mari mutter, and he held in a chuckle. The thought of a lifetime laughing with her was so very appealing.

"So how did you know about my position in Chalnikan?" he asked quietly as he led her out of the hot sunshine into a solar, seating her on a chaise.

She shrugged as she made herself comfortable. "You said you were a diplomat, but not where. So I did a Google search on you. Sit down, Lysander. I don't like being at a disadvantage."

He mock-groaned, but sat beside her. "You did a *Google* search on me? I feel violated. I wish I'd never told you we had net access here."

The smile in her voice made him smile in return. "Even commoners have their ways."

He tilted his head and checked her out. "I hadn't realised how much of a snob you are until today." Ignoring the indignant flash of her eyes, he went on, "My life isn't a fairy tale, Mari. Much of the time it's like walking a tightrope of expectation. I'd have thought Charlie's new life would have shown you the reality of the life of the upper classes. Every member of the nobility still has to eat, sleep and use the bathroom. They still need to find love, get married and have children. And that's what I want with you."

"It's only been six days," she retorted with clear asperity, and he knew he'd upset her by calling her on her delusions. "We both know this isn't real."

Sander wanted to smile again. She sounded hunted, which meant she was tempted. He struggled against calling her a liar. He was a diplomat—he knew when to call a spade a spade and when to be tactful. A woman on the run did *not* want to hear she was being a coward. "I know it seems insane. It's too soon. I can't possibly love you—but the thing is, in these few days you've shown me a new way to look at the world," he said softly, taking her hand in his, feeling happiness pierce him with almost knife-edged beauty. "You've made me see things differently, Mari. You've made me think, kept me laughing—and when you touched me, kissed me, you bowled me out. Completely. I spent last night imagining a lifetime of laughing with you, of learning from you—" he grinned "—and, of course, of kisses that make me melt. And I saw at least four little boys and girls who'd teach me not to take life too seriously. I saw my children with milk-chocolate eyes and gorgeous curls."

"No, eyes like the sun sparkling on the Aegean and a smile that makes my insides flip," she replied absently, her gaze focussed on his mouth. Then she inhaled sharply. "I didn't mean to say that."

Sander was no fool. As a famous king once said, there was a time to speak and a time to be silent. She'd been dreaming of him, she loved his eyes and smile, saw her children with those attributes; it was enough. It was a weapon to fight with until she was so desperate for him she'd wave the white flag of surrender willingly and say the words he'd spent a lifetime running from. Words he was now desperate to hear from only one woman's mouth.

Oh, that sweet mouth…

It was time for the best kind of battle—a fight without words. He leaned into her and brushed his mouth over hers.

One, two, three butterfly kisses, waiting for her response—and then her hands were in his hair, she was falling back, bringing him with her as he took the kiss deeper, hotter, loving the rightness of lying on her, hearing her soft moans of joy, feeling her frantic hands touching him everywhere she could.

He kissed his way slowly down her throat and

along her collarbone, hearing her murmur, "Lysander, *Lysander*," as if she couldn't get enough of him.

He'd never liked his full name before, but from the first time she'd said it he'd been hooked: a private whisper of her passion for him. When they were together, when they touched, it didn't matter that they'd only met days before, or that they were Duke and commoner. Right now they were just a man and a woman, so right for each other it seemed ridiculous to let a title, or even his people, get in the way.

Finally he understood why a king would abdicate for the sake of the woman he loved...

"Don't go, Mari *mou*," he whispered in her ear, feeling her shiver. "At least stay long enough to know if this is real, if we can make it."

She stilled beneath him. "I can't be a duchess."

He lifted his head from where he'd been exploring her ear with his lips. "Yes, you can," he said softly. "You *care,* Mari. All my people want is someone to care for them."

She shook her head, her mouth set stubbornly.

"I realise there are more things to think about than you and me alone. If you come to Persolis and decide you can't be Duchess, maybe you can be my love, my wife, and let me do the work." And then, no matter how she might promise to stay out of political life, within weeks she'd be questioning his every decision, giving him the human side of every problem. And when she did, he'd be the happiest duke in the world—because he needed her wisdom as much as he needed her smile, her laugh and her touch.

"I *can't*," she said again, a mulish look to her chin even as she wriggled beneath him—not trying to make him get off her, judging by the languid look in her eyes.

Oh, she wanted him—how she wanted him—but he saw the battle being lost through a lack of knowledge of his life. He changed tactics. "Just come to Persolis with me. See what you're turning down before you go back to your exciting life."

She pulled a face at his reference to the job she'd told him she hated on one of their island tours. "I'll lose my job."

He moved against her as he curved a hand around her cheek, and saw her forget what she'd been talking about. "I can see how tempting it would be. Receptionist or duchess—continue living with your parents..." her expression was indescribable at that "...or living with me, sharing my bed, my kisses..." He punctuated each word with a lingering kiss, making her moan and move beneath him.

"Stop it, Lysander," she whispered, even as she turned her face to take in another kiss. "You—you're trying to seduce me into it..."

"And totally without shame, too," he whispered back, finger-drawing down the inside of her arm, feeling her body quiver in sweet, honest response.

Air was expelled from her lungs in a rush. "You don't know me. It's only been a few days."

He was skilled in word analysis. He heard the fear and the longing, the wistful wishing and her terror that the love they both felt would go belly-up as fast as it had come to them. The dreamer fought the practical woman, sword to battleaxe, and not even Mari knew which was winning.

"We'll never know if you leave," he murmured, kissing her ear, loving the sensual squirm she gave. "Stay with me—a few weeks, a few months—until we know. It's not merely about how we are together when we touch, as wonderful as that is. It's about your laughter and your sunshine, your principles and your honesty, your caring and your refusal to back down. You have so much courage, Mari. Don't lose it now."

She buried her face in his neck. "Lysander…"

She was melting—but even while he felt the surge of masculine triumph, he knew this decision was too important for her to be seduced into it. "I can tell you I've never felt like this with any woman, but how can you believe it? You need time to know it won't change—and I need time to convince you. Stay with me here in Hellenia, Mari—give us time to know this is real."

"How can you not be angry? You lost your job because of me," she whispered.

He closed his eyes at his stupidity. Of course she'd think he'd resent her for that. "Actually, I've been offered a better post—if I decide to take it. Even if I don't, all you and Mikhail have done is eased a decision that was too hard for me. I've been avoiding it since Konstantinos joined the monastery. I've been telling myself it was best to stay on a while longer, to foster good relationships in the European capitals to benefit Persolis—and it was the right decision. But you're right—it's time for me to take my place in Persolis and let my mother retire." When she didn't answer, he said, "Why aren't *you* angry? I didn't tell you who I worked for, or why I took you away to separate you from Mikhail."

She nodded, her eyes sincere. "There's no point in my being offended. Mikhail's insistence was causing an embarrassing situation for everyone. I'm grateful you helped me, and that you didn't judge me or think me a mercenary woman out for what I could get."

She was so innocent and wise, his lovely Mari—and he wanted to smile, as he always did when he was in her company. He held her closer. "Nobody could have looked at you, heard you that first day, and thought the worst of you, Mari."

Her eyes shimmered, and he saw yearning and caring there—then they closed over. "I need space, Lysander. I need time to think."

A good diplomat knew when to push and when to retire. "Of course," he murmured, and moved off her body—it felt as if he'd left something behind as he stood. Maybe his heart. "All I ask is that you give us a chance…and listen to your heart, Mari."

He saw the doubt in her face—the self-doubt. She needed to convince herself—which she'd never be able to do if she were a runner.

Such a shame for his sweet love that she was fighting someone with the best diplomatic contacts in the Corps.

Sander grinned, anticipating each and every battle…

CHAPTER SEVEN

A month later

"Is THIS a joke? You've had my passport for a month now, and the problem isn't fixed?"

Mari glared at the plump, middle-aged woman behind the glass counter at the Australian Consulate, who smiled apologetically. "I am afraid not, madam. The irregularity with your passport is an unusual one, and it has to be sorted out at the London office. Until your passport returns here you can't travel."

In other words, *you can't leave Hellenia until a certain diplomat removes the unusual irregularity he created especially to keep you here.* She knew the unspoken terms: *Come and see me. Come to Persolis.*

Right then Mari wanted to see Lysander, all right—to throttle him. This woman was like Sergeant Schultz from *Hogan's Heroes*—she knew *nothing.* And those who could help her, the Ambassador and all his aides, were all far too busy to get her home.

Too busy to see the King's cousin, were they? When they'd been fawning over her until now? Did Lysander have the entire diplomatic staff on his side, as well as her family?

Everyone wanted her to stay in Hellenia. Her parents weren't going home, and neither was Stavros. Her dad, having toured Hellenia for three weeks as a resident expert in green solutions, had gone to Persolis five days ago at Lysander's invitation, giving unorthodox solutions to the age-old problem of garbage storage.

"What? You think the entire country turned out their garbage in an effort to keep you here?" her father had asked indignantly, when she'd tried to blame Lysander for her dad's sudden elevation in status to First Assistant to the Minister for the Environment.

And Stavros was finishing his medical studies at the University of Orakidis.

"How can you call it nepotism?" he'd protested, when she'd questioned his sudden scholarship for his final years. "They *need* more doctors here, Mariela. There's been war here for decades. I can speak the language, I have family connections, and I came in the top ten percent in all my exams at Sydney Uni. For the first time I can study full-time, instead of working my way through."

When she'd kept trying to make him see what was really going on, Stavros had mocked her.

"Oh? So Sander arranged my good marks over the

past five years to keep you here? When did you become so self-important, little sister?"

"Go to him, Mariela," was her mother's unvarying advice. "Go to Persolis and judge for yourself whether or not you can make a difference."

Her parents and Stavros had gone deaf without warning, refusing to interfere or even listen to her reasons for not marrying Lysander. Jazmine was full of stories about the Duke, making him appear a cross between a saint and the loneliest man in the world. And Charlie's schedule this past week had been too full for him to help on the matter of her passport issues.

"Is the Duke of Persolis here?" she asked the woman, wondering if he was listening in somewhere, waiting for her to ask for him.

"Yes, madam, he is here currently—attending an important meeting. Would you like to see him?" The woman's searching look was answer enough: Lysander wasn't at any meeting. He was waiting for her to ask for him, even if all she wanted was to tear him limb from limb.

Steam almost pouring from her ears, she snapped, "Yes, please."

Moments later she was ushered into a functional office. The door closed behind her—and Lysander stood up behind the desk he sat at and smiled at her. "I've missed you so much," he said simply, his arms held out to her.

Oh, how unfair was it that he'd said that, making

her melt when she was so furious? "Don't distract me, Lysander. Play fair!"

Yet, confused, filled with turbulent hunger, she took a step closer…

"I can't afford to." He moved towards her, slow and cautious, with that fascinating smile. "You'd only run away if I did. You wouldn't give us a chance."

Her cheeks heated in unspoken acknowledgement of his words. "I can't stay," she cried, feeling wretched. "Don't you see it will never work?"

"All I can see is you. I'm dying to touch you," he said huskily. Those eyes…that smile…

And she was in his arms. "Lysander."

The kiss was everything she'd been dreaming of during the long, lonely month without him. She forgot all the good reasons to leave. She forgot she was mad with him—or maybe the negative passion fuelled the other, more primitive need.

"Tell me you've missed me," he mumbled through hot kisses down her throat.

She didn't have to, because it was so pathetically obvious—but she gasped, "You know I have. Lysander…" She tossed his tie, unbuttoned his shirt, spread greedy hands across his chest.

He shuddered and groaned. "I have to be back at that meeting in ten minutes. I'm going to totally humiliate myself."

She stilled. "I'm sorry, I shouldn't have come to see you, but I was so angry." Her hands still caressing his body, she forced her gaze to his. "I need my passport back."

His eyes met hers, unflinching. "And I need you to give us a chance—at least see what it is you're turning down before you play the coward."

Like the swinging of a pendulum, her ardour became anger again. "I lost my job. My parents are selling the house and staying here. My brother's studying here. You've made sure I have no life to return to. You're not giving me a chance to make a fair decision."

"You can't make a fair decision without coming to Persolis!" he snarled.

"I can't *think* when I'm near you!" she cried. "How can I make a fair decision if all I feel for you is this?" She dropped her hands. "And anger that you've put me in a cage? It's dysfunctional, Lysander. Nothing can be right between us if I resent you!"

He stilled, and slowly nodded. "You're right—again. But I can't let you go, Mari. My life's been *grey* the past month. I can't stand thinking you're half a world away from me!"

Yearning and something dangerously tender filled her, body and heart. "Wouldn't you rather I went and came back to you of my own free will, knowing how I feel?"

He wheeled away, breathing hard. "I think you already know how you feel about me, Mari. What you need to know is how you feel about my life. You need to come to Persolis *before* you go to Sydney." When she didn't answer, he added harshly, "I won't be there, if that makes it easier for you. Go and meet my mother and my people as Charlie's cousin—you've done that before, visiting Toby and Lia in their duchy, Malascos. We don't have to go public if I'm not there. Your passport will be waiting when you return."

It wasn't a request, and Mari knew two things: he wasn't going to give way on this, and he was right—she was being a coward. Slowly, she said, "All right." She moved away when he turned back with a blazing smile. "I'll play fair if you will."

That wasn't a request either.

Two weeks later

At the steps of the ducal residence, Mari stood waiting for the limousine, her hands in the Duchess's. "Thank you for making my time here so wonderful, Kat."

The dragon of her nightmares had become a purring kitten, if an elegant one. The Duchess—*Call me Kat,* she'd said the first day—lovely and well-spoken, was as warm and open-hearted as Lysander, with the same dancing in her eyes. She'd encouraged Mari to look on her as another aunt from the start, and by now Mari had almost forgotten her title. It was just like being with Charlie, Lia or Toby. She was so…ordinary. So *real.*

Kat squeezed the hands she held. "Thank you for giving me the chance to know you, darling girl. I've always wanted a daughter. Now I feel I have one…almost."

The last word was added hastily, with a comical look of guilt. The silent agreement that neither of them would speak of Lysander, apart from about his childhood, hadn't been broken.

Mari giggled, and kissed the Duchess's cheek. "Now I know where he got his audacity from."

Kat nodded, her dimples flashing. "The car's here."

Mari hugged her, and turned to pick up her bag.

"Mari, if I might give you one piece of advice?" Kat said softly.

Feeling fatalistic, Mari turned back to face her.

"The title is just a word, you know. I think you've seen that with me, with your cousins, but you're blinding yourself against my son. Beneath the job, and the robes for state occasions, he's just a man in love."

Mari pushed her lips together hard, to stop the foolish rush of tears. "I need space to see that, Kat— especially when he's been using his power against me. I have to go."

Sadness and acceptance filled the older woman's eyes. "I'll talk to him."

Another hug, fierce and loving, and she snatched up her bag and ran down the stairs.

Ten months later

From the middle of the long receiving line where the royal family greeted their guests, those especially invited to watch the new Earl of Haridis and his Countess receive their formal titles, Sander watched the new Lady Mari Mitsialos, daughter of the Earl, with subdued hunger. It had been so long since he'd even seen her—longer since they'd been alone.

She was dressed for the occasion in a deep claret silk ballgown, her hair pulled up in a smooth chignon; she wore rubies and diamonds about her ears and throat; an IWC watch worth ten thousand euros adorned her wrist. She looked perfect—but she didn't look like his Mari any more, and he wondered if he'd created a monster in his efforts to win her.

Taki, Maria and Stavros had taken to their new lives like ducks to water. And though Sander had been the one to first propose the title, Taki had become an earl based purely on his brilliance in science and his dedication to his new country. The Minister for the Environment, a bored viscount, had gratefully relinquished the position when Taki had invented a toxic waste blanket that increased decomposition, making a cleaner country and improving the health of the villagers and townspeople living near toxic rubbish dumps. Taki had won the admiration of the press and the people without any help from Sander.

Stavros led his year at the university, and had everyone's respect.

Mari was the only member of the family who didn't come regularly to Persolis, or accept her place in Hellenia without reservation.

Her passport "problem" had cleared the day she'd returned to Orakidis City, and she'd left immediately for Australia, staying there six agonising weeks. Charlie had sent him a terse e-mail the day she went.

Mari needs space. Give her time or she'll never come back.

Much as he'd hated the dictum, he'd known Charlie was right. He hadn't contacted her in all that time—apart from one red rose delivered to her friend's apartment every week, with a card simply saying: *I'm waiting.*

He hadn't even known she'd returned to Hellenia until his mother had mentioned Mari's "latest call". So Mari was calling his mother...so she'd returned...so she'd visited Malascos, met the people there, as well as in in Orakidis City... She'd visited Malascos, but she only visited Persolis when ambassadorial business took him from home. She wanted space, but he was suffocating without her.

He'd won his people's approval. He now performed all his duties, knowing Mari had been right—

this was real life, and running from that basic truth hadn't made him a better man. So he'd turned down the post with the United Nations, taking the post of Second Assistant to the Ambassador on the condition that Persolis came first. Sometimes he felt stretched to his limits, barely finding time to sleep…if only she was here, sharing his load…

For the past six months she'd only left the palace in Jazmine or Charlie's company, or to make her visits to Lia and Toby in Malascos. Jazmine's and Lia's pregnancies had given Mari an opportunity to help Charlie with affairs of state, and she'd shone. From formal affairs to visiting villages and towns in need of royal help, anything Charlie asked her to do she did—and she was winning the admiration of his people on her own merits.

Her father had been elevated to Hereditary Lord without dissent. Stavros was hailed as the new Viscount, heir to the new Earl, with enthusiasm, especially after a stint in Orakidis Hospital, when he'd saved a child's life. But Mari refused to see she deserved anything. "I'm only doing what anyone would do," she'd said the last time they'd met, at an official function a month ago. A night when she'd refused to see him privately, had barely glanced at him.

As he reached the royal family now, he bowed deeply before Mari. "My lady." He lingered a moment too long over her hand. He couldn't make his lips leave her gloved skin.

"Your Grace," she murmured, and tugged her hand.

He couldn't let go—not yet. "Mari *mou*," he whispered into her knuckles.

"Your Grace," she murmured again, her voice filled with meaning. He glanced up. She looked composed, even with a light blush staining her lovely honey-cream skin. She tilted her head at the long line of people waiting to greet her.

"Your pardon, my lady," he said softly, his fingers trailing over hers as he let go. "It's been too long since I saw you." *Since I touched you.* "My hands won't obey my mind."

"Stop it, Lysander," she whispered, her eyes reflecting her longing and her exasperation. "I'm not *ready*."

The next person in line was listening avidly to their conversation, under cover of meeting Stavros—but Sander no longer cared who knew how he felt for Mari. Right now he'd take any chance to talk to her he got. "When will you be, *eros mou*? It's been a year. I still love you and you still won't believe it."

Her chest lifted and fell with the quiet dragging in of her breath. She leaned into him, whispered in his ear. "The antechamber…after the ceremony."

His heart soared and his rebel body, anticipating the reunion, went into overdrive. He adjusted his ducal cape so his excitement wouldn't become public knowledge. "I'll count the minutes, *eros mou*," he whispered in her ear, touching the pearly skin with his mouth.

She shivered, made a tiny sound—and he moved on at last, satisfied, to greet Toby, waiting for him with twinkling eyes.

"Sander, my almost cousin," the gentle giant murmured with wicked humour. "Making assignations with your lady in the palace? Ah, those were the days. It makes me feel nostalgic."

Sander grinned and shook hands with the commoner turned Grand Duke and Prince after his marriage to Lia. Everyone knew of Lia and Toby's unorthodox courtship in the secret passageways of the Malascos palace, right under the nose of the autocratic old King, who'd wanted Lia to marry Max, the Grand Duke of Falcandis. Old King Angelis, confined to his room now, had totally forgotten his former dislike of the Australian firefighter turned Grand Duke. He adored Toby, loved the baby son born two months before, and firmly believed he'd manipulated events to make the marriage possible.

The minutes moved like snails as the ceremony droned on and on. An hour became two, while Taki, Maria and Stavros revelled in their new positions and Mari smiled like the Sphinx, gracious, mysterious—accepting what she couldn't change, but not seeming to share her family's shining happiness.

Not for the first time Sander felt doubt creep into his heart. He'd believed she loved him, hoped she truly wanted life with him. What if he'd been wrong? What if she still missed her free, anonymous life in Australia? Her family title now made that life almost impossible for her—and he'd been the first to suggest Taki's elevation. In making her worthy of him, he'd ripped her life, her choice, from her.

He barely made it through the four hours of the reception without his hungry gaze following her around the room. He couldn't remember what he'd eaten or drunk, what he'd said to his dinner partners. He could barely remember if they'd been old or young, male or female. All he'd known were the moments *she'd* stopped at his table, talked to him: precious seconds that had ticked by too fast.

Now the time had come. Watching, he saw her turn her gaze to him; her head tipped and she vanished into the crowd.

Moments later he made his way to the door at the other side of the room, walked down the deserted hall and back into the reception room and slipped inside the door of the private antechamber.

He closed the door behind him, ignoring the rich appointments in the gold-and-white room, the Persian rug and Chippendale desk. He drank in the sight of her, shoes kicked off and swinging in her hand. Ah, *that* was his girl, his Mari, and he was alone with her at last…

Her head, lowered at first, lifted and turned to him. "Don't," she said softly, before he could smile or whisper her name with the hunger he couldn't restrain. "We need to talk, and I can't think when we touch."

Her honesty robbed him of breath or thought. He nodded, and waited.

"You said you'd give me space, but your manipulation went on—the roses, the title for Dad," she said quietly, looking him in the eyes. "You still haven't given me free choice."

Pain and guilt pierced him. "I know." Hoarse words, honest admission. "I thought I was helping to make your decision easier."

Her eyes narrowed. "Make it easier for me to choose you, you mean," she replied, with weary anger. "I lost my life. I lost my job. Mum and Dad sold the house. And—I've changed. I'm not who I was a year ago. You've left me nothing to go home to."

"Is it so bad here?" he asked, his throat ripping as if broken glass had lodged there.

Her sad glance tore through his heart. "You don't know how big the choice is for me. You're not only the Duke now—you'd be Ambassador to the United Nations but for me, wouldn't you?"

Taken aback, he stared at her. "Only in the sense that you made me see that ignoring my duty was as wrong for me as it was for my people. I turned the position down because I had enough to do."

"How can I believe that?" she cried.

"I might have manipulated events around you, withheld the truth from you at the start, but I've never lied to you. I didn't want the position," he said quietly.

She dropped the shoes and snapped, "How would I know? All I know is since I came into your life you've given up an exalted position. How can I not think that it's because of me—that I'm holding you back?"

"I did it for the right reasons, Mari," he said, through a tight jaw. "I'm tied to my land, my people—but I don't think that's your deepest problem. Your problem is with yourself."

"I'm a commoner," she said slowly, her nostrils flared.

"Not any more."

"You can't change what I am." Her face hardened. "*Lady* is a word, Lysander. All I am is a commoner, with a word tacked on in front of my name."

"As am I—and Lia and Charlie. It's all any of us are. I'd have thought Charlie, Lia and Toby's experience would have taught you that."

She stared at him. "Nothing will change my upbringing. I'm a commoner. You're a blue-blood."

"My mother said you were blinding yourself to who I really am." Impatiently he grabbed at a letter-opener from the exquisite Chippendale desk behind him and pierced his thumb. "What colour is that?" he snarled, pointing at the droplet of blood welling from the cut. "If it was *blue,* I'd be dead."

Mari sighed and shook her head.

"The problem was never the title, was it?" he
asked, a vast sadness filling him. "I've done all I can
to prove to you that we're not so far apart as you
think, but in the end it's down to you. When did you
first feel you weren't as good as anyone else? When
did you start to believe that no matter what you did
you were replaceable, unworthy of love and a happy
life?"

In her sweet eyes there was honest bewilderment.
"It isn't that, Lysander. I want to be loved, to be married—but I miss my life at home. I miss Australia,
and the freedom to be me, to make mistakes without
being watched. If I marry you, I'll never have it back.
How could we visit *my* life, the life I still love and
will always miss?"

The grey mists filling him suddenly parted as he
understood. "The same way the Crown Prince and
Princess of Denmark do. They didn't build themselves
a palace in Tasmania, did they? They stay with her
family and eat at the local pubs, visit her old haunts."

"With the press there with them all the way," she
sighed.

He nodded and shrugged. "I'm sorry, Mari, but
that's a fact of life for you for the rest of your life—
no matter who you marry. You're the King's cousin.
But you can either run from it—pretend it doesn't
exist, as I did with my life—or you make it work for
you, as Frederik and Mary do, by making everyone

love you. The press love Mary's origins, and the fact that she's never tried to be anyone but herself." Slowly, he added, "As they love Charlie, Lia and Toby. The ordinary royals—the fairy tale come to life. The people and the press lap it up, because it makes the nobility human." One step, two; he lifted a hand, and as if mesmerised Mari took it in hers, bringing it to her lips, kissing his skin with tender hunger. So long since she'd been so close, so loving… The thrill of joy that always came at her touch ran through his whole body. "The people love your family, Mari," he muttered, husky with his need for her. "And they love you for all you do for the country—always giving, without asking for anything in return. Has anyone mentioned your origins to you when you help the country? Has anyone said you don't deserve your title, or that you're not good enough for me?"

Mari frowned. "No, of course they haven't. I'm the King's cousin."

Her palm-kisses were making him crazy to have more. Impatient with her lack of self-worth, he retorted, "It has nothing to do with Charlie. They love you for who you are—just as they love your whole family. The whole country knows by now that I want to marry you, yet there hasn't been one word of dissent. They're all waiting for the announcement, to join in the celebrations. You're my duchess already, in everyone's eyes but your own."

Still kissing his palm and fingers, she glanced up, startled. Rethinking her life. He waited for her to readjust.

"Lysander," she whispered, clinging to his hand. "Is that true?"

He understood what she hadn't asked. "My mother's waiting outside with the family ring, *eros mou*—the Persolis engagement ring. She adores you, and can't wait to welcome you to the family." When she didn't answer, but stood there dazed, he wound his fingers through hers. "Can I ask her in?"

Mari bit her lip, trying to dampen the hope that leaped into her eyes.

It was time to give her a tiny push. "All I have to do is call her phone once."

A breath shivered out of her. She frowned again. "Lysander... I don't know..."

It was his turn to lift her hand to his mouth, kissing her palm, her fingers, with lingering, loving sweetness as he said the words he'd fought against for months. He had to say them now, for her sake, because he truly loved her and wanted her to be happy.

"Tell me you don't love me, Mari. Look in my eyes and tell me you don't love me, that I'm not worth the life changes you'd have to make for me, and I'll make it all go away. You'll have your quiet life back in Australia. I'll never see you again."

Her eyes squeezed shut, and he held his breath,

counting the moments. Did she love him as he loved her? Had he gambled her life on an empty premise?

Then, finally, she spoke. "I adore you," she whispered, "but if you ever manipulate me like that again I'll have to kill you."

With a shout of happiness, Sander snatched her into his arms and kissed her, hard and hungry. "I won't have to," he murmured between kisses. "You think I don't know you're going to arrange the rest of my life?" he added with a wicked grin.

She laughed and snuggled in to him. "Did you really have to rope in all my relatives, as well as the Diplomatic Corps?"

He chuckled and kissed her hair. "What can I say? You're a strong-minded woman. It only took over a hundred against one for an entire year before you finally gave in." He lifted her chin, making her look at him. "Say it, Mari."

She didn't pretend to misunderstand. "I love you, Lysander. I'll marry you, have your children… and, yes, I probably *will* run the rest of your life," she added, eyes twinkling with happy self-knowledge.

"My mother will be very relieved to know that," he said solemnly, his eyes dancing.

"Your mother *is* very relieved." An amused voice came from the doorway. "I beg your pardon, but I've been waiting for you both to notice me these past few minutes."

Mari ran to the Duchess. "Kat," she whispered, and hugged her.

Kat held her tenderly. "Good girl. I'm glad you didn't make it easy for him. Lysander needs a real woman with strong principles. You chose well, Lysander." She smiled at her son, then turned back to Mari. "Now you really have become my daughter."

"Thank you," she whispered into the floral-scented embrace.

"No, I thank *you*, darling girl. Thank you for making this past year worthwhile, for becoming the Duchess he needs before you said yes." The old Duchess smiled at her. "That's what you were doing the past year, wasn't it—taking royal lessons as your cousins did, making sure you could sustain the life and the pressures that would come with being Lysander's wife?"

Startled by her insight, at her ripping aside all the other issues to find her core insecurity, Mari nodded and flicked a glance at Lysander. The pride and love in his smile turned her insides to honey-mush. Glad as she was for such a loving mother-in-law, she couldn't wait…

"What am I thinking?" the Duchess laughed, and hugged her again. "A newly engaged couple want to be alone, and I keep talking. Here you are, son." She pressed a small box into Lysander's hand. "I'll keep your secret for exactly an hour. If you're not out and announcing your engagement by then, expect the room to be invaded."

She closed the door behind her; Lysander gave her *that* smile, and Mari ran into his arms. "Fifty-nine minutes of kissing," she murmured. He laughed and set the alarm on his watch, and neither said anything more—for exactly fifty-nine minutes.

EPILOGUE

The Summer Palace, four months later

IT WAS enough to make her believe in fairy tales…but this was *her* happy ending…

"Are you happy, *eros mou*?" Magnificent in a dark tuxedo, Lysander put his arm around her waist as they stood on the balcony usually reserved for royalty only. The intense interest of the people and press in the Duke and new Ambassador (he'd eventually decided to take the posting, at Mari's urging) and his commoner Duchess—already gaining the respect of the diplomatic world with her caring and her need to help—had led to this unprecedented move.

"I don't think I could possibly be any happier." Mari stood beside her husband of one hour in a wedding gown made by Europe's foremost new designer, emeralds and diamonds at ears, throat, wrists and fingers. They were on the balcony where she'd watched her cousins greet their people. Now she was the one waving and throwing flowers down to the smiling, cheering crowd, and she knew they were her people too.

She, Mari Mitsialos, was a duchess, an ambassador's wife—but though both those things were important, they paled beside the core truth: she was going to be beside the man she loved for life.

The past four months had taught her how true it was: titles didn't make people; people either made a title or lowered it. She'd worked hard—learning diplomatic language, meeting the people of Persolis and discovering their needs. She was still learning how to be a duchess from Kat, but she'd had the intense satisfaction of seeing her parents and her mother-in-law having fun meeting in the middle of their different lives. And though she and Lysander were both busy, they made time for each other every day, working in and around each other's schedule. She'd learned to treasure a brief glance, a moment's touch of hands—but for the next month, on the royal island, they'd just be a couple in love, and finally alone...

"Mari! Mari!" the people chanted, throwing roses to her. One made it high enough; Lysander caught it and, with a loving smile, handed it to his bride. She kissed the crimson bloom and laid it against her heart. The cheers deafened her; the popping of flashes grew more intense.

"You know what they want—exactly what I want," Lysander murmured, pride and love in his voice; and, in the joy overflowing from a heart bursting with happiness, she laid the rose on the balcony and turned into his arms.

As they kissed the roar of the crowd grew, and then went quiet—or maybe it was just that she couldn't hear anything, see or feel anything but Lysander. Duke or Ambassador, he was just Lysander to her—the man she adored—and she was his bride, his wife.

She was truly blessed.

* * * * *

0410/25/MB272

BRIDES OF BELLA LUCIA

A family torn apart by secrets, reunited by marriage

Two fantastic collections containing four full-length stories each, following the scandalous Valentine family and their exclusive Bella Lucia restaurant empire

FREE ONLINE READ!

Brides of Bella Lucia:
Unexpected Proposals

*Available
5th March 2010*

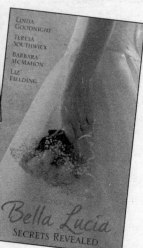

Brides of Bella Lucia:
Secrets Revealed

*Available
2nd April 2010*

www.millsandboon.co.uk

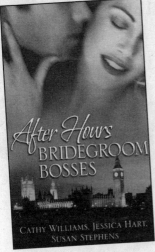

BLACKMAILED TO HIS BED – BUT HE CAN'T BUY HER LOVE!

millsandboon.co.uk Community

Join Us!

The Community is the perfect place to meet and chat to kindred spirits who love books and reading as much as you do, but it's also the place to:

- **Get the inside scoop from authors about their latest books**
- **Learn how to write a romance book with advice from our editors**
- **Help us to continue publishing the best in women's fiction**
- **Share your thoughts on the books we publish**
- **Befriend other users**

Forums: Interact with each other as well as authors, editors and a whole host of other users worldwide.

Blogs: Every registered community member has their own blog to tell the world what they're up to and what's on their mind.

Book Challenge: We're aiming to read 5,000 books and have joined forces with The Reading Agency in our inaugural Book Challenge.

Profile Page: Showcase yours. ... o a record of your recent community activity.

Social Networking: We've added bu... he end of every post to share via digg, Facebook, G... Yahoo, technorati and de.licio.us.

www.millsandboon.co.uk